last chorus

A PERFECT SONG DUET: PART TWO

L.M. HALLORAN

dedication

For you. Yes, you.

Thanks for letting me break your heart.
As promised, I'm about to put it back together...
after I mess with it a little more.

Ready? Let's go.

author's note

Your mental health matters, so please review the following content warning. If you have no triggers, skip this to avoid spoilers.

This novel contains the following mature themes: heavy emotional angst, anxiety disorder rep, depression rep, neurodivergence rep, insomnia, emotional/psychological abuse (not by MC), PTSD, references to grooming and assault of a teenage girl, mention of miscarriage (not FMC), explicit M/F sex including anal, and degradation/praise kink.

last chorus

"We all make mistakes, don't we? But if you can't forgive yourself, you'll always be an exile in your own life."

CURTIS SITTENFELD

transition

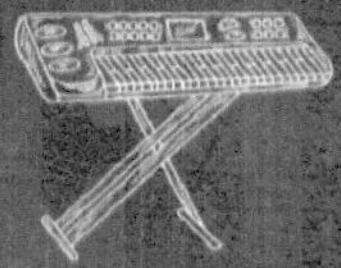

transition : *a rhythmic or melodic interlude between sections of a song*

CHAPTER ONE

wilder

SIX AND A HALF YEARS LATER

WILDER 31 | EVA 29

The doorbell's soft, bell-like tone echoes through the house. Even expecting it, my chest tightens and my pulse accelerates. I lower my mug of tea to the counter and close my eyes.

A normal stress response.

Breathe.

Focus on physical anchors.

My lungs push against the pressure around them as I inhale, hold the breath, then blow it out in a rush through my mouth. As I continue the exercise, I tap firmly beneath my collarbone until my nervous system calms and my heart rate slows.

Even with over six years of practice under my belt, I'm still amazed when the simple technique works. Gratitude fills me for the freedom I have now that I'm able to manage my anxiety.

The doorbell rings again.

"Coming," I mutter.

I leave the kitchen and walk down the hallway toward my visitors. The click and hum of the central heating and the creak of floorboards under my bare feet are familiar, grounding sounds. Late December, mid-morning sunlight cuts through trees on the property, diffusing through double-paned glass on my right and making the wood and white walls glow. After weeks of gray, it's a welcome sight.

As I pass the two platinum albums hanging in frames on the hallway wall, I breathe deeply again and remind myself that everything is okay, that I can handle this. That I've handled *a lot* without a drink or a drug, like writing and recording five albums back-to-back. Months upon months on the road. Sold out stadium crowds and festival fields around the world. Screaming, crying fans who have no concept of personal boundaries. Live interviews under glaring lights. And the most personally challenging career requirement: industry events and award shows where seeing *her* is unavoidable.

But the real proof I can handle anything sits in my chest: a broken heart that still, somehow, keeps on beating. That I've learned to accept, even embrace, as the ultimate proof that nothing, *nothing*, has the power to send me back into the darkness.

My fingers trail lightly across the leaves of a potted fern beside the front door, and I use the physical sensation to focus my mind on the present. One more breath, then I flip the deadbolt and pull open the door. Frigid air swirls around me and I relish the shock of it.

The couple standing on my porch regard me with starkly different expressions. Matt Sullivan is frowning deeply, hands stuffed in his pockets, shoulders high and tense beneath his coat. His wife, on the other hand, beams at me with a smile so familiar I have to make myself return it.

"Hi, Wilder," Sophie says warmly. "Thanks so much for letting us come by."

"Of course. How was the ferry?"

"Just fine," she answers as Matt grumbles, "Fucking crowded."

I glance at him—he doesn't meet my eye—before standing back. "Come on in."

Once they're inside, I close the door and lock it, then wait as they remove their coats and hang them on hooks in the foyer. As I study their body language, it occurs to me with faint amusement that of the three of us, I'm the calmest.

Sophie turns first, clearing her throat as she smooths flyaway, dark blonde hairs from her face. "How was your Christmas?"

Since she's best friends with my mom and they talk daily, it's obvious she's attempting to fill the awkward silence. I don't know exactly why they're here, but whatever the reason, it's becoming apparent that it's not a good one. My jaw clenches against the urge to ask the question that's haunted me since my mom called two days ago with their request.

"It was great," I answer, my voice steady despite clanging nerves. "With River living in London and the twins down in San Diego, it'd been a while since we were all under the same roof. How was yours?"

"Just fine, thank you." Her smile falters as she glances at Matt, who's still frowning as he stares at the floor. She nudges his arm and he finally looks at me.

What I see in his light blue eyes has me struggling not to take a step back. The familiar resentment I was expecting is nowhere to be found. He looks sad and lost.

My stomach drops.

"Thanks for seeing us," he says mutedly.

I nod, then shift back on my heels and pivot, suddenly knowing I need to be sitting down when they reveal what brought them to my door. "Come on back. Can I get you guys anything? Coffee? Water? Tea?"

"We're fine, thanks," Sophie replies.

They follow me silently down the hallway, but as we enter the heart of the house, Sophie gasps. "This is absolutely stunning, Wilder."

The open-concept living space is dominated by huge windows along the back wall that showcase a private beach and water beyond. The view is framed by the assorted pines and deciduous trees that crowd the six-acre property. One particular tree snags my gaze like it always does. It stands alone, thick trunk supporting a multitude of long, crooked branches, pale and bare for the winter.

A sycamore.

Sophie turns to me with a bright smile. "Rose showed me before and after pictures, but they didn't do this place justice. You guys did an amazing job."

A smile comes more easily this time. "Thank you. I'm pretty proud of it."

With my touring schedule, it took close to three years to finish the remodeling since my dad and I were committed to doing most of the cosmetic work ourselves. I'm more proud of this house than I am of my career success. It's my sanctuary, the first place where I've felt completely at home since I was a child. More than that, though, it's a physical embodiment and affirmation of the effort I put into rebuilding my life on a solid foundation.

Matt walks past us, his gaze trailing over the arched ceilings, sunroom-inspired dining space, modern kitchen, and adjacent living room. He doesn't say anything as he veers toward a couch and sits. Posture rigid, he stares blankly at the waterline. Sophie trails after him, perching at his side and taking one of his hands in hers.

My skin buzzes as I follow and settle on the opposite couch. It takes conscious effort not to mirror Matt's tension. I keep my arms relaxed, my hands folded loosely over my stomach.

No amount of breathing is going to help my heart rate at this point, so I do what's sometimes necessary and simply sit with the discomfort.

To my surprise, it isn't Sophie who breaks the silence.

"You're probably wondering what we're doing here." Matt laughs shortly, dragging a hand through his pale hair. *Her* hair.

Since he's cutting to the point, so do I. "I am, yes."

His throat moves. "I owe you an apology."

I wasn't aware I was fidgeting until his words sink in and every muscle in my body stills.

Sophie gives him an encouraging nod, and he continues, "I've said some really fucked-up things to you over the years. Things you didn't deserve."

Is this why they're here? The notion relaxes a knot inside me. Maybe this isn't what I was afraid of, after all.

Smiling slightly, I tell him, "Nah. I definitely deserved them."

Matt studies my face, then smirks. "You definitely did."

Expression aghast, Sophie smacks his shoulder. Matt chuckles. Surprising everyone, including myself, I join him.

Sophie glances between us, mystified. "I think what my husband is trying—and failing—to say is that we're extremely proud of you and the man you've become."

A surge of embarrassment makes my voice gruff. "Thanks, Sophie."

"That's what I said, isn't it?" Matt jokes before sobering. He pins me with a stare. "In all seriousness, I *am* sorry for the things I said. You needed support back then, but I was too caught up in my head to give it. I'll always regret that. I'm grateful you made it through, Wilder."

The gravity of the moment settles on my shoulders —not the heavy, clawed feeling of the past, but a light, comforting shroud. Goosebumps roll gently down my arms, and an old, internal scar fades.

"I appreciate that," I murmur.

Sophie squeezes Matt's hand, her eyes glassy as they shift to me. Her chin trembles, then firms. "For what it's worth, we know you didn't mean to hurt our daughter."

I've barely processed her statement when Matt adds, "We know you loved her very much."

Surprise forces air from my lungs too fast, leaving me dizzy. I lift my gaze to the ceiling, seeking an anchor, and see a knot on one of the beams. In the lumpy, imperfect circle, I find a modicum of calm. And in that calm is an instinct I can no longer ignore.

Lowering my gaze to Evangeline's parents, I ask the question that's become a nonstop irritant the last two days.

"She's not okay, is she?"

Sophie's expression crumples. Matt's hardens defensively, his pale eyes impossibly bright. "No, she's not," he answers.

A thousand questions crowd my mind—*what, why, how*—but what comes out is, "I'm assuming you've talked to Rye and Lily?"

They nod, and Sophie says softly, "They've tried.

We've tried. But she's..." She trails off, a vacancy in her eyes I'm all too familiar with. Matt puts his arm around her and she leans into his side.

"No one can get through to her," Matt informs me. "Even knowing what fame can do to people, it's surreal. She's like a different person."

I think of the last time I saw Evangeline, in a media clip last week. She was walking into a restaurant in Los Angeles with her boyfriend. In the five seconds I managed to watch the video, I'd been focused on how much I wanted to rip his fake-tanned hand off her back.

Now I force myself to confront the image of *her*. Too thin. Too much makeup. High heels. Fake nails on the hand lifted toward the flashing cameras. Winning, superstar smile. Long hair tamed into perfect waves. A designer mini-dress in some bland color.

"I want my daughter back," whispers Sophie.

The crack in my heart widens, more debris falling silently into the abyss of Evangeline's absence.

Matt's agonized eyes hold mine. "We need your help. *She* needs your help."

Potent emotion floods me—twisted, irrepressible hope at the prospect of being close to Evangeline again. Despite knowing the hope is false, it feels too fucking real. I need to recenter myself in reality. Remind myself and them of the truth I have to live with every day.

"I want to help," I say as gently as I can. "Of course I do. But let's be realistic here. I'm the last person on the planet she'd listen to. There's an album that won five Grammys detailing exactly how she feels about me."

Matt's eyes narrow, flashing with determination and stubbornness. I see so much of Evangeline in his expression that for two seconds, I can't fucking breathe.

"So that's it? You're giving up on her?"

Sophie's head lifts, anxious eyes flying from Matt to me.

I tense. "I'm respecting her wishes—the ones she screamed at me outside your house when I came home from treatment? I'm sure you remember." I pause, reining in the emotion that bled into my voice. "It's been years. We've both moved on with our lives."

Matt scoffs. "Don't give me that bullshit. You still love her." I flinch, and he goes in for the kill. "If you don't, explain why you don't publicly date anyone, ever. Why you still write songs about her. Why *that*"—his arm swings toward the painting over the fireplace—"is on the wall."

I don't follow the line of his finger. I haven't looked directly at the painting since it was hung up on the day the house was finished.

I shift in my seat, my skin crawling. "I honestly don't know what you're asking me to do."

"I think you do," he challenges.

Standing, he draws Sophie to her feet. I rise, too, frustration punching through my veneer of calm.

"She won't talk to me. I fucking tried, Matt."

The aggression leaves his face as he sighs. "I know you did. But that was then and this is now." He pauses. "When she does answer our calls, it's like talking to a stranger who body-snatched our kid. But there's one word—just one—that gets an authentic reaction from her. Even if it guarantees she hangs up on us."

I frown, but he doesn't make me wait.

"Your name."

They turn toward the hallway.

"What the hell? How is that a good thing?"

Matt stops and looks back. I recoil when I see tears in his eyes. "It means she's still in there somewhere. *You're* still in there somewhere. You might be the only one who can bring her back."

He strides down the hallway while Sophie lingers. "I'm sorry, Wilder." She glances at Matt's dwindling form and sighs. "We're both a little out of our minds. Just tell me you'll think about it? Maybe try reaching out to her again?"

She looks so heartbroken, I can't help but nod. "I'll try."

"Thank you." She smiles softly before following Matt.

By the time my leaden feet reach the foyer, their car is headed down the driveway.

I drop my forehead to the door and breathe.

Just breathe.

wilder

Late afternoon, my doorbell rings again. This time I rush toward it and throw it open. "About fucking time."

"Language," chirps Lily.

Rolling my eyes, I step back. "Give me a break, she's not even two."

Lily strolls past me, Rye following with my goddaughter. After closing the door behind them, I hold out my arms. Rye acquiesces to my silent demand and hands me Emma, who's already reaching for me.

Her tiny fingers immediately start tugging my hair as she chants, "Why-Why, Why-Why."

The first time Emma called me the nickname Evangeline used when she was a toddler, it felt like a knife in my gut. But exposure therapy is a thing for a reason.

After hearing it innumerable times, it's now one of my favorite sounds.

"Fair warning, she's cutting molars," Rye says as he pulls off his coat. "Prepare for drool."

"Oh yeah? Show me the goods, Ems." I tickle her belly and she giggles, mouth dropping open and showcasing her collection of tiny teeth and red gums. "Ouch. That looks like hard work."

Saliva dribbles from the corners of her mouth, a thick stream dripping off her chin to my bicep. "You're so gross," I coo at her, "but I still love you."

A silicone toy shaped like a giraffe appears between us. Emma grabs it and starts gnawing on the head like a rabid animal.

"You know, if you wanted to see the baby, you could have just said so. No vague, alarmist demands necessary." Lily's light tone is at odds with the frown on her delicate features.

I look from her to Rye, whose concerned expression finally registers. "Shit. Sorry. I didn't mean to worry you guys." I adjust my grip on Emma. "Matt and Sophie came to see me today."

Comprehension sweeps across their faces. They exchange a look before Rye sighs. "We were kind of afraid they would but didn't want to say anything in case nothing came of it."

"They were talking about Evangeline like she needs either an intervention or an exorcism. What the hell is going on?"

Another loaded glance passes between them.

"Can we at least sit down before hashing this out?" asks Lily. Without waiting for an answer, she sweeps past me toward the kitchen. "You're making us dinner, by the way. One of your fancy recipes, please and thank you."

Before Rye can walk away, I grab his arm. "Just give me a scale or something. How worried should I be?"

He grimaces. "Man, I wish it were that easy. A big part of the problem is we can't get close enough to her to find out. I have better odds surviving Lily's cooking than I do getting a call back from Eva."

"I heard that!" Lily hollers from the kitchen.

Rye and I share a smirk. As we walk down the hallway, he continues in a low voice, "Do I think she's in an intervention-level crisis? No. Unless bad taste in men qualifies."

I open my mouth, then close it. Is that what Matt and Sophie were indirectly asking me to do? Break up Evangeline and her boyfriend? The idea is as wild as their assumption that I still have any effect on their daughter whatsoever.

On the other hand, the Sullivans aren't stupid. Matt

especially has been in the music industry for a long time, and he's definitely heard the rumors about his daughter's boyfriend.

Clay *fucking* Eaton.

Entertainment lawyer, media golden boy, and unequivocal dirtbag who groomed and seduced his sixteen-year-old stepsister when he was twenty-three. The latter isn't conjecture, either. His stepsister, Kendra, is my ex-girlfriend, and she told me everything.

I can't even think Clay's name without wanting to break his face. Even harder to accept? That I told Evangeline he was morally bankrupt and not only did she fall for his fake charm, she's been with him for *two years*. The reason I didn't tell her about his fucked-up relationship with Kendra was because at the time, I hadn't wanted to give her nightmares. Now I wish I had.

The only reasonable—and gut-wrenching—conclusion I've come to is Evangeline must have decided that because I lied about my drug use, I lied about everything else, too.

All this time, I've clung to the silver lining that at least she had Lily and Rye. Only now I'm not sure she does.

The remainder of the walk to the kitchen is spent naming three things I can see, three things I can hear, and three things I can feel.

It barely takes the edge off.

Rounding the island, I hand a squirming Emma to her mom. Lily gives her a smooch on the head before swapping the teething toy for a sippy cup of milk. As Rye opens the fridge to hunt for his favorite Kombucha, I head to a couch and flop down to wait for them.

They eventually settle in the same spot Sophie and Matt occupied earlier. Emma curls into her mom, drinking lazily from her cup and blinking slowly. In spite of my tension, I smile.

"She's gonna pass out."

Lily nods, smiling softly as she smooths dark hair off Emma's forehead. Her mom's touch pushes her over the edge into dreamland. Rye extracts the sippy cup from small, twitching fingers and puts it on the coffee table, then turns his attention to me.

"All right, tell us what they said."

It doesn't take long to recount the conversation. When I'm finished, Lily blows out a heavy breath.

"That's kind of messed up." She looks down at Emma. "On the other hand, I can understand their desperation."

Rye studies my face, correctly interpreting my expression—namely, how close I am to losing my shit. "It's not fair that they put this on you. Eva is different, sure, but she hasn't been body-snatched or whatever. She's still the same person, just..." He shrugs.

"Meaner," mutters Lily.

Rye counters, "She's under constant scrutiny and pressure."

From the looks on their faces, it's obvious they've had this argument before. I've never been privy to it because of the unspoken rule that they don't talk about Evangeline in front of me. I've also never pried, respecting their choice and, frankly, my own mental health. Plus, I've always assumed the rule came from Eva herself.

Lily's dark eyes throw sparks. "And I'm not under scrutiny or pressure? Really?"

"Babe, that's not—"

She cuts him off. "Last time I checked, there are two members in Glow, but only one of us is making huge decisions about the future without speaking to the other."

I frown. "What does that mean?"

Rye winces. "The Indigo contract expired a few months ago and Eva turned down a new one. Lily found out after the fact. It's been kept on the down-low so far."

My eyes widen. "What the hell?"

Lily's laugh is humorless. "My thoughts exactly. After

everything Indigo has done for us? I got my hands on the new contract they offered, too. She turned down an obscene amount of money, not to mention ownership of all masters and publishing rights. It makes zero sense. And you know what she said when I confronted her? That I was being small-minded. She basically called me an idiot."

"I don't think—" Rye starts.

"Stop defending her! You weren't there."

Emma stirs with a mewl of protest. Lily visibly struggles, then relaxes with a dejected shake of her head, whispering, "It was horrible."

Rye's expression falls. I look away as he wraps an arm around her. "I'm sorry. You're absolutely right. It's not okay that she went to the meeting without you or said that to you. None of this is okay."

Lily sniffs and whispers, "Thank you," then returns her focus to me. "Obviously I'm not done being angry with her. I've also started to consider this might be the end of Glow."

More shock reverberates through me. "Seriously?"

She shrugs. "Our tour at the beginning of the year was challenging, to say the least. If Rye hadn't been able to come with Emma, I don't know how I would've managed. Our parents are getting older, too, and we want more kids. It would be nice to focus on family for more than a few months at a time, you know? Maybe even finally plan a wedding."

She and Rye share a wistful smile before she continues, "If Eva does want to call it quits, I'd be fine with it. I just wish she'd come out and say it instead of giving me some avoidant bullshit about 'waiting and seeing' and 'weighing our options.'"

Rye's tight expression tells me he heard the same undercurrent in her voice I did: denial. Lily wouldn't be fine with saying goodbye to Glow forever any more than I'd be fine with never playing guitar again.

What she wants is what many artists our age—or really, people in general—want. The best of both worlds. Family and career. And she could have it, no question. While smaller artists might suffer financially from touring less or putting out fewer albums, Glow has reached a level of success very few do. Night Theory included.

Eva and Lily have done exactly what journalist Alex Illoka first predicted. What *I* predicted. Worldwide superstardom and a fanbase of millions that grows daily —check. Over two hundred industry awards, including twelve Grammys—check. Thousands of young artists emulating them—check.

All before either of them turned thirty.

My head swimming, I ask, "Do you think she wants to go solo?"

Lily smiles weakly. "If you'd asked me that two years ago, I would have said not a chance in hell."

"What's so significant about two years ago?" As the last word leaves my mouth, realization strikes. "You think *Clay* is behind this?"

"It wouldn't surprise me. He's obsessed with her fame and what it can do for him. I've never liked him, and he's never liked me. It's not a huge stretch to imagine him pushing her to break ties."

The notion of anyone, but especially *him*, having that much influence on Evangeline nauseates me.

"Does... does she love him?" I ask hoarsely.

Rye looks ten types of uncomfortable as he shrugs. "She says she does."

Lily scoffs. "Yeah, in the same tone you use when you tell my parents I'm a great cook." Her fierce gaze moves to me. "I realize we've had a *don't ask don't tell* policy about this for years, but I'm officially over it. What happened between you guys messed her up big time."

"I know," I whisper.

Her head tilts. "Do you? Do you know that while you went to rehab, did all that therapy and figured your shit out, she was sitting awake in a dark closet all night, every night?"

Dizziness hits me as blood drains from my head. A familiar prickle rolls down my spine. Imaginary fists squeeze my lungs.

Rye shifts. "Lily, maybe—"

"It's okay," I say, sucking in a deep breath. "I'm ready to hear it."

Lily's eyes soften. "You know I love you, Wilder. I'm so glad you're sober, and you're the best godfather Emma could have. But you also broke my best friend, and a part of me will never forgive you for that."

Sharp pain slices through my chest. Rye shifts in his seat, giving me a pained look.

"You think this is my fault," I murmur.

"God, no!" She sighs noisily. "I'm sorry. I don't mean it that way. What I'm trying to say is I don't think Eva dealt with what happened between you guys. At least not in a healthy way. She pulled it together, sure. Glow was obviously a great distraction. From the outside, it looked like she'd transferred all her pain into an album and was fine. Great, even. Right?"

My tongue too thick for words, I nod.

"I thought the same." She gives me a sad smile. "Like the rest of the world, I bought the act she put on. I was convinced she'd tell me if she wasn't okay. If I'd paid more attention or asked more questions, maybe—"

"Don't do that to yourself," I interject. "Even if you'd known the right questions to ask, there was no guarantee she'd answer."

Rye cups her shoulder. "He's right. She's always been that way, always hated showing weakness. Or whatever she perceives as weakness, I should say."

My heart squeezes. "Remember the eyepatch?" I ask, and Rye laughs shortly. I tell Lily, "When Evangeline was five, she made an eyepatch out of cardboard and yarn for her gray eye."

Rye grins at the memory. "She used black and green crayons to draw an eye on the cardboard, but it was all misshapen and freaky-looking. I ran away screaming when I saw it."

I crack a smile. "You were a wuss."

"I was four, asshole."

We chuckle.

Lily sighs. "Is the point of this story coming anytime soon?"

The moment's reprieve passes, heaviness sliding back into my chest. "Sophie called my mom freaking out because Evangeline wouldn't tell her why she wanted an eyepatch. She asked for the number of the child therapist I was seeing."

Lily's jaw drops, and I wave dismissively. "Yeah, I was already a mess at seven. Anyway, that weekend I cornered Evangeline and got the truth out of her. Some kid at school had called her a freak and hurt her feelings. I made up a story about how her gray iris meant she was related to fairies. It worked and she took off the eyepatch. But the point is, she's always locked down her emotions. Compartmentalized them."

"That's when you started calling her Fairy," she surmises.

I swallow the sudden knot in my throat. "Yeah."

A loaded silence falls, broken only by the soft, rhythmic whistles of Emma's deep breathing.

Rye's stare narrows thoughtfully on me. "Except with you."

Lily looks between us, frowning. "What?"

He turns to her. "Eva has always locked down her feelings around everyone *except Wilder*. Think about it. In all the years you've known her, has she ever really lost it in front of you? Like full-blown emotional meltdown?"

Lily sucks in a breath, glancing at me. She doesn't have to say anything. I know exactly what day she's thinking about.

I'd relapsed the night before and hid it as best I could from Evangeline. But she still knew instinctively that something was wrong. The next afternoon, I walked into her house full of shame and crippling fear. Lily was there. Evangeline had been crying, her eyes swollen and bloodshot.

After Lily left, she told me she was afraid of the dark, both tangibly and metaphorically. That when I'd shut her out the night before, I'd felt like a darkness she couldn't find her way out of.

I was too desperate to keep her to tell her she was right. I *was* the dark, and I was swallowing us both.

Memories and regrets clatter inside me. Fighting for calm, I look up at the knot on the ceiling beam. The afternoon shadows make it look like an eye. I squint, and it seems to wink at me.

Inhale—two, three, four.

Exhale—two, three, four.

I repeat the exercise until my body lets go of the fight-or-flight response. Until my heart stops racing. Until my disjointed thoughts blend and finally ring with a single, harmonious note.

Everyone close to me knows I don't carry a mere torch for Evangeline.

My entire soul burns for her.

Like I told her when we were kids: everything else, *everyone else*, will always be background noise. At least for me.

I've kept my distance for over six years out of respect

for the very clear boundary she set when I came home from treatment. It was the only form of amends she'd accept. But something else is equally true: my distance was dependent on the conviction she was okay. Healthy and happy. That not only did she not want me, she didn't *need* me.

After today, that conviction is smoke.

I lower my gaze from the ceiling. "If you tell me where Evangeline will be on New Year's, I'll teach you how to make the best Nikujaga your parents will ever taste."

Lily blinks in surprise, then smiles. "Deal."

CHAPTER THREE

evangeline

Your love was overrated

Way too complicated

A trap to force compliance

Numb all of my defiance

Now that I've seen through you

You can take your pretty words

Stuff them in your throat

And choke

Lying on my side in bed, I watch the digital clock on the nightstand creep slowly toward 4:00 a.m. Outside of its muted blue glow, the bedroom is swathed in velvety black. The dense, textured heaviness would have terrified me years ago, but now it's as familiar as the keys of a piano.

As I gaze into the dark, I think about that famous Nietzsche quote. How if you stare long enough into the abyss, the abyss stares back at you. Reaches out and touches you.

Perhaps he's right, and in some obscure way, I've become what I fear.

I can't find the energy to care.

3:36 a.m.

With twenty-four minutes before I can get out of bed without garnering suspicion, I roll over. Clay lies in his usual position facing away from me. I stare at the slope of his shoulder under the coverlet, tracking its rhythmic rise and fall.

The three feet between us might as well be a thousand. We only traverse the space during sex, something that's become an increasingly rare activity over the last six months.

I may be perpetually sleep-deprived, but I'm not blind. More than our sex life has changed since we moved in together. Outside of weekly date nights—always in public with the pressure of paparazzi watching us—we don't spend time together like we used to. No more casual nights just the two of us, chatting and laughing and enjoying each other's company.

I thought living in the same city, the same house, would bring us closer. But the opposite has happened. He works late most evenings. When he does come home at a decent hour, after dinner, he disappears into his office or our home gym. In the last month especially, the time we do spend together is set to a soundtrack of his passive-aggressive disappointment and my apathetic avoidance.

I know I should care more. Feel something... *bigger*. About him. About my life and its current trajectory. But I'm insulated underwater, dark and cold. Everything around me is slightly distorted, colors and sounds muted.

I roll over to face the clock.

3:45 a.m.

Fifteen more minutes until I can make coffee and sneak out to the pool house where I've hidden caramel creamer in the mini-fridge. Two hours until I have to choke down egg whites and toast with a smear of avocado. Four hours until—

Sheets rustle, the sound jarring in my silence-attuned ears. I wait for Clay to settle again, but instead, the mattress behind me dips with his weight. I suck in a startled breath as his arm slides over my waist. He draws my back against his front and kisses my shoulder.

"I know you're awake," he whispers. "I could hear you thinking in my dreams."

There's a smile in his voice.

I relax against him, my worry dispersing. He's not going to leave me, and I have no reason to leave him. Besides, no relationship is perfect. Intimacy ebbs and flows over the years. What we have is reliable, and that's what matters.

Deft fingers slide down my stomach and lift the hem of my nightgown. "How about an early New Year's gift?" he murmurs.

In reply, I cover his hand with mine and guide it between my legs. His touch doesn't incite overwhelming need, but that's okay. Passion isn't all that important in the scheme of things.

I can pretend.

The little lies don't matter, anyway.

♪

WHEN I STEP out of the shower an hour later, Clay is shaving at the bathroom sink. His lean torso is on display, tanned and toned. Hazel eyes track me as I towel dry.

"The stylist should be here around two so we can pick out your dress for tonight." His gaze lowers to the sink as he rinses his razor. "Hair and makeup start at four, and the car will be here at seven. Drink lots of water today, and make sure you take a nap this morning. Ten to twelve would be a good time for it. I have to do a little work, but we'll have lunch together at twelve-fifteen."

I make a sound of agreement, then trade my towel for a robe and move to the second sink to brush my teeth. As I squeeze toothpaste onto the brush, I wait for a reminder to floss. When it doesn't come—he's distracted rinsing his face with cold water—I'm almost disappointed. Not because I actually enjoy his micro-managing, though most days it doesn't bother me. Sometimes it's even a game. *If I do this, or don't do that, what will he say?*

Lily hates that Clay is so controlling. I understand her concern, I really do. It makes perfect sense why she and Rye don't like him. What they can't see, can't possibly understand, is the lure for me. The relief I feel being taken care of—and the necessity of it.

When I ran into Clay at an awards show afterparty two years ago, I was floundering. Flickering like a dying light. Eminently close to giving up on... everything.

He saved me from myself.

I spit out toothpaste, making sure to rinse all the froth from the porcelain, then use a hand towel to wipe droplets of water from the surrounding countertop. Clay snorts and shakes his head. He thinks it's a waste of time to clean up after myself when we have a housekeeper who comes daily. But he's used to it now and doesn't bother saying anything.

As I start my skincare routine, he dries his face and tosses the towel on the floor. Pausing behind me, he lifts a tendril of my wet hair and rubs the strands between his fingers.

"Did you use that new hair mask I got you?" he asks, smiling when I nod. "Thought so. Feels silky."

With a pat on my ass, he leaves the bathroom.

I wait until I hear him exit the bedroom, then grab his towel off the floor and clean the mess he left in and around his sink.

evangeline

I've spent a lot of time in Los Angeles over the years —it's an inescapable leviathan of the music industry—but living here has made me lose appreciation for the climate everyone else loves.

Case in point, it's New Year's Eve and a balmy sixty-four degrees. I don't even need a coat. Which, given the minuscule dress I'm wearing, is unfortunate. It's also deeply unsettling, like my body knows something is wrong. I felt the same way waking up on Christmas morning and eating breakfast outside in the warm sunshine.

Clay says it will take time for me to adjust. Maybe he's right. But while the barely changing weather disturbs me, I doubt I'll ever get used to the migraine-inducing smog and constant traffic, or the fact there's more dirty cement here than trees or actual dirt. Or the dreaded Celebrity Tax, a joking term that really isn't funny.

While the price of celebrity certainly isn't unique to L.A., in my experience, it's more acute and constant here than in Seattle, Austin, or even New York. Anonymity is next to impossible thanks to the weather and further exacerbated by the city's culture of exploitation. Not only does the public have the right to stalk, dissect, criticize, and confront me every time I leave the house, but I'm supposed to be immune to it or at the least, never complain.

Even among those who experience the same daily pressures I do, there's no respite. Every conversation is inherently dangerous. Laden with hidden agendas and context.

Like the one I'm having right now.

Poppy Cole is a twenty-year-old pop star. Blonde hair. Piercing blue eyes. Unquestionably beautiful. Our fanbases have minimal overlap, so her barely veiled animosity makes no sense. I've literally never exchanged words with her before tonight.

"My stylist showed me that dress as an option for tonight," she says, her heavily made-up eyes flickering down my body. Her smile is fixed and completely fake.

Maybe it's the dry winds blowing across the crowded

outdoor patio and irritating my eyes, or the uncomfortable heels Clay insisted I wear, but I can't summon the polite pretense required for this game. The one where I pretend we're hitting it off for the sake of appearances.

Another thing I've learned about L.A., or at least Hollywood: it's high school all over again. Cliques and social climbing and nonstop cattiness.

Poppy's eyes glitter with annoyance, probably because I'm not rising to her bait but merely staring back at her.

She makes a second attempt. "I'm glad I didn't wear it."

I take a small sip of champagne and say mildly, "It's definitely not a style that suits everyone."

When her smile freezes, I suffer immediate guilt. Fame in this city is a designer toxin for young, ambitious women. I was spared the worst of it living like a recluse in the Pacific Northwest, but apparently the smog is slowly sucking out my kindness.

I open my mouth to apologize in the usual way, by complimenting her dress, but she speaks first.

"We should do lunch sometime. I'll introduce you to my esthetician. She's amazing at..." She twirls a fingertip around her face, eyes radiating false sympathy.

Ah, age-shaming. Nice.

"Oh, look! It's Olivia. I have to say hello. So great

chatting with you, Eva. Call me!" She gives me a little wave and sashays away.

I don't bother saying goodbye.

Around me, forty or so people mingle or lounge on stark-white furniture in the cement backyard of an ultra-modern Hollywood Hills mansion. I hear Clay's laughter and track the sound to a nearby group of men. The tableau could be the intro to a joke: a lawyer, a judge, and an actor walk into a bar...

Clay glances at me, the skin around his eyes pinching when he sees I'm alone. I instantly hear his voice in my head reminding me of the importance of networking.

I paste a pleasant smile on my face, then wish I hadn't when the stretch of my facial muscles activates an urge to yawn. My scheduled nap today was a bust, and even the IV drip of vitamins, antioxidants, and electrolytes I had after lunch failed to dent my fatigue. Gritting my teeth, I overcome the reflex and look around for a friendly face. Or at least a familiar one.

What I really want is to ask Clay if we can go home. Ring in the new year on the couch in our pajamas. But I know better. He isn't a homebody like me—this is his happy place. Asking him to leave would not only ruin his night, it would worsen his growing concerns about my sleep. Or rather, my lack of it.

If I don't get a handle on my insomnia soon, I'm afraid history will repeat itself. I'll be given a choice between a stint at a private clinic or sleeping pills at home that give me nightmares and make me feel like a zombie all day.

Tension tightens my shoulders as I glance at Clay again. He's still watching me, body language projecting an intent to excuse himself and come over. If he does, I'll be stuck to his side the rest of the night, guided from group to group until my head spins.

I look around again, a bit more desperately, and sigh with relief when I spot a familiar man sitting on a couch on the other side of the patio. Maybe I *do* have one friend in this city. Seizing the opportunity, I walk toward him. If it weren't for the icepicks on my feet, I might even run.

Even surrounded by fashion-obsessed partygoers, Martin Page stands out. He wears a shimmery silver vest with no undershirt, the pale color highlighting his warm brown skin and trim physique. Snug, matching pants with fringe down the sides and white cowboy boots complete his ensemble. On anyone else, the look could easily be kitschy, but on Martin it's effortless high fashion. I'm probably the only one here who knows he likely found the outfit at one of his favorite resale shops.

When he spies me approaching, a smile overtakes

his face. "Eva!" He shoves at the man next to him, who gives him an annoyed look but scoots down to make room for me.

After depositing my half-full glass of champagne on the table, I sit carefully, keeping my legs sealed so I don't flash the party. Bending as much as the restrictive dress will allow, I rub at my ankle where a tiny strap has cut into my skin. When the sting only gets worse, I give up and lean against Martin's shoulder.

I whisper, "You hate my dress, don't you?"

"It's hideous," he whispers back.

I laugh over an abrupt urge to cry. "I miss you."

He drops his head against mine. "Same."

Martin was the up-and-coming stylist who took Lily and me under his wing six years ago. The instincts of our publicist, Anita, were right when she surmised we'd be perfect for each other. Over the following years, Martin became more than a friend. He was family.

My heart still aches at the memory of the day last year when he tearfully informed us he needed to part ways. Lily and I were blindsided, heartbroken, and confused. Friendship aside, our professional relation-ship had always been mutually beneficial. After dressing us for our first Grammys, Martin became one of the most sought-after stylists on the West Coast, and since then his name has been synonymous with edgy elegance. Until last year, his name was also synonymous with Glow.

But despite the lingering pain of his sudden departure and vague reasonings, there's no world in which I wouldn't be happy to see him.

"How are you?" he asks softly.

A lie sits on my tongue, but the truth leaps over it. "Tired."

Martin drops a hand to my knee and squeezes gently. "Come down to my place in Baja for a week. We'll drink margaritas and float in the pool all day. How about next month?"

I suck in a breath, my first instinct a resounding *yes*. But then I picture Clay's reaction and my chest deflates. There's no way he'd be okay with it, not with so much up in the air.

Before I can think of a way to say no, the man seated on the other side of Martin asks, "Is that who I think it is?"

Martin straightens and looks around. "Who? Is it Miley? Because if it's not Miley, I don't care."

"I can't believe it," someone else murmurs, while a woman on a nearby love seat slaps her friend's arm and says, "I knew tonight was going to be epic. Where's my phone?"

The energy of the party shifts fast, conversations

dying off or lowering to murmurs as more and more people turn to observe the newcomer. I still can't see them, my line of sight blocked.

Whoever they are, I'm both grateful for the distraction and feel sorry for them. I've been in their shoes more times than I can count. While fame can be thrilling, especially at first, eventually it gets old being treated like a product instead of a person.

Lost in my thoughts, I jerk in surprise when Martin swivels toward me. His eyes are wide, lips pursed in distress.

"Honey, you're not going to like this."

"Huh?"

Frowning, I glance over his shoulder right as a small group disperses, revealing the man standing near the back door of the house.

A fiery, pins-and-needles sensation crawls over every inch of my skin.

"What's he doing here?" I whisper.

Martin squeezes my burning fingers. "Not a clue."

It's been years since I've seen Wilder in such close proximity, my exposure intentionally limited to glimpses at fifty feet during award shows or the occasional, accidental sight of him on social media or in a magazine.

I want to look away, *need to*, but I can't. I can't even

blink. The sight of him has frozen every inch of me, skin to marrow.

Clearly his stance on conformity, and fashion in general, hasn't changed. He still dresses like he's twenty-five. I wish I could say the forever-casual look isn't attractive anymore, that it makes him appear immature or slovenly. But it doesn't. In a sea of sparkling silverfish, he stands out like a tiger shark. Unapologetically unpolished. Magnetic, sensual, and irreverent.

Worn jeans hug his lean hips and long legs above combat boots. A faded black T-shirt showcases the sculpted contours of his chest and arms, the latter's surface almost fully obscured by tattoos. Unruly dark waves frame his face, enhancing his striking features. I'm grateful I can't see his eyes—until I see the woman he's looking down at, who's suctioned to his arm like a frilly pink octopus.

Poppy.

My jaw grinds and a spark of pain erupts behind my right eye. Through a veil of static, I register snippets of conversations taking place around me.

"...even hotter in person."

"...definitely my hall pass."

"She doesn't look so good..."

"...clearly not over him."

"...you blame her? He's a god in flesh."

I finally drag my eyes from Wilder to see people staring at me. A *lot* of people, with expressions ranging from pity to pleasure.

"Let's go inside," Martin says urgently.

When I nod, he stands and pulls me to my feet, then guides me away from the couch. I barely feel the throbs of protest in my ankles. I'm a marionette, relying on his arm around my waist to keep me upright and moving. People scatter from our path as we make our way toward the house. Thankfully, there's another entrance closer to us, so we don't have to walk past *him*.

Then, like a different puppeteer takes control of my body, my head snaps to the left. From twenty feet away, dappled-forest eyes bore into mine.

I hate you.

And like he heard my silent scream, Wilder nods.

I know.

pre-chorus

pre-chorus : *the section of a song that builds anticipation for the chorus.*

CHAPTER FIVE
wilder

Ten reasons to forget you

Twenty lies that were true

A hundred ways out

A thousand through

Even if I could (really should)

Won't ever walk away from you

I scan the faces around me, ignoring the rising chatter and focus of L.A.'s rich and bored. Let them stare and gossip. I don't care about them.

Nor do I care about the woman who attached herself to me like we're old friends—the intimate kind—the moment I stepped outside. She's been chattering in my face for less than a minute and I've already stopped listening.

Talon-like nails pinch my bicep. "Did you hear me, Wilder?" she asks with a little laugh. A laugh that says, *Of course you did because you can't possibly be ignoring me.*

I pause my search for Evangeline and frown down at her. Her face is familiar, but I don't know her name because she didn't bother telling me. Like she can't imagine a world where every man she meets hasn't jerked off to her photograph.

"You have such pretty eyes," she says breathily.

I extract my arm. "Thanks. What did you ask me?"

She arches her back, trying to draw my attention to her breasts. I keep my eyes on her face.

"I asked if you wanted to get out of here," she says with a sultry smile. "Celebrate New Year's our own way."

I'm almost, *almost* impressed by her nerve.

"No, thanks."

Her shocked expression makes me want to laugh. It also makes me want to buy her six months of therapy. In lieu of suggesting she consider how propositioning a stranger might not be healthy, I go back to ignoring her.

She doesn't like that, her breasts pushing against my arm. "Fine by me. We can just find a bedroom here."

Now I'm annoyed. I open my mouth to tell her to get lost, but no words come. Because in that moment, my roaming gaze finds Evangeline's profile, downturned as she walks toward the house on the other side of the patio. Martin Page is with her, his arm around her waist. He's staring at me, dark eyes glimmering like he's trying to telepathically communicate. My brows lift in question, and he shakes his head.

Utterly confused, my gaze falls to Evangeline. The second it lands on her, her head jerks up and turns. Mismatched eyes lock unerringly on mine.

My breath stills.

My heart seizes.

It's the first time in over six years she's looked directly at me and nothing has changed.

She hates me.

I swallow. Nod in acknowledgment. She and Martin disappear into the house.

♩

WHEN LILY and Rye asked me what my plan was for tonight, I told them I didn't have one beyond seeing Evangeline for myself, maybe observing her for a minute before bailing. It was true—*was* being the operative word.

Now that I've seen her, I'm incapable of walking away.

Even harder to swallow than her gaunt cheeks and the almost brittle way she moved was seeing the absence of what always made her *her*. That intangible aura that ensured she was the center of every room even when she was hiding in a corner.

She didn't look like someone at the peak of professional success, whose lifelong dreams have come to fruition.

She looked empty.

The only thing familiar about her were her two-toned eyes and the loathing in them. In every other way, she barely resembles the girl I grew up with. The woman I loved, whose heart I irreparably broke.

I wander the party in a daze, waiting for Evangeline to come back outside or for an ability to leave to manifest. People talk to me. I talk back. Smile and nod and fulfill the demands of small talk.

"What brings you to L.A.?"

"Just escaping the rain for a minute and visiting some friends."

"Did Night Theory break up?"

"Don't believe everything you read. We'll be back in the studio soon."

All the while, I fight the instinct to find Evangeline.

When I reach my absolute limit of socializing, my smile a grimace and my ears buzzing faintly, I retreat to the shadows at the edge of the patio where a waist-high fence separates the home's backyard from a terraced hillside. In the distance, downtown L.A. shines like a gold-dusted circuit board.

I look up at the sky, clear but disturbingly starless, like even the air here holds dreams just outside of reach.

She doesn't belong here.

"Wilder?" asks a tentative male voice. "Can I talk to you for a minute?"

I turn, a polite refusal ready, but choke the words back when I see who it is. "Sure."

Martin Page approaches the fence a few feet away from me. He doesn't say anything right away, just stares outward much as I'd been doing. Tucking my hands in my pockets, I wait, braced for him to tell me off on Eva's behalf.

"I don't know if you remember me, but we've met in passing a few times."

The thread of nervousness in his tone makes me blink and swiftly reassess. "I remember you, Martin. Good to see you."

His head turns, eyes scanning mine, and he gives a little laugh. "It's so weird. I feel like I know you, but this is the first time we've had a conversation."

For a second, I think he means Evangeline talked about me over the years, but then he continues, "When my little sister was first getting clean, about three years ago, I went with her as support to a sobriety convention in Seattle. You were one of the main speakers."

All I can manage is a weak, "Ah."

I remember that convention well. How I'd wanted to refuse the invitation, but my sponsor convinced me—or rather, bullied me—into doing the forty-five-minute talk. I'd been nervous as hell leading up to it, the task of sharing my story with a ballroom full of recovering addicts seeming infinitely harder than performing for thousands.

In some ways, it had been. But there's also nothing quite like having hundreds of people from all walks of life nodding and laughing in solidarity as you talk about the most fucked-up time of your life. More than any therapy or one-on-one conversation, the experience convinced me that I'm not alone—or even remotely unique—in my struggles with addiction. And there's massive relief in knowing that.

Afterward, I was glad I'd done it, but I've also never accepted another invitation to speak at a large event. As much as I've grown to appreciate the sense of belonging I feel when I'm with other sober people, I'm still not much for group activities or crowds. Without a guitar in my hands, that is.

"I didn't mean to make you uncomfortable," Martin

says. "I know it's all anonymous for a reason. I swear I've never told anyone about seeing you or shared what you talked about."

I smile wryly. "It's all good. My sobriety is an open secret, anyway. But I do appreciate the discretion. How's your sister doing?"

His face lights up. "Amazing. Still clean."

"I'm glad to hear it."

Martin glances toward the house. "So, uh, there's another reason I wanted to talk to you."

My pulse kicks inside my throat. "You want to dress me, don't you?"

His laugh is a tad shrill. "Talk about a dream come true. But no—I can't because... well, you know."

I nod slowly. "Because of Eva."

He gives a wincing smile and a nod. "She's actually who I wanted to talk about. I realize this is insanely presumptuous, so feel free to tell me to fuck off."

"Not gonna do that," I murmur.

Whatever he sees on my face seems to encourage him, but then his gaze darts anxiously toward the house again. It belatedly occurs to me that he's worried we'll be seen together, that it will get back to her.

Where we're standing is pretty dark and a good fifteen feet from the closest person. It's also past eleven and from the increasing sounds of revelry, everyone's pretty trashed. But I still shift a few steps back until Martin's shorter, slighter frame is blocked by mine.

When he realizes what I've done, he looks embarrassed but also relieved. "Thanks. If she finds out I'm talking to you, she'll never speak to me again."

I should be used to hearing confirmations of her continued enmity, but I'm not. Every one is a fresh blow to my chest.

Before I can think better of it, I ask, "She still hates me that much, huh?"

"I don't think it's you she hates," he says with a sigh.

My brow furrows. "What does that mean?"

Martin shakes his head like he either doesn't have an answer or can't tell me. He clears his throat. "I stashed her in a bedroom and told her I'd look for Clay. But I don't see him. Do you?"

Confusion deepening my frown, I turn and scan the throngs of people. I haven't seen Clay at all tonight. While wandering the party, I was half-expecting him to appear and try to get me to leave. I can't say I'm not glad I've avoided him so far, but...

My gaze snaps back to Martin. "What are you getting at?"

His jaw firms. After a few seconds of internal struggle, he says tensely, "He went inside before you got here.

I didn't see him in the house, which means he's probably in a different bedroom."

"What—" I start, then stop as the words click. Rage unfurls under my skin. "He's cheating on her at a party they're attending *together*?"

Martin gives an agitated shrug. "Even if he isn't, he's still the piece of shit who threatened to end my career if I didn't quit working for Glow. More to the point, he's a toxic asshole who doesn't deserve Eva."

Reeling, I open and close my mouth a few times before managing to speak. "Does Eva know? About him threatening you?"

Martin shakes his head. I'm somewhat relieved until he says, "I've been where she is—with a partner like him —and knew there was no point in telling her. That's not to say I didn't try early on to get her to dump his ass. The red flags were waving from the beginning, if you know what I mean."

Cold snakes down my spine. "I don't, actually."

His eyes probe mine. "Do you still care about her the same way you did when you gave that talk?"

"Yes," I say without hesitation.

His sad smile makes me think he can see the fractured heart beating in my chest. "I figured when I saw the way you looked at her tonight. You've got the whole broody, pining thing down pat."

I huff a humorless laugh, and his gaze shifts to the lights of downtown.

"I'm ashamed to say it took me a while to see what was happening. Clay is really good at camouflaging control as care. Better than my ex, that's for sure. But after months of perfect behavior, he started slipping up when I was in the room. Making comments about her diet, clothing, who she was spending time with."

"What the fuck," I whisper, but Martin doesn't seem to hear me, his gaze turned inward.

"Eva started second-guessing herself over the littlest things. Withdrawing from me, from Lily and Rye, and relying on Clay's opinion for everything." His haunted eyes find mine. "She doesn't see it because she can't. He spun his web around her so slowly she didn't notice, and now she's wrapped up tight. Dependent on him. I don't know what to do."

Mud replaces blood in my veins, making my heartbeat sluggish. I stare at the lights of downtown, wavering like a mirage—like my entire reality.

This is a lot fucking worse than I thought. Than Lily and Rye thought. And Sophie and Matt's distress suddenly makes a lot more sense.

"I just spoke to Lily and Rye a few days ago," I murmur. "They're not fans of Clay's, but they have no idea it's as bad as you say."

Martin hears my unspoken question. "When Clay came into the picture, Lily was about to pop out a baby. She was nesting and shit. I was around Eva a lot more." His mouth pinches with guilt. "When I saw them in Seattle last year, before I quit, everything seemed great. *Eva* seemed great. I convinced myself it was all in my head, that I was projecting my own trauma onto her. And I stupidly let it go, forgetting how good these motherfuckers are at playing the long game."

Dipping his chin, he makes a choked sound. "I didn't even know Eva moved down here until I read it online. She hasn't returned my calls for months. When I saw her tonight, I wanted to throw up. She looks unwell. There's no spark in her eyes. And that dress and those heels? Come on. My Eva would never. God, I don't know what to do." He covers his mouth, muffling a sob.

Bouncing thoughts coalesce into a roiling mass of fear. My scalp prickles in warning right before vertigo hits. I swing forward, bracing my hands on my knees.

Breathe in. Hold. Breathe out.

Miraculously, my panic stalls at a rolling boil instead of overflowing into a full-blown attack.

"Oh God, are you okay? Shit—I'm an idiot. I was already planning on calling Lily tomorrow, but then I saw you..." He makes a shrill, distressed sound.

"I'm okay," I grunt.

Martin pats my back. Hesitant, light taps like he's afraid I'll take a swing at him. The thought brings a burst of caustic hilarity, which in turn dials my anxiety down another notch.

Waving him off, I straighten my spine one vertebra at a time. When I'm upright, I dig my fingers into my hair, clenching them and concentrating on the slight burn until my mind clears.

"I'm really sorry, Wilder. I shouldn't have dumped all that on you. Especially since—"

"I'm fine. Just got dizzy."

He doesn't look convinced but thankfully doesn't continue his thought, which I'm sure was something along the lines of, *Especially since there's nothing you can do or say to help her because she can't even stand to look at you.*

My breath hitches in my still-tight chest. "I'm only here in the first place because you're not the only one worried about her. So I came to see for myself. What you've said is a lot to take in. What I *saw* is a lot..." I trail off, unable to put words to the tangled knot of guilt and worry inside me.

"Hey. This isn't your fault. You know that, right?"

I'm surprised for the few seconds it takes for me to remember he heard me speak at the convention. I might not have said Evangeline's name, but I shared candidly about the guilt I carry—will always carry—for hurting the girlfriend I loved deeply. And like my sobriety, Evangeline's and my shared history is an open secret.

I look away from the knowing glint in his eyes.

"Left down the main hallway. Second door on the right." Martin's voice is low, vibrating with sudden fervor. "I left her wrapped in a blanket on the bed and half-asleep. I'll run interference if I see Clay."

My head whips toward him. His brows lift expectantly, an unmistakable challenge in his eyes.

I bark a disbelieving laugh. "Are you for real? She literally fled when she saw me. Better that I bring what you've said to her parents, to Lily and Rye, and they—"

"Maybe you're right," he interjects, his expression torn between worry and conviction. "But can you really leave without trying?"

I huff and drag a hand through my hair again, no doubt making it even more chaotic than usual. "Think you know me, huh?"

His lips twitch. "Pretty much."

I look at the house, at the door leading inside.

To her.

"Fuck it."

As I stride away, Martin calls, "Thatta boy!"

I flip him off over my shoulder, his startled laugh swallowed by voices as I part the crowd with my steps.

evangeline

Curling further into an unfamiliar blanket on a stranger's bed, I bring my fists against my breastbone and press toward the ache beneath.

I don't actually hate Wilder.

I wish I could.

Maybe if he were still a drug addict, leaving the wreckage of his selfishness scattered in his wake, it would be easier. But since I'd never wish a relapse on him, I'm left instead in the itching intersection between a grudge I can't let go of and a maudlin longing that time has reshaped but not erased.

At least the years have granted me *some* clarity. Enough that I know it's not him I miss so much as the person I was before I fell in love with him. Seeing him just reminds me of that loss.

But as with everything tied to Wilder, even my clarity on the matter isn't simple. It has depth and weight. A history full of tangled shadows and glimmers of inescapable light.

No matter how much I might want to at times, I can't pull up the roots he planted inside me when we were young. They're too deep. He'll always be the boy I worshipped as a child. The teenager who read my poetry, picked up a guitar, and changed the course of our lives. The unique, complex man who opened my world with equal parts conflict and communion.

He'll always be a part of me.

I can't *not* be happy he got the help he needed and turned his life around. That his career took off and his music has garnered both success and acclaim. That he's sober, stable, and by all accounts thriving.

But feeling happy for him from afar, buffered by the life I've built for myself, is one thing. Being close enough to see the freckles in his eyes is, as tonight proved, drastically different.

It took years for the high, piercing note of my heartbreak to fade. For me to let go of Wilder, of who I thought I was to him—who I thought we were to each other—and move forward with my life.

But I did. I fucking did.

Didn't I?

My erratic thoughts clash and reform, providing a new, unwelcome dimension to my acceptance that Wilder will always be a part of me. Because if that's true, then parts of *me* were displaced as he grew. I'll never be able to heal the gaping cavities his roots dug inside me.

He'll always be my weakness.

My forever wound.

A small, pained moan shocks my ears. My gaze flies around the room for a good five seconds before I realize the sound came from me. When I do, I make another one—a hoarse laugh.

I'm officially losing it.

I have no idea how long it's been since Martin left to find Clay. There are no clocks in the room and my phone was left at home. Is it close to midnight yet? Why hasn't Clay come?

Please get me out of here.

Despite my desperate desire, when I finally hear the soft creak of the doorknob, it's not relief I feel but panic at the thought of Clay seeing me like this. Heady adrenaline shoots through my veins. I wrench upright, throwing my legs off the bed and tossing the blanket to the side.

My stomach swoops as the door swings inward, then drops like a lead weight when it isn't Clay who steps inside but a stranger paradoxically more familiar than my own reflection.

Wilder gives me a slight, close-lipped smile and shuts the door behind him. "Hey."

Speechless, I watch him sidestep a few paces before sliding to the floor. He braces his arms on his bent knees, drops his head back to the wall, and closes his eyes. The thick tendons in his forearms jump beneath black-and-gray tattoos as his long, elegant fingers move restlessly, playing a song only he hears.

Less than five feet of carpeted floor separate our toes.

"I fucking hate parties," he mutters.

I blink hard, half-expecting him to disappear, but instead he becomes more real. *Excruciatingly so.* Airbrushed memories of him collide with reality and tear something deep in my chest.

At twenty-five, he was almost ethereally beautiful. Now he's... devastating. Somehow both rougher and more refined. Potently masculine, mature, and *healthy.* Smile lines crease the skin around his eyes, the shadows of his dimples now permanent fixtures, the slope of his clean-shaven jaw even sharper. His body has changed, too, still lean but more densely muscled, his light olive skin radiant.

Movement brings my gaze to his throat. As he

swallows, the wings of a gorgeously detailed moth ripple in mimicry of flight. He shifts against the wall, sighing, and a hint of his midnight-rainstorm scent reaches me. Seductive and threatening. A siren's haunting call.

I want to light him on fire.

I want to suck him in like water and drown.

He's thirty-one years old.

It's unbelievable, suddenly. So wild a notion that I choke on the urge to giggle, the pressure of holding it in nearly unbearable.

"W-what are you doing?" I finally ask. My voice is ragged. Breathy and dismayed.

Dark lashes parting, his gaze lowers to my face. His expression is inscrutable, but there's a glimmer in his eyes. One that sends more adrenaline into my system.

"Taking a break from all the drunk, annoying people outside. What are *you* doing?"

The casual familiarity in his voice pulls the plug on my thoughts. They pour away in a torrent, leaving a buzzing silence behind.

Wilder's lips curve to one side, deepening the adjacent dimple. "Better close your mouth before you catch a fly." His eyes flicker down. "Legs, too."

I snap my knees together, simultaneously grabbing the discarded blanket and bringing it over my lap.

Embarrassment sears my face and chest—another shock, nearly nauseating in its intensity.

I can't remember the last time I blushed.

"Get out," I whisper.

Head tilting, he cups a hand behind his ear. "What was that?"

My teeth clench. "Get. Out."

He stretches his legs, crossing them at the ankle, and folds his arms over his chest. "Nah, I'm good here." He smiles slightly. "How's life these days?"

I can't speak.

Can't think.

Air rasps in and out of my lungs. My arms tremble uncontrollably.

"Did you know Emma is cutting molars?" he continues, eyebrows arched inquisitively like I'm not having a fucking aneurism five feet away. "She's the coolest. I still can't believe she calls me Why-Why. Such a trip."

My breath stills. "She does?"

"Yeah." His eyes turn so soft and warm, I have to look away. "Gotta say, though, I kind of miss her calling me Poop."

A strangled sound leaves me. "Poop?"

He hums in confirmation. "No idea how that one started." I arch a brow and he chuckles. "Fine, there was an incident. I might have had an adverse reaction that

Emma thought was hilarious. In my defense, it was my first experience with explosive baby diarrhea."

I grimace. "Gross."

"The grossest. But at least she decided on calling me Poop instead of picking one of the other words I used in the moment. Lily would have freaked if she started calling me Fuck."

I bite my cheek. "She's definitely militant about the no-profanity rule."

At the thought of Lily, my flash of humor dies. My relationship with her, Rye, and Emma has changed over the last year, most drastically in the last six months. I want so badly to fix what's broken, but I don't know how. Not without making a sacrifice I'm not sure I'll survive.

Wilder's stare is heavy and probing. I look down to hide my expression, but it's too late.

"You don't belong here. This city is a vampire sucking you dry. Come home."

Anger roars through me, the welcome firestorm burning away my melancholy. "You have no idea where I belong. You think you have the right to say that? Why? Because I followed you around as a kid or because we fucked for a few weeks a million years ago? Get over yourself, Wilder. You're a footnote in my life."

His jaw hardens, arms falling to his sides as he sits up and leans forward. For a moment, I think he's going to spew equal vitriol back at me. I *want* him to—want him to say something as awful as what just came out of my mouth so I don't have to acknowledge the stinging precursor of guilt. So I can hate him again, if only for a moment.

What he says instead, in a dangerously soft voice, is worse.

"Lie to yourself all you want. I'll *always* know you. You're inside me forever, just like I'm inside you. And you belong where you always have, with your feet in the dirt between water and giant trees, moonlight shining in your hair."

The absurd words shatter like glass inside me. Tiny, bleeding wounds open all over my heart.

My belated scoff sounds alarmingly close to a sob. "I don't know what your angle is, but let's get one thing straight—you're deluded if you think I'll ever fall into your bed again."

He laughs.

The motherfucker *laughs.*

Then he stands up, stretching his arms over his head and bending from side to side like we're in a goddamn yoga class. The hem of his T-shirt rides up, exposing a few inches of skin above his belt. I tear my eyes away, but not fast enough to prevent the sight from burning itself into my brain. Two sharp, shadowed valleys of muscle arrowing toward his groin. Tattoos I've never seen before. That trail of coarse, dark hair I wish I didn't remember the feel of grazing my belly.

When he stops flaunting his stupid, ripped body, I shift my glare back to his face. He wears a knowing smirk that makes me want to kick him in the nuts.

"You thought I was flirting with you?" *Tsking*, he shakes his head, eyes bright with laughter like the joke's on me. "You've never even seen me flirt. In any case, I think we can agree that ship has sailed."

My jaw drops.

His devilish grin widens. "It was good chatting with you. Happy New Year." He opens the door, then glances back at me. "See you around, Evangeline."

He's gone before I can gasp my next breath.

evangeline

New Year's Day dawns bright and clear. Not unexpected. What *is* unexpected is the fact I missed dawn for the first time in months. I'd blame champagne for knocking me out, but I didn't even finish my first glass.

For the last half hour, I've been sitting at the glass-top table on our terrace, nursing my second cup of coffee and picking at half of a tart grapefruit. Neither has dented my grogginess.

The kidney-shaped pool we never use glitters in the sunlight, smaller reflections dancing off damp blades of grass beyond. For once, there's an actual bite in the air. Occasional currents of cold slide beneath my robe and coil around my bare legs.

I'm still too hot.

Fuzzy-headed and floaty.

A bird lifts from a nearby palm, its passage bringing a flash of memory. Inked wings moving on golden skin. A rough shake of my head sends the errant thought away.

Focusing on the pool, I fantasize about jumping in. The water can't be more than fifty degrees, and my Pilates instructor is always talking about cold plunging and how beneficial it is. Would it feel invigorating or terrible? More importantly, would it wake me up?

My musings are derailed by the crisp, measured clicks of designer men's shoes on tile. Smoothing my expression, I turn my head toward the house. Clay approaches me, his attention on the tablet in his hands. While I have yet to change out of my pajamas and robe, he's dressed in his typical winter casual wear: pressed slacks and a lightweight cashmere sweater.

A greeting dies on my tongue when he lifts his head, revealing the scowl on his face.

I should have jumped in the pool.

"I'll get dressed in a minute. Just finishing breakfast."

Without saying a word, he sets the tablet on the table beside my plate with its listing grapefruit husk. I blink down at the screen, my pulse jumping when I see the side-by-side photographs at the top of an article from a popular magazine.

Suddenly, I'm more awake than I've been in months.

The photos are red carpet shots from the Billboard Music Awards a few months ago. One photo is of me. The other is of Wilder.

In reality, we didn't cross paths that night, and I made sure to be using the restroom when Night Theory was onstage. But whoever picked and aligned these particular photos did a masterful job at manipulating perception. We look like a couple, both in all black, similar faux-serious expressions on our faces. Even our bodies are angled toward each other, giving a subtle impression of togetherness.

My already erratic heartbeat rattles as I read the headline.

Music's Favorite Star-Crossed Lovers Spotted Together New Year's Eve

I read the opening paragraphs, my stomach dropping further with every word. Multiple people apparently saw me go into a bedroom and Wilder slip inside after me. There's no mention of Martin, who was in the room with me far longer than Wilder was, or the fact Clay found me just minutes after he left and we shared a public kiss at midnight. Because facts have no place in clickbait.

I open my mouth to say as much, but Clay snaps, "Keep reading."

The back of my scalp tingling in trepidation, I continue scrolling and realize this isn't some short fluff piece with no purpose but to generate website traffic to ads. The article is long, dense, and annoyingly well written.

First is the expected regurgitation of history: our fathers being best friends and founding members of Breaking Giants, how we grew up together and formed Night Theory in our teens. The moderate success of our first album and tour. Our electric stage chemistry and how I shocked fans when I suddenly left the band. That I didn't leave because of creative differences like our label said but because of rising conflict with Wilder. How after a three-year estrangement, we had a brief, intense affair followed by an explosive breakup. Wilder went to treatment for drug abuse. I cut him out of my life.

The accuracy of it all is jarring but not really surprising. For better or worse, we're both autobiographical songwriters and public figures. Anyone with access to the internet and time to kill could piece the same story together.

But then the article takes an unexpected turn, going from annoying to a *fuckmylife* level of alarming.

According to the author—someone named Angie Irving, though it's likely a pseudonym—Wilder and I are still in love with each other. How does she know? Well, apparently every album we've written and released since our breakup is part of an ongoing love letter between us. Her theory is backed up with a shockingly thorough analysis of our individual discographies over the last six years.

It's both complete bullshit and perfectly crafted to be convincing as hell.

Fuck. This is really bad.

I lower the tablet to the table, making sure it connects silently with the glass. My senses return slowly. I become aware of my cold fingers and toes. An itch on the back of my neck. Gusting breezes whispering through bushes and trees. Birdsong and the neighbor's sprinklers. Water gurgling through the pool's filtering system.

"I've already talked to Anita," Clay says in a monotone. "A retraction isn't likely, but I might slap the magazine with a suit anyway just to make their life miserable."

When he doesn't say anything else, I know it's my cue to explain myself. But right now the only coherent thought in my head is that I hope Angie Irving and her so-called credible sources from last night are stricken with incurable rashes on their assholes.

I take a few sips of cold coffee, ignoring its bitterness, and try to come up with something to distract Clay. I need to buy myself some time to get my thoughts in order.

"I really loved that dress," I finally say. "The one from the BBMAs."

I wore the long, edgy black number against his wishes. He was pissed for days and has yet to overlook an opportunity to remind me of how ugly he thinks it was.

Sadly, he doesn't take the bait.

"Don't make me ask, Eva."

As I set down my mug, I remind myself to stick to general facts and avoid sounding defensive.

"He walked in uninvited. We had a brief conversation about Emma before I questioned his motives for speaking to me. He reassured me that he has no romantic interest in me and was merely taking a break from the party. He left. You came in a few minutes later."

There's a weighted pause. "Look at me."

Forcing myself to remain relaxed, I shift my gaze to his face. Even expecting the coldness in his eyes, it still shocks me. They used to be warm all the time.

"Is that all?" he asks.

"Yes."

He frowns at me for another moment, then looks across the backyard. "Maybe that's the spin. Childhood friends catching up." Nodding to himself, he adds decisively, "If I can't figure out a faster fix, at least we have The Golden Globes next weekend. I'll ask Anita to find out who's working the carpet and prep some questions for them. We'll rehearse your responses."

I have zero interest in attending The Golden Globes, in being photographed and dissected for consumption by the masses, but there's no point trying to get out of it. Clay's social standing, cultivated meticulously over a decade, means he's invited absolutely everywhere. Last week, he was invited to a ribbon-cutting ceremony for a butcher shop. So I guess I should be grateful he's selective about our appearances.

I make a noncommittal noise and fiddle with my robe, pulling the fabric over my knees.

Another heavy sigh floats over me. "You should have told me last night." His voice is soft now, thick with hurt that makes my blood instantly boil.

Before I can stomp the impulse, I retort, "I was distracted by the taste of someone else's lip gloss during our New Year's Eve kiss."

We both go preternaturally still.

I can't believe I said that.

Fingers grip my chin, lifting and turning my face. His eyes scan mine. "It was a forgettable mistake."

His version of an apology, as well as a reminder of how discreet he is normally. Like the fact he doesn't routinely wave his infidelities in my face means I don't have a right to be offended.

To him, our dynamic is normal. He's merely repeating patterns he witnessed between his parents when he was a child and again between his father and stepmother during his teens. Even among his colleagues and friends, I don't know of a single relationship that's monogamous.

There have been times recently that I've even wondered if what I saw growing up, what I've always wanted for myself, is nothing more than a fantasy. An aberration of modern love.

Clay's grip on my chin tightens. "Maybe if you actually enjoyed sex, I wouldn't need to find relief elsewhere. Have you considered that?"

The fire inside me burns brighter. The flame is black, though. Toxic. Biting my tongue so hard I taste copper, I roughly pull my chin from his hold and scoot my chair back. I stand and gather my plate and mug.

"I'm going to take a shower," I say as I move past him.

"Do we need to discuss this further?" he asks sharply.

What I hear instead is what he really means: do I need to be reminded of how well he takes care of me?

I shake my head, my shoulder blades squeezing together as he follows me inside. I set my dishes beside the sink, knowing that if I rinse them and put them in the dishwasher, it will set him off. There's no way I can handle one of his rants right now.

As I walk toward the hallway, he asks, "Did you take a sleeping pill last night?"

Caught equally off guard by the question and the lack of animosity in his voice, I look over my shoulder. "No."

Familiar and seductive warmth sparkles in his eyes. The sight of it ruptures my psyche, half of me relaxing while the other half remains hyper alert.

A smile curves his lips. "That's great news. How do you feel?"

Like the blade of a serrated knife, thanks.

"Good," I lie.

He tilts his head. The smile stays, but the warmth in his eyes disappears. "I hope that means you're feeling up to calling Lily today."

My stomach turns to lead even as I smile back. "Maybe."

Turning on my heel, I walk from the room.

evangeline

I have no questions left

No air to feed my breath

Emptiness the price I pay

For the love you took away

After my shower, I throw on old sweatpants and a T-shirt without thinking. Halfway across the bedroom, I come to my senses and change into a gray athleisure set Clay gave me for Christmas. I'm not a fan of the style, but at least the fabric is soft.

In the hallway, I hear his voice coming from his office at the opposite end of the house. Lighthearted, charming tone. Infectious laugh. It's the voice he uses to seduce clients... and women.

It certainly worked on me.

The thought causes a flare of uncomfortable, sticky heat beneath my skin. My teeth clench.

I need to calm down before I face him again, and there's only one room in the house that's truly mine. Walking lightly so he doesn't hear my steps, I quickly head downstairs.

The bulk of the lower level is a lounge with game tables, a bar, and a widescreen TV that Clay and his friends use for their bi-weekly poker nights. Down a hallway to the left is a movie room, complete with theater seating, as well as our home gym, a guest suite, laundry, and a full bath. But tucked off a smaller hallway to my right is my studio.

Formerly a storage room, Clay had the space remodeled before I moved in. I think I've been in it a grand total of four times in six months, a fact he likes to weaponize whenever he perceives me as ungrateful.

I slip inside the room and flip on the lights, dimming them immediately when the brightness makes me wince. The door thumps closed behind me. I swiftly lock it, and my lungs expand with a deep breath. Possibly my first of the day.

The space is pretty bare-bones. Soundproofing

panels. Low-pile carpet. Some basic recording equipment, none of which is plugged in. A desk, laptop, standing mic, audio interface, speakers, a mixer. My keyboard, still packed away in its giant case. Three guitars, two acoustic and one electric, likewise collecting dust.

The back wall is lined with boxes I haven't unpacked and don't care to. Bubble-wrapped, framed album art, articles, and accolades. All of Glow's awards, including a dozen Grammys.

In the living room upstairs, Clay has empty glass shelves ready to display the gold gramophones. He bugs me about unpacking them once or twice a month but hasn't demanded it yet. I'm dreading the moment. I would have left them in storage in Seattle if he hadn't personally packed them.

I can never tell him why I don't display them. Why I don't even like looking at them.

Because of Wilder.

"I can't wait to remind you of this moment twenty years from now when I'm putting up yet another shelf for your awards."

The memory makes me flinch and focus elsewhere. Unfortunately, what my eyes land on next are three boxes stacked beside the desk. They're older, the cardboard wrinkled, the tape peeling. They were definitely supposed to end up in storage, but I'd forgotten to mark them with the right label before the movers came.

Without permission, my feet carry me to them. I finger the tape on the top box, then peel it off.

Haphazardly stacked journals stare up at me, all different colors and sizes, all filled front to back with my teenage ramblings. My heart pounding, I pull a few out and set them on the desk. Then a few more. Before I can stop myself, I've removed them all to reveal what's hidden at the bottom.

Memories drift around me like distant music as I stare at the black, sticker-covered memento box. My fingers tremble as I lift it.

An unsteady step backward brings me to the desk chair, the leather sighing as I drop my weight and settle the box on my knees. The lid is warped from sitting under the combined weight of the journals. I tug until it comes free, then toss it on the desk and look inside the box for the first time in close to a decade.

There are loose, lined pages folded in fours, covered in messy words. An assortment of ticket stubs. Paper napkins littered with bleeding ballpoint ink: doodles and notes and disjointed lyrics. Sycamore leaves in various stages of life preserved by thick, yellowing tape.

Cheap guitar picks and curling band stickers. The very first Night Theory fliers, which Eddie and I printed on bright pink paper to annoy Wilder. A few of our demo CDs, the plastic casings cracked and the labels faded.

My eyes land on a palm-sized, dark green journal tucked against the side. The edges are worn, softened by countless hours spent in backpacks and purses and pockets.

I grab it without considering the consequences, opening the cover to read the first page.

THIS JOURNAL BELONGS TO WILDER AND EVANGELINE. IF YOU AREN'T US, FUCK OFF.

You're so dramatic.

I close it fast, my shuddering exhale fracturing the quiet. My fingers curl, clenching until the journal curves. When the binding crackles ominously, I throw it back in the box. Shoving the lid on, I waste no time loading it and all my journals back in the original box.

If I had packing tape, I'd reseal it. If I had a blow-torch, I'd burn them all.

Jerking to my feet, I walk around the room a few times. Consider and discard the idea of setting up my keyboard. Pause to open a guitar case, then close it when the sight of my custom Gibson acoustic makes my stomach bottom out. All while the pressure inside me builds and builds.

I resume pacing, back and forth from desk to door, faster and faster until I feel the claustrophobia that was missing when I entered the room. My thoughts churn with my legs, thrashing against their containment. Against walls I knew were there but for the first time can actually *feel*.

God, it fucking hurts.

Thanks to opening that stupid box—thanks to last night and Wilder's goddamn mouth, his unbelievable arrogance in telling me where I belonged—I *remember*. The girl I was. The girl I wanted so badly to protect but ended up caging and muting instead, little by little, over the course of years.

In hindsight, it's clear how my prison was crafted, another brick added every time I felt too much—too vulnerable or uncertain, hurt or angry or lonely. More bricks after each brief, disappointing attempt at a relationship. After lackluster sales reports, poor reviews from respected sources, a particularly vicious media cycle, a flood of critical comments online...

Every time I smiled when I wanted to scream. Said I was fine when I was flailing. Pushed forward when I wanted to rest. Avoided when I wanted to confront.

I built my mental cage to protect myself. To *save* myself. But now I'm trapped inside. Cut off from the bonds that used to give my life depth and vibrancy—my friends, my family. I'm disconnected from my own voice. From *music*.

There's only darkness and silence inside me now.

I know Lily believes I rejected the Indigo contract because of Clay's influence, but I did it out of desperation. Out of deep fear and shame for what I've been hiding from her.

The only person who knows I haven't written new material in over a year is Clay, but my confession didn't faze him. He said it doesn't matter. That when I go solo, the best songwriters in the business will jump at the chance to write for me.

When I told him I'd rather give up music altogether than perform other people's songs, he laughed and said I needed to grow up. *"Stop thinking of yourself as an artist, Eva. You're a business."*

More walls shift forward in the fog around my mind. Different dimensions of the same prison demanding acknowledgment.

I suddenly see it—who I've become. Who Lily and Rye see. My parents and brother, too.

But mostly, I see myself through Wilder's eyes.

And I hate her.

wilder

Frank Clarke wipes a napkin roughly over his mouth, causing his bushy gray mustache and surrounding beard to expand like porcupine quills. With an exaggerated groan, he leans back in his chair and belches. Disgusted looks are thrown our way from the nearest table, but Frank just grins at me and winks.

I roll my eyes at his antics. I'd wanted to meet at the house I'm renting, but he'd breezily suggested lunch. After years of him pulling this exact shtick whenever we're both in town, I didn't bother trying to dissuade him. At least the restaurant he chose this time doesn't have a dress code and didn't require renting a plane.

The quaint, Santa Monica café may be casual, but in keeping with Frank's tastes it's highly exclusive. I hadn't even bothered with calling for a reservation myself, knowing they'd think I was lying about who I was, and instead texted my PA to do the honors.

Normally I get a kick out of bringing the burly, aging biker into social spheres he wouldn't otherwise be able to access. But the last hour has been a struggle. I'm bent out of shape about last night, exhausted and impatient. So while he's decimated his food and talked nonstop, I've barely touched mine and most of my responses have been monosyllabic.

Frank slurps his Americano contentedly. I continue pushing food around my plate, ignoring curious stares from teenagers whose wealthy parents have dragged them out for New Year's brunch.

After a few more minutes of torture, Frank finally sets his cup down and folds his hands over his belly. "Okay, champ. Why don't you tell me what's on your mind?"

I glance around one more time, reassuring myself that the closest tables are actually pretty far from us and no one is pointing a phone in our direction. I still speak softly and don't use names as I tell him everything from Matt and Sophie's impromptu visit to what happened last night.

Even without names, Frank knows exactly who I'm talking about, having been on the receiving end of my verbal vomit more times than I can count. Sober himself for three decades, he's been a drug and alcohol counselor almost as long.

I met him at Oasis, the desert treatment center where I spent three months and where he works as a group therapy facilitator. In my first week there, he took a liking to me. Apparently how deeply pathetic and ornery I was reminded him of himself at my age.

Our unlikely bond grew and was solidified when, a few days before leaving Oasis, I had a severe panic attack. Despite all the work I'd done, despite feeling mentally stable and even hopeful about the future, the impending leap back into my life—and all it signified—hit me like a train.

What sent me spiraling wasn't the impending start of Night Theory's delayed world tour; I was amped to play music again. Nor did I really care about what the press was saying about me. The problem was everything else. All the consequences of what I'd done to Evangeline, to my family, to my supportive but rightfully resentful bandmates, and the fact I'd have mere days to start repairing all my relationships before touring for months with temptations everywhere.

I was still shaking from the effects of the attack when Dr. Chastain called for Frank to join us in his office. I didn't know what was happening until Frank appeared like a prison-tattooed Santa Claus and in his usual, gruff way said, "I haven't been a roadie for forty years, but if you want some company on tour just say the word."

And that was that. With Chastain's support, Frank took a leave of absence from Oasis and came on the road with me for seven months. He's been my sponsor ever since. By the end of that tour, I'm pretty sure my bandmates and our road crew liked him more than me. My family, too. Not really surprising in hindsight. I was legitimately fucking nuts for the first year of my sobriety, on a daily rollercoaster of emotional highs and lows.

Kind of like right now.

When I've finished unloading the chaos of the last week on him, Frank studies me in silence, his lips working against the scraggly ends of his mustache. The objectively nasty habit is his tell that he's about to impart some wisdom I don't want to hear.

"She's not yours, Wilder." When I stiffen, he lifts a hand. "Before you get your panties in a twist, I'm not saying you shouldn't care or even that you shouldn't try to help, but if you only want to help her because she might fall in love with you again... well, that's selfish as shit, isn't it?"

My abdominals clench against a blow that bypasses them and lands deep in my gut. Rubbing my hands over my face, I mumble, "What am I supposed to do?"

"The only thing I'm qualified to give you advice about is how to stay sober and not be a dick."

I drop my hands to glare at him.

He heaves a sigh. "I won't sugarcoat this for you."

"I don't want you to."

He shifts in his seat, wrinkles deepening around his eyes. "Your friend seems to be in a tough spot. Between what the man last night told you and what you observed, there are a lot of markers pointing to psychological abuse." He pauses for another round of mustache chewing. "Statistically, it takes an abuse victim seven times to leave their abuser for good. Do you know if she's tried to leave him before?"

I shake my head, my stomach roiling. "I don't. I guess I can ask..." I trail off, thinking about my phone call with Lily and Rye this morning. Their stunned silence after I told them what Martin said and what I saw with my own eyes.

They judged Evangeline harshly. Had all but written her off. And now they're sitting with the knowledge that her withdrawal and hurtful behaviors might have been cries for help.

All I could do was tell them it wasn't their fault. How were they supposed to know? Evangeline has always been a fortress, and they aren't mind readers. It's no one's fault but Clay's—and maybe mine.

Logically, I know I don't have that kind of power. But I still *feel* responsible. What if what I did to her made her more susceptible to Clay's abuse somehow?

I'm haunted by the image of her when I walked into the room last night. How she sat so still, pale and rigid on the bed. Like a broken doll, her eyes lifeless.

Frank grunts, and I realize I've curled my fingers around a knife on the table. I release it so fast it spins and clanks against my plate.

"I want to hurt him," I confess.

"I know, bud, but you won't. Because you want to help her more."

"How?" I demand. "How do I help her?"

He shakes his head sadly. "I know you want a straightforward answer, but I don't have one other than don't confront her. Given your history, I can guarantee it won't end well."

"Agreed," I grumble, thinking about what triggered her anger last night—my ill-conceived comment about how she didn't belong in Los Angeles. I can only imagine her reaction if I told her she should leave her boyfriend because he's an abusive piece of shit.

God, the irony. It fucking *stabs*.

I was her abusive boyfriend once. Lying to her. Manipulating her to keep her at my side.

Dark emotion coils and tightens around my heart. I

see it in my mind as a thick, black-scaled snake. Old and tired but still powerful. Selfish. Covetous and borderline amoral.

I'm not a perfect person just because I'm sober. Far from it. Last night I did something I swore I'd never do again—I lied to Evangeline. I told her I wasn't interested in her anymore, pretended that the idea of me seducing her was laughable.

In the moment, I hadn't wanted her to see me as one more person who wanted something from her. But I do want something. I want *everything*.

A handful of times, most recently when I heard she was dating Clay and freaked out, Frank has asked me to consider the possibility that my feelings might collapse in person. That they're not actually real. That maybe I've been holding onto the idea of us all these years to avoid facing vulnerability with someone else.

He isn't the only one who's suggested it. My parents have voiced similar concerns. Jax, Eddie, and Zander have as well. And it's been implied in one way or another by every person I've been romantically involved with over the years—usually accompanied by anger— when they invariably realize I'll never fall in love with them.

But after last night, I know they're all wrong. Ten seconds in the same room with Evangeline was all it took. No matter how much she's changed, how much I've changed, my feelings haven't. I felt the same old fire in my gut, my bones, my cock. In my fingers, itching to touch her. My tongue, burning to taste her.

I still want her. All of her. Her secrets and truths. Every thought and word, sigh and gasp. Every smile and frown and tear. If anything, my obsession is *more* now. Clearer. Purer. Unsullied by my inner conflict of the past. By my addiction, my self-hatred, my demons.

And she still wants me, too. She'd no doubt deny it, but I saw the proof. The goosebumps on her arms. The fevered intensity in her eyes as they roamed my body. Her expanding pupils. The thumping pulse in her neck. The blush that billowed like a rosy cloud over her chest and face.

Our bodies and souls still sing for each other.

Like Frank is privy to my thoughts, he says softly, "Be careful, Wilder. These situations are delicate and volatile. They're not dissimilar to the progression of active addiction in the sense there needs to be a rock bottom situation of some kind. Something that activates an urge to seek help. The only thing you can do is the same thing I'd counsel loved ones of an addict to do. Don't enable but don't judge or shame. Maintain healthy boundaries while providing a safe space for them to come when they're ready for change."

My mind latches onto two words: *safe space*. I want to be that for her so fucking badly. Can I? Is there a way to become again what I once was, before all the pain and hurt? Her confidant... her friend?

Frank drops his fist against the table. Not hard enough to alert other diners but still hard enough to jolt me from my thoughts. My gaze flies to his face. Twitching mustache. Knowing eyes.

"Stop scheming," he says gruffly.

The admonishment lands like an anvil. Annoyed by how easily he pinned me, I quip, "Yeah, yeah. The only person I have control over is myself. Can't help anyone if I take my oxygen mask off. Stay on my side of the street, et cetera."

Frank only huffs in amusement, stroking his beard with thick fingers before draping his arms on the table and leaning forward. His expression turns grave.

"Your friend didn't choose this, not like we chose drugs and alcohol. You get me?"

I nod weakly. "She's a victim."

"That's right." The sudden worry on his face makes my heart beat faster, and I know what he's going to say before he says it. "It's been a long time. Your feelings may not have changed, but..."

My mind fills in the blanks.

...but her feelings might have.

...but you're setting yourself up for heartbreak.

...but you're risking a relapse if this spirals.

...but she isn't yours.

I drop my gaze, unable to hold his. "I hear you."

Frank clears his throat. "I hate to bail on you like this, but I've gotta get back to Oasis." He shakes his head in mingled exasperation and fondness. "For fuck's sake, next time let me know right out of the gate that you need a serious one-on-one. I wouldn't have dragged you out to lunch or yapped so much."

I crack a smile. "Fair enough."

Part of me wishes I could go to Oasis with him. Back to the place and time when all I had to worry about was putting one foot in front of the other. Eating three meals at set times. Walking a dusty, rock-lined labyrinth at dawn and dusk. Swimming laps until my muscles burned. Learning about my anxiety, the root causes and triggers, and how to manage it sober.

In many ways, those three months were the hardest of my life. Dr. Chastain tore my head and guts apart before helping me put myself back together. But despite how painful it all was, there was a beautiful simplicity to the process.

Best of all, back then I still had hope. Naive, selfish hope that my broken heart was temporary. That when I got out, I'd make amends to Evangeline and in time she'd forgive me. Because surely our love was too big and perfect for her to walk away from.

Only it wasn't.

I thought I'd learned that lesson when I returned to Seattle, when she said all that shit on her parents' front lawn. When she took the pieces of my heart and stomped them to dust.

But apparently I'm hardheaded as fuck. Or a master of denial still clinging to a single remaining sliver of hope.

Still addicted to her and unable to let go.

"It's going to be okay, Wilder."

I nod, not meeting Frank's eyes, and signal for the check.

wilder

I follow Frank to the front of the restaurant, where he pauses near the host station to chat with the woman there. I stop as well but don't pay attention to their conversation, distracted by all the notifications on my phone that weren't there an hour ago.

There are texts from pretty much everyone I know, but what spikes my blood pressure are the missed calls and voicemails. Two are from Night Theory's manager—concerning because Mack is currently in Barbados with his longtime girlfriend and his last words to me were, "Have a nice break and don't fucking call me unless someone dies."

But far worse are the six missed calls and three voicemails from our publicist.

Shelley isn't known to overreact.

My heart racing, I unlock my phone and open my text messages, bypassing my sisters and mom in favor of Jax.

His most recent message reads,

> Anything you want to share with the class? Did she actually talk to u??

Attached is a link to an online article from a big gossip magazine. The preview shows side by side images of Evangeline and me from the BBMAs, along with a headline that makes my eyebrows jump. A flare of satisfaction warms my chest, smothered almost immediately by alarm when I think about Clay reacting to this.

Has he seen it? Has *she* seen it?

Given the calls from Shelley, my guess is yes and yes.

Fuck.

Before I can click on the link, a voice asks, "Mr. Ashburn?"

I look up at Frank and the woman, who wears a gold pin on her black button-down that says MANAGER. Frank's lips are folded inward, his eyes laughing. The woman, conversely, looks like she's ten seconds from a mental breakdown.

"Yes?"

Before she can answer, the heavy front door opens and a familiar man slips inside. Sam is my usual driver-slash-security when I'm in the city. He's ex-military, mid-forties, with biceps as big as my head. His normally placid expression is intact, whereas mine has no doubt shifted to horror after what I just glimpsed outside.

Hell in the form of a swarm of hungry, buzzing paps.

Double fuck.

"Good timing," Sam drawls at me. "I was just coming in to discuss the situation. Car's out front already, but there's fifteen feet of exposure between the door and the curb."

He doesn't have to tell me they're here for me. I can hear them shouting my name now. Someone must have seen me when the door opened.

The woman steps toward us, wringing her hands nervously. "On behalf of the entire Rhubarb family, I'm so sorry about this, Mr. Ashburn. Rest assured, we're already investigating to make sure no one on our staff is responsible. If you'd be willing to wait a few more minutes, more security is on the way to assist you to your vehicle."

Frank pats her shoulder. "Don't worry, Belinda, he's not going to blame you. Ain't that right, Wilder?"

"Yeah, that's right," I say, then look away, uncomfortable with the acute relief on her face. It was probably one of the teenagers inside posting to their socials, anyway. "Is there another exit?"

Sam answers for her. "They've got that covered, too."

I sigh. "All right. Let me make a quick call, then we're out of here whether or not we have backup. I can make it fifteen feet."

He nods and shifts so he's blocking the front door. Technically, as members of the public paparazzo have the right to enter a restaurant, though they rarely do because of harassment and privacy laws. I'm still glad Sam is in the way. I'll have to deal with the vultures soon enough.

Frank claps me on the shoulder. "My bike's parked around back, so Belinda's gonna show me out. Call me, okay?"

"Will do. Thanks, Frank."

"Good luck, champ."

When he's gone, I skirt around the host station into a short hallway and dial Shelley. She picks up on the first ring, not bothering with hello.

"Happy New Year, right? Good news and bad news. The bad is that I'm hungover and my phone won't stop ringing, so thanks for that. The good news is the article is flattering. Well, maybe not flattering since it implies Eva cheated on Clay Eaton with you last night. But as I see it—"

"Hold up," I bark. "Cheated? We barely spoke for five minutes. Who the fuck said this?"

There's a minuscule pause and an equally short exhale. "You haven't read the article. Okay. In summary, unnamed people saw you and Eva sneak off to a bedroom last night. There are no photos, which is good. Also good, streaming numbers for both Night Theory and Glow have skyrocketed—"

"Nothing about this is good, Shelley," I say through my teeth. "You know there's a double standard for this shit. Even a rumor of Eva cheating will follow her in the press for years."

Her tone softens. "I know. I have more news on that front. I spoke to Glow's publicist, Anita Allman. Super weird convo, to be honest, but the moral of the story is she wants our help redirecting the narrative. I have a feeling you won't like the ask, though."

"What is it?"

"She wants you to have lunch with Eva and Clay tomorrow at Café Doux in Beverly Hills. The spin is that last night was childhood friends running into each other and catching up. Vibe for lunch is smiles and laughs all around—documented, of course. Voilà, heat's off and cheating rumors are dead in the water."

As her words sink in, my skin starts crawling. The mere thought of having to sit across from Clay and pretend like I don't want to murder him has me slumping against a wall. What if he touches her? *Kisses* her in front of me?

I don't think I can do it. I'm not that good of an actor.

When I'm silent too long, Shelley says softly, "From a PR standpoint, I have no problem with you declining. We can mitigate the backlash another way. Release a statement of our own, accept a few interview requests. Whatever you feel comfortable with."

I press a thumb to the spiking tension in my forehead. "Are you sure Eva's on board with this? With lunch?"

Shelley's voice lowers again. "That's the weird part. With the history between you guys, I was surprised she agreed. No offense."

I grunt. "None taken. Why is it weird?"

"Well, since I was so surprised, I fished a bit. Anita was cagey at first but cracked. She didn't speak to Eva at all. This is coming from—"

"Clay," I finish, his name a bitter burst in my mouth. "He's definitely orchestrating this. Dude hates me. He's probably hoping I say no so he can blame me for any fallout."

"Huh. I didn't realize you had history with him, too."

I almost smile at the poorly veiled curiosity in her voice. Knowing the details won't leave our phone call, I offer, "I dated his stepsister years ago. Around the same time, she stopped sleeping with him. He blames me for her change of heart."

Shelley chokes on air and coughs for a good ten seconds, then finally gasps out, "What in the daytime drama?"

"Less soap opera, more *Dateline*." I bite my cheek before I tell her the whole truth. "Trust me, he's not a good person."

"He sounds like a nightmare," she says seriously. "My call with Anita suddenly makes a lot more sense. She definitely doesn't like him. Is this one of those toxic-boyfriend-becomes-manager situations?"

I wince, regretting opening my mouth. "Maybe. I honestly don't know. Can we move on?"

"Of course," she says gently. "What are your thoughts about tomorrow?"

Movement down the hall turns my gaze to Sam, who jerks his thumb toward the front door. "I have to go," I tell Shelley. "Leaving a restaurant surrounded by paps."

"Ah, how delightful. Not that you need the reminder, but—"

"Neutral expression and keep my mouth shut," I say dryly.

"Exactly. Call me in ten?"

I move toward Sam. "My brain doesn't work at your speed, Shelley. Give me an hour to think it over."

"You got it. Oh, and don't worry about calling Mack. That was my mistake. I forgot he was on vacation when I was trying to track you down. Talk soon."

She hangs up just as I reach Sam and two nervous, rent-a-cop-looking guys, presumably from the restaurant's security company. The noise from outside has definitely increased in volume. I wince when a woman's scream confirms that the crowd now includes fans—rabid ones who will drop everything and risk speeding tickets to get wherever I've been spotted.

Belinda hovers before the archway leading to the dining room, a forced smile on her face. Standing beyond her is a family clearly waiting to leave. The kids gape at me while their parents give me double stink-eye.

"Sorry about this," I tell Belinda. "I'll be out of your hair in a sec."

She rejects my apology with another one of her own, but she's clearly frazzled and wants me gone.

The security guys introduce themselves to me as the four of us approach the door. I forget their names as soon as they're spoken, a hundred percent of my mental effort focused on preparing myself for extreme sensory overload.

Inhale. Hold. Exhale.

When Sam looks back at me, I nod. He opens the door and pandemonium erupts. Shouts and screams and bodies rushing, pressing, shoving. Every step toward the black car at the curb feels like a mile-long sprint. My breath is shallow, muscles tight, heart racing, but my face reflects none of my inner turmoil.

"Wilder! Wilder, over here!"

"Are you in L.A. to see Eva?"

"Look this way!"

"What happened in the bedroom last night, Wilder?"

"MARRY ME, PLEASE!"

"Wilder! Is Eva leaving Clay Eaton for you?"

When the car's back door opens, I manage to slip inside calmly instead of diving. Sam forces his way around the hood while a crying woman yanks on the handle of my locked door and people jostle each other to get a good camera angle through the windshield.

Sam makes it inside, cursing as someone tries to crawl in with him. When he finally gets his door closed sans interloper, his eyes meet mine in the rearview.

"We'll have to take the long way home."

Meaning, he'll have to lose however many cars are already waiting to tail us or risk leading them to my rental.

I want to tell him to take me straight to the private airport in Van Nuys. Every instinct is screaming for me to go home. But I can't. If I bail now, it means abandoning Evangeline to deal with the mess I unintentionally made in her life last night. Poisoning her mind further against me. Leaving her at the mercy of Clay and the rumor mill.

So instead of taking the easy way out, I smile faintly. "Figured. Thanks, man."

"You got it."

The security guys clear the crowd enough for us to pull away from the curb. It's slow going for a block, the main road congested by people slowing to gawk. As soon as traffic opens up, Sam takes advantage and does what he does best, taking our followers on a merry chase until, close to an hour later, we're in the clear.

By the time he pulls through the gate at my rental, I've read the article several times and cycled through an emotional spectrum ranging from joy to despair. I also texted with Jax and Rye and called my mom, who I shamelessly tasked with updating Evangeline's parents.

When I walk inside the house, I finally call Shelley back with an answer about tomorrow. She isn't thrilled but neither is she surprised.

No part of me is looking forward to sitting under the scrutiny of cameras while pretending I'm happy to share a meal with the woman I love and her abuser.

But for Evangeline, I'll do it.

I'd do much worse for her.

A few minutes after I hang up with Shelley, she

emails me two documents bearing the logo of her PR firm. *Smalltalk Prompts and Socializing Tips for Introverts,* and *Body Language in the Public Eye.*

The attached email is brief and almost makes me laugh.

No, these weren't written with you in mind.
Okay that's a lie. They're totally about you.

You'll do great. Just be yourself.

Being myself tomorrow will mean leaving the restaurant in handcuffs. Since I'm not down to spend a night in jail—or more likely, the rest of my life—I guess that means I'll have to be someone else.

I'll have to lie. Again.

And hope someday Evangeline will understand why.

evangeline

We're going to be late.

Since Clay is never late unless he intends to be, it's a power play. He wants Wilder to have to sit alone and wait for us. I have no idea what advantage he thinks it will bring, but either way it's asinine.

Not that I'm in a hurry. But I also want to get this over with.

"You didn't come to bed last night."

They're the first words he's spoken to me since we left the house and the third sentence today. No concern evident in the tone, just reproach. Like I'm a defiant child who intentionally stayed up past bedtime.

I'm not the only one who picks up on the immediate tension in the car. Our driver, Phillip, glances at us in the rearview before turning on the radio to give us an illusion of privacy. The Escalade is spacious but not *that* spacious.

With an internal sigh, I turn from the window to face Clay. He doesn't look at me, continuing to scroll through sports statistics on his phone. But he's waiting.

"I lost track of time in my studio and crashed in the bedroom downstairs."

I don't care whether or not he believes me. It's his fault I couldn't sleep in the first place, since he agreed to this insanity on my behalf. There was no way I was going to be able to turn my head off last night, so I didn't even try.

I ended up watching mindless television for hours to avoid thinking about this ridiculous PR stunt. About Wilder. About the flood of messages and voicemails on my phone since the article came out. From Lily and Rye, Martin, my parents, my brother. From my publicist, manager, and my PA, Sandra.

Most of all, though, I needed distraction from the disquiet I've felt since opening that box in my studio—the eerie feeling that maybe my insomnia isn't actually an inability to sleep, but sleep of a different kind. One I can't wake up from. One that has slowly taken me so far from myself I no longer know who I am.

Clay tilts his head at my answer but otherwise doesn't respond. If I wasn't adept at reading his micro-expressions, I'd believe he was relaxed right now. Ambivalent about going to lunch with Wilder. But there's strain around his eyes and his left pinkie twitches intermittently against his phone.

He's just as anxious as I am.

"This is pointless," I mutter, tugging on the hem of my too-short dress. "I'm honestly shocked Anita suggested this."

I'm likewise shocked Wilder agreed to it. Six years ago, he wasn't a fan of Clay's. I don't quite remember why, only that he told me he didn't like him on the night of Glow's first showcase. Maybe something to do with his ex, Kendra, and the fact Clay is her stepbrother?

That whole evening is a blur in my memory. Mostly because it was so intense for Lily and me, but partly because it exists in a padlocked mental closet along with the majority of that month of my life.

Maybe Wilder doesn't care one way or the other about Clay these days, but I know for a fact Clay despises him. I also know why.

Despite their seven-year age difference, Clay and his stepsister were extremely close growing up. They remained that way until Kendra met Wilder. She fell in love with him. He got her hooked on painkillers before dumping her... for me. Not long after, Kendra left Seattle. She hasn't spoken to anyone in the family for years. All Clay knows is that she's been in and out of rehabs since and is living back East somewhere.

If there's anyone who has a reason to hate Wilder, it's Clay. Which means he isn't doing this for himself. He's sacrificing his peace because he thinks it's best for me, for my reputation.

My irritation softens and fades. I reach across the back seat and touch his thigh. He finally lowers his phone, shifting cold eyes to my face. I ignore the instinct to retract my hand.

"We don't have to do this, Clay."

"Yes, we do," he says, his voice low and rigid.

I make myself smile. "This will blow over soon enough. Tomorrow there will be a new story, a different drama."

He scoffs. "I won't be cuckolded by the media, Eva, and definitely not by the waste of oxygen that is Wilder Ashburn. So put a smile on your face and play the part. Consider it your due for landing us in this situation to begin with."

Dumbstruck, I recoil to my side of the back seat. He returns his attention to his phone. I study his profile, searching for *something*, but he's wearing his courtroom expression. Perfectly composed and aloof.

Another one of my mental walls crumbles. More awareness floods in.

I swim through tangled, murky thoughts until Phillip pulls up to the entrance of Café Doux. Then I shove the mess in my head behind a mental door and slam it closed.

By the time I exit the car and walk inside with my arm wrapped around Clay's, I've become who I need to be. The transition is surprisingly easy, fueled by the adrenaline pouring through my veins. The incessant butterflies in my stomach are just a side effect.

It doesn't mean anything that those butterflies multiply exponentially when the hostess leads us to a private, shaded patio and I see the man sprawled in apparent ease at a corner table. A man who turns his head as we approach. Who rises gracefully to his feet, a welcoming smile on his face.

Wilder's smile never falters as he shakes Clay's hand. They exchange pleasantries, and several people stationed discreetly around the otherwise empty patio take photos. The men laugh. Camera shutters click rapidly.

This can't be real.

Wilder turns to me with an easy grin. It looks so effortless, so *unlike him*, that for a moment I'm convinced I'm asleep. The feeling intensifies when I blink and see a flash of light—an instant sunrise behind my eyes—and hear leaves rustling in an imaginary wind.

"Great to see you, Eva."

His hands cup my shoulders, twin flashpoints of heat. His kiss to my cheek is there and gone, the flutter of passing wings after a midnight rainstorm.

Still not convinced this isn't a nightmare, I smile at him with counterfeit joy. "You, too. I'm so glad we could squeeze in a lunch while you're in town."

There's a flash of wry amusement in his eyes, so fast I wonder if I imagined it, then he's sitting back down. We're all sitting. Ordering iced teas and appetizers. Chatting about the weather and traffic, about the city's ongoing efforts to rebuild after the devastating fires a few years ago.

Clay holds my hand. Touches my back. Strokes my thigh. I ignore the way my skin hums with discomfort. When he nuzzles my ear and kisses my cheek in the same spot Wilder did, I smile like his casual affection is normal and welcome. Like it doesn't rub against the emotional bruise left by our conversation in the car.

Wilder tells a story about remodeling his house and a family of ducks that put construction back months.

We laugh.

Clickclickclick go the cameras.

Over our meals—steaks for the men, a dressing-free

salad for me—Clay brings up the Grammys next month, congratulating Wilder on Night Theory's nomination for Best Rock Performance for their song, "Gray Matter." Then he asks if he thinks they'll win.

Wilder's eyes sharpen; Clay's smile widens. I stiffen, my gaze flickering to the nearest cameraman and the phone sitting on the table beside him. We all know our conversation is being recorded, that whatever Wilder says could very well end up in print.

I hold my breath until Wilder says offhandedly, "We're up against some of my favorite songs and artists from last year, so I'll be happy no matter the outcome." Forest-toned eyes slide to me and soften. "Glow's up for three, right? Ready to add another shelf?"

My heart cartwheels in my ribcage, elevating my pulse and sending a wave of warmth up my neck. In my head, a locked door rattles ominously.

As I suck in a breath, I finally accept that I'm undeniably and unfortunately awake.

Clay's fingers tighten on my thigh to the point of pain, eliciting another gasp. Wilder's eyes narrow. He opens his mouth, but Clay interjects brightly, "You'll be thrilled for whoever wins, won't you, my love?"

"Absolutely," I intone, then place my napkin beside my plate. "If you'll both excuse me? Too much iced tea."

I push my chair back, forcing Clay to release me or

risk an awkward struggle. He flashes me a sharp grin. "Hurry back."

I nod.

Smile.

My thigh throbs as I walk away.

CHAPTER TWELVE

wilder

Evangeline's act is flawless, but I see right through it. Maybe because I learned how to behave through observation and mimicry as a child, I'm able to recognize when someone else is presenting a false front. Pick up on subtle cues others would miss. But I think the truth is both simpler and more convoluted.

I just know *her*.

The broken, angry woman on New Year's Eve was miles closer to the real Evangeline than the version striding away from our table.

Four-inch heels clack expertly over tile, the muscles in her calves bunching starkly on each step. Shiny, white-gold hair bounces in its high ponytail.

In no world can she be comfortable. Not in those shoes. Not in that tight white dress that does nothing to conceal the jut of her ribs. And the fact she ordered a salad without dressing? Iced tea with no sugar? It's beyond disturbing. Like seeing a snow leopard declawed and defanged, brainwashed into thinking they're a gazelle.

But then I recall her gasp and the flash of pain in her eyes when I asked about Glow's Grammy nominations. The clenching of her jaw when Clay answered for her.

She's still in there... somewhere.

"We're done for today."

Clay's words are for the photographers, who obediently pack their equipment and file from the room. I watch him warily as he lifts a finger to beckon our dedicated server.

"Scotch on the rocks."

The man's eyes move to me. "And for you, sir?"

"Nothing, thanks."

With a polite nod, the server turns to leave, but Clay stops him with another arrogant lift of his finger.

"Hold the drink for five minutes and close the doors. If she tries to return, have the chef give her a tour of the kitchen or something."

"Very good, sir." Eyes lowered, he slips across the patio on silent feet. On his way out, he closes glass-paned French doors.

Here we fucking go.

Clay wastes no time dropping the pretense of friendliness, shifting instantly into what Eddie would call Yacht Guy Dickhead Mode. Draping an arm over Evangeline's empty chair, he manspreads in his designer slacks and sighs like his balls are relieved. But the key to the personality type—which Clay nails—is looking relaxed *and* like there's a baseball bat shoved up his ass.

As I wait for whatever intimidation tactics he has planned, I'm extra grateful for my hour-long meditation this morning and the phone calls with Frank and my dad. But what really allows me to stay calm in response to his smug smile and air of superiority is the primal, unspoken communication between our egos.

We both know my dick is bigger than his.

Eventually Clay realizes he won't win a staring contest with me. His chin lifts imperiously. "I hope you know what's happening here."

I smirk. "Aww, are you trying to thank me?"

His smile vanishes. "I should have known you'd be too stupid to understand."

I roll my eyes. "Why don't you enlighten me."

Lowering his arm, he leans forward. "This will be the last time you speak directly to Eva. She belongs to *me.*"

Rage unfurls in my gut. I let it out in a slow exhale so

it doesn't taint my next words. "Wow, Clay. Join us in the current century. These days we don't own women." I tilt my head. "I wonder how Eva would feel about what you just said?"

"You actually think she's capable of thinking for herself? That's precious."

Even aware that he's baiting me, I still tense. "If you believe that bullshit, you don't know her at all."

With an unnerving smile, Clay relaxes back in his seat. "To the contrary, it's you who doesn't know her. Let me let you in on a little secret. Eva thinks and does whatever I tell her to because unlike you, I have her best interests in mind. I know exactly what she needs."

My molars grind. "Is that right? Let me guess, she needs you dictating her career like you already dictate her personal freedoms. You want to launch her as a solo act. Turn her into another boring, overproduced pop star. I bet you already have the Big Three chomping at the bit to sign her and a dozen brand deals in the pipeline, huh?"

He doesn't bother faking offense, instead shrugging casually. "What can I say? I have a gift for the big picture, and I've had my eye on this particular one for years. Thanks, by the way, for removing yourself from view early on. A little disappointing how long it took her to get her shit together afterward, but it worked out in the end. In fact, you primed her quite well."

I hate him. I really, really fucking hate him. And he knows it, his smile turning even more smug.

"Realistically, Eva has another four, maybe five years of peak marketability. I plan to use them. Then, of course, there will be residencies and other ventures. Who knows, maybe a Glow reunion album or two. And let's not forget the two kids raised by nannies and the vacation home in Turks and Caicos."

Fury and helplessness bleed my thoughts red. My knuckles itch to punch the smarmy look off his face.

I need to end this before I end *him*.

"Does she know all you care about is objectifying and commodifying her?"

His eyes glitter with malice. "What she knows is her place, which is doing exactly what I fucking say. And it's past time you learned your place, Wilder. Let me put this in plain terms: if you come near her again, I'll gladly destroy your reputation and end your career."

And... I'm done.

I hit Stop Recording on the phone in my lap, then tuck the device into my pocket and stand.

"Threats from an Eaton, how tediously familiar. Sorry to cut this short—really, I'm enjoying myself—but your five minutes are up."

I saunter around the table, forcing Clay to either stand or be at eye level with my crotch. He shoves his chair back and rises, then plants his feet and puffs up his chest like he's a tough guy.

I invade his personal space until I'm close enough to smell his overpriced cologne and hair wax. Close enough for him to be painfully aware of our height difference, how I'm looking *down* at him. Then I let my mask drop, revealing how close I am to letting myself off the leash. That if it weren't for Eva, his physical health would be in serious fucking jeopardy right now.

When I brush imaginary lint off his shoulder, he flinches.

It makes me smile.

"Speaking of Eatons, how *is* Kendra these days?" I pause, enjoying the vein that begins to pulse in his temple. "Ah, that's right. You wouldn't know, would you, *big brother*? Well, I'm sure you'll be relieved to hear she's doing great. She's happy, and more importantly, she's safe."

At the unmistakable ring of honesty in my words, the blood drains from his face. Then rage brings it right back in an unflattering flush.

"You piece of shit," he spits. "Tell me where she is."

Grabbing the top of his shoulder, I slowly increase the pressure of my grip as I angle my mouth to his ear. "I will never fucking tell you where she is, but I'll let *you* in on a little something. She still has the Eaton box of secrets. So how about this? You never threaten me or tell me what to do again, and I won't send Eva the recording I made of our fun little conversation... today, at least."

He jerks, muscles bunching as he tries to break my hold. I just squeeze harder, slapping his hand away when he tries to grab my arm.

"Do we have a deal, Clay?"

"Fine," he hisses, "but mark my words, you're going to regret this."

I chuckle darkly. "That's just one of the many differences between you and me. I'm not afraid of bad press. And we both know there's nothing you can throw at me that I can't return doubled. *With receipts.*"

Releasing his shoulder, I give it a final pat, hard enough to make him stumble back. I watch dispassionately as he struggles for composure, his nostrils flaring, chest heaving, hands clenching and unclenching. Sadly, this is likely one of the few times in his pampered life that he's felt powerless.

At the sound of the patio doors opening, I look up and smile at Evangeline. She pauses on the threshold, her eyes narrowing on us. Our server shifts nervously behind her, Clay's scotch in his hands.

"What's going on?" she asks, her gaze sliding to

Clay's back. He doesn't turn around, likely because his balls are in his armpits and his face still resembles an eggplant.

My smile softening, I walk toward her. "Just thanking Clay for lunch. I have a flight to catch."

The closer I get to her, the more her body reacts. I relish the small hitch in her breath, her subtly dilating pupils, and the ribbons of rose that sweep across her cheekbones.

For the first time today, her control over her expression falters. Vacuous neutrality vanishes. Bemusement shifts to wariness, which turns into a scowl of defiance. Her chin juts up, eyes flashing as I stop right in front of her.

There she is.

A sense of rightness warms my chest. I'm still the only one she can't hide from. The only one who can read her music.

She knows it. I know it.

The whole fucking world knows it.

Giving in to impulse, I gently cup her head and place a soft kiss on her brow. She tenses. And when I drop my mouth to her ear, she stops breathing.

"410 Coves Lane, Madrone Island," I murmur. "Anytime, for any reason. No expectations or strings attached. I will always be here for you, as a friend, no matter what."

Releasing her, I allow myself a final glimpse of her face: searching eyes, flushed cheeks, lips parted in shock.

Then, against every instinct, I walk away.

PART THREE

chorus

chorus : the section of a song that encapsulates the lyrical message.

evangeline

Turned out the lights

Lost all my lessons

Sunk into shadows

And now here I am

In the darkness

In the empty

Again

In the weeks since that excruciating lunch, things have been different between Clay and me.

Clay has been different.

I was on edge for days afterward as I waited for him

to share all the flaws in my performance. For him to accuse me of smiling too often, talking too much or not enough, or not hiding my disgruntlement at eating a dry salad while the men had juicy steaks.

My biggest fear, though, was that he'd demand I tell him what Wilder said to me right before he left. I crafted a dozen potential responses. A dozen ways to deflect. But he's only brought up lunch once, and that was an offhand comment about the success of our ploy.

Instead, from the moment we got in the car to drive home, he's been kind. More than kind—he's been warm and charming and engaged, just like he was when we first started dating. There have been no critiques of my body, clothes, or sleep habits. No coldness, indifference, or disdain.

When I come down with a horrible cold right before The Golden Globes, he shrugs it off and stays home, plying me with medicine, tissues, and soup. When I have a particularly painful period and spend all day in pajamas in front of the television, he doesn't insinuate that I'm lazy. He brings me my favorite chocolate and a heating pad.

There have been other changes, too. He's started coming home from work in time to have dinner with me. He hasn't dragged me to parties or events. He doesn't bring up Glow or my standing appointment with a Sony music executive.

I'm not proud of it, but I test the boundaries of our new peace a few times. But nothing ruffles him. Not when I tell him I'm tired of toast and want more breakfast options. Not when I go shopping and come home with a bunch of black clothes.

Even though part of me stays wary and waiting for the other shoe to drop, as weeks pass, I begin to relax. My sleep improves, which does wonders for my energy, stability, and clarity. Slowly, I step back into my life.

My parents are overjoyed when I begin calling them a few times a week. Receptive to my unwillingness to talk about myself, they stick to safe topics like my brother's newest girlfriend, the painting my mom is working on, and my dad's new whittling hobby that will last, at best, another month or two.

One day, I impulsively send Rye a meme. He sends one back, and before I know it, we're exchanging them daily. Around the same time, I ask Lily for photos of Emma, which become routine video calls. At first, my goddaughter doesn't seem to know who I am—a fact that hurts more than it should since she's literally a baby. But it doesn't take long for Lily to start sending me videos of Emma asking if "Aun-jelly" can sing to her.

I start playing guitar again, too. For a few minutes a

day at first, then a few hours. My calluses reform. Soreness in my arms and back peaks and fades.

The more I play, the more I *listen*, the more I come to understand that music never left me. I was the one who turned my back on music. And with that realization, a floodgate opens.

I overflow lyrics and melodies.

Mixed with my relief is guilt over keeping the news from Clay. I tell myself it's because I don't want to jinx the return of my muse, but it's really because I'm not writing solo pop songs.

I'm writing the next Glow album.

Telling him would be more than a test of our relationship—it would be a crucible. And although there are moments wherein I sense the crossroads ahead of me, I'm not ready to face it. Not yet. Not even as every song I write pulls down another wall inside me. Opens another door of memories.

I'm remembering myself, who I was before I became the very thing I was most afraid of—the endless, uncaring dark.

And if I'm remembering someone else at the same time? Seeing our past anew through a wide-angled lens? Finding comfort in his promise the last time I saw him?

There's nothing I can do about it.

He is, after all, a part of me.

♪

TUESDAY EVENING, the week of the Grammys, begins like every other recent night. Clay comes home from work, spends forty-five minutes in the gym, then showers and joins me in the formal dining room with its too-large table and uncomfortably stiff chairs.

Over salmon with mushroom risotto—I hate mushrooms, but it's Clay's preferred Tuesday meal—he tells me about winning a copyright case in court today. I respond exactly as I'm supposed to, with effusive praise, while ignoring the dread and determination sitting side by side in my chest.

When Clay finishes eating, he signals to our chef, Paul, who moves forward to clear dishes from the table. I shift in my seat, uncomfortable as always with the power differential.

In his late sixties, Paul works tirelessly for us every morning and most evenings. On Sundays, he's here almost all day, prepping lunches for the week. He does his best to make my restrictive menu flavorful, sneaks me chocolate chip muffins a few times a month, and chats with me whenever Clay isn't home.

Lifting my plate, Paul eyes my untouched pile of risotto like it personally pains him. Before he can ask to make me something else as he does every week, I smile warmly and shake my head. It's hard enough sitting here while he waits on us; no way am I making him work more than he already does. No matter how hungry I am.

"It was delicious Paul, thank you," I murmur, and he gives me a soft smile. "Have you thought any more about a vacation? I bet Laurie would love a trip to see your grandkids."

He glances furtively across the table. "I haven't, no." Before I can respond, he beats a hasty retreat.

"Inciting rebellion among the staff?"

Clay's smile is teasing, but there's a coolness in his eyes I haven't witnessed for a few weeks. The sight is oddly comforting, like slipping back into a familiar, if painful, reality.

"Just making sure they're happy," I say flippantly, then continue before I lose my nerve. "I know it's game night and the guys will be here soon, but can we talk about this weekend for a minute?"

His smile brightens. "Have you changed your mind about Friday night?"

"Ah, no. I haven't."

Goodbye smile.

"I'm disappointed to hear that. You already turned down the invitation to perform, but skipping the gala, too?" He shakes his head. "Terrible decision, not to mention lazy of your manager to allow it."

I have no idea why, but I want to laugh. His tone is so autocratic it's theatrical. Resisting a childish urge to mock it, I reply, "Regardless, I haven't changed my mind."

Clay lifts his wine glass, swirling the dark liquid before taking a sip. "This casual throwing away of free publicity... is it going to become a habit?"

My internal levity disappears. "I've worked myself to the bone for years. I've earned some rest. Mallory knows this."

He sniffs. "Moving on. What did you want to talk about?"

Steeling myself, I forge ahead. "As I've already mentioned, Lily and Rye are renting a house at the beach this weekend. I've decided to spend Sunday with them and get ready there. You're welcome to join us, or if you'd rather not, we'll be ready for the limo at three."

For five long seconds, he doesn't say anything. While I can't see his anger, I can feel it, clawing and crawling all over me. I sit still, my heart pounding in anticipation of an argument.

But then he smiles and shrugs. "That's fine. Send me the address, and I'll pick you guys up at three."

I don't relax.

Not when he tosses his napkin on the table and stands. Not when he drops a kiss on my head, squeezes my shoulder, and tells me he's going to get ready for game night. Not even when he leaves the room.

As Paul returns to clear the silverware, I stare at the woodgrain surface of the table and ignore his worried glances. I wait to feel what I *should* feel. But there's no sense of victory. No relief.

Instead, a memory slips into my mind. The voice of Wilder's great-aunt, Katherine, speaking to five-year-old me after I fell and hurt myself playing outside.

"Did you know that when dams are built, they have to have outlets and spillways? No? Well, I want you to imagine a very bad storm, or even just lots and lots of rainy days. If there are no outlets for all that unexpected water, the reservoir behind the dam will overflow and flood the area. Eventually, the dam itself will crack under the pressure of everything it's holding back."

I'd barely understood what she was saying, but I remember vividly how I'd felt. Pressurized and overfull. Poised on the cusp of violent expansion.

I feel the same way now.

But unlike back then, no tears come. There's no spillway. No parents waiting to fuss over my skinned knees and face, no seven-year-old Wilder to tell me I'm going to have cool scars and make me laugh.

I'm alone at my breaking point.

"Eva?" asks a gentle voice. "Can I get you anything else?"

I blink up at Paul. "I'm fine, thank you."

He hesitates, radiating fatherly concern, and I manage a smile. "You should take a vacation, Paul."

He winks. "I will if you do."

I laugh, and though it's mostly for his sake, when he leaves the room, he goes unknowing of the gift he gave me with those few kind words.

A tiny spillway—a reminder I'm not alone. Or rather, that I don't have to be.

wilder

Tell me you feel this

Hear me screaming

As I carve our names

In the sycamore tree

"I should leave before she gets here, right?"

Rye throws a handful of peanuts in his mouth, chomping them as he tracks me with squinted eyes. "First, you've gotta stop pacing. You're making me dizzy and blocking my ocean view. Second, where are you going to go? You're literally staying in the house with us."

"The guys have suites near the arena. I can go hang

with them." I stop at the corner of the couch he's sprawled on. "Hasn't anyone told you it's gross to talk with your mouth full?"

Lily's disembodied voice answers, "A million times, Wilder!"

Rye rolls his eyes, brushing peanut dust off his chest. "Hilarious, my love," he calls back, then says to me, "Don't trust her. Last week she put leftovers in a cabinet instead of the fridge, then freaked out when there was an unidentified smell in the house. She wanted me to call nine-one-one because she was convinced it was a gas leak."

"I heard that," Lily says as she chases a giggling Emma into the living room.

Rye's mom, Kat, follows the pair. With deft precision, she circumvents her daughter-in-law to pick up the nap-escapee. She murmurs to Lily, then gives us a cheerful wave before carrying a squirming Emma back down the hallway.

Lily flops onto a love seat. "Your mom is a godsend, full stop."

Rye, his mouth full of peanuts again, wisely nods instead of speaking.

Lily rolls her eyes, then yawns so hugely her jaw cracks. "Sleep regression is brutal."

My mind still mid-spiral, I squint at her. "Sorry, sleep-what?"

"Regression. Remember when you watched Emma last week and she refused to nap? Imagine that twenty-four seven. We're a minimal-sleep household at the moment, hence the leftovers in the pantry."

"And why we told you to pick the farthest bedroom from us," adds Rye. "You're welcome, by the way."

"Ah. Thanks." I glance at my watch. "Not to be totally self-centered—sorry about your parent life—but can we get back to my question? I don't want to make Evangeline uncomfortable. Do you think I should leave?"

Rye grins. "No way. If you bail, it'll be super obvious to everyone that you're a big baby chicken."

"Wow," I deadpan.

Lily snorts. "Stay, Wilder. She knows you're going to be here. And you want to see her, don't you?"

I palm the back of my neck, squeezing to relieve the tension that's been there since I woke up. "Of course I want to see her."

Rye sits up, finally realizing I need him to take me seriously. "What are you worried about?"

"I just have a bad feeling," I admit. "I know you said she's been acting more like herself the last couple of weeks. Sophie and Matt told me the same thing. But you guys heard the recording—all the foul shit Clay said about her. And now suddenly she's writing Glow's next album, wants to come up to Seattle to record this summer, and is hanging here solo all day? Something isn't adding up. What's changed?"

Lily chews her lip. "I don't know. I haven't asked about Clay because I haven't wanted to scare her off. At the risk of sounding naive, maybe she's finally realizing what a monster he is and is gearing up to leave him?"

"Maybe." Though I try, I can't keep the skepticism from my voice.

Rye glances between us. "Let's hope for the best."

Not wanting to kill the mood any more than I already have, I nod a few times before turning to gaze out a giant picture window at the ocean.

When I heard Evangeline was reaching out again to her friends and family, that she was working on Glow songs, I was initially optimistic. Unfortunately, over-thinking is my brain's default mode. It wasn't long before I was chewing on other, darker possibilities, the worst of them being that because of my meddling, Clay changed tactics. I know damn well he didn't trip and land on how to be a good person. What worries me is that he's pretending to be one and she's falling for it.

Beyond the glass, the Pacific glitters in the morning sunlight, blue water mottled by stretches of foam, seaweed, and darker currents. I follow a set of waves, tracking its transformation from distant swells to white-water on the beach. Then I find another set and another.

My awareness of the room fades, the vastness and rhythm of the ocean reminding me that I'm one fleeting, fragile life on a planet four and a half billion years old. Measured against the scope of time, my worries are minuscule and absurd.

But I guess that's part of being human—the intrinsic struggle between irrelevance and ego. Even though I can accept that my emotions aren't facts, they often feel tangible. Powerful and overwhelming, like a never-ending set of waves pummeling my shore.

Lost in a mini-meditation where I imagine that instead of sand, I'm a wave indifferent to fear or heartache, I miss the soft chime of the doorbell. I don't notice Rye and Lily leaving the room. Nor do I hear a single set of footsteps approaching me.

But then, like my cells are coded to react to Evangeline's nearness, I sense her. My skin vibrates, the hairs on my neck lifting. My lungs instinctively expand to bring her closer.

My missing piece.

Her advance is tentative, with several long pauses during which I struggle not to turn around. As hard as it is, I wait.

Come here, baby, I coax silently. *I won't bite.*

When she finally appears a few feet away, I give myself permission to look at her. Baggy sweatpants, white T-shirt, and flip-flops. Hair in a messy bun, no makeup covering the sprinkle of freckles on her nose. Arms crossed tightly over her chest. Eyes on the ocean. Chin slightly uplifted. Lips lightly pursed.

You're so fucking gorgeous, Fairy.

Like she hears my thought, her gaze flickers to me. The moment our eyes meet, hers snap back to the window.

"Great view," she says.

My face spasms as I hold back a grin of triumph. "Yep. Pretty much the only thing I like about this city."

"Hating L.A. is such a cliché. What's not to love? We have sunshine and beaches. Oh, and don't forget smoothies and avocados."

The thick sarcasm in her voice has the unfortunate side effect of sending blood rushing to my cock. I quickly tuck my hands in my pockets to minimize the evidence, grateful I traded sweats for jeans this morning.

"I don't actually hate it here," I murmur. "I probably just resent that I can't experience it. I wish I could hit up a taco truck and spend an afternoon at the beach." I pause, wincing. "That probably sounds super whiny and ungrateful."

Surprising me, she shakes her head. "No, I get it." She hesitates, and I hold my breath until she continues. "Do you think if our dads weren't our dads, we still would have felt the compulsion for all this? The career, the fame, this… life?"

Facing her, I lean a shoulder on the window frame. Casual, like this is no big deal. Just your average, deep-as-fuck conversation between lifelong friends.

Inside, I'm exploding.

"I think so," I say carefully. "I've wanted to make music from the moment I first held a guitar, and I vividly remember you singing before you could even talk. That being said, it would have been a lot harder for me to make it to this level."

She gives me a dubious look. "How so?"

"If certain doors hadn't already been open because of my dad, I think we both know my personality would have been a major roadblock."

The glimmer of humor in her eyes makes me glad I'm already leaning on something.

"You seem to do okay with the whole *peopling* thing nowadays."

I grin at her. "Are you agreeing I was an asshole?"

Her gaze returns to the window, but her lips curl in the cutest little smile. "Maybe."

My chuckle reaps an immediate reward: her

answering shiver of awareness. It's a challenge not to entertain a fantasy of mapping her goosebumps with my tongue. Good thing I'm a pro at abstinence.

Pulling my gaze from her, I find a wave to focus on. "That compulsion you mentioned—I think everyone has it. We all want to be known and heard, validated and loved. As artists, we simply have a public, defined space to ask for that feedback. The key to staying happy, at least for me, is maintaining perspective. My music is a reflection of me, sure, but it's also just one part of the whole. So I try to remember that no matter how loud a million strangers are, their feedback isn't nearly as valuable as the voices of those who see all of me."

Feeling Evangeline's stare, I glance at her and immediately tense. She looks horrified.

"What is it? What did I say?"

To my shock, she laughs. "Nothing. That was really profound, is all."

The stranglehold on my lungs releases, then reclamps twice as hard when she *fades* right in front of me. Her smile falls, shoulders curling inward. Her eyes turn distant right before she looks down.

When she speaks, her voice sounds *wrong*. Timid and sad. "I'm happy you're clean and sober, Wilder. I'm sorry I've been too cowardly to tell you that." She makes a soft, derisive sound. "Let's be honest, I've been too much of a coward to even acknowledge you for the last six years."

My ability to speak is shredded, her name a puff of air she doesn't hear. She hugs herself tighter, making herself even smaller, and closes her eyes.

"In the beginning, I avoided you because I was angry and my heart was broken. But even when I didn't feel that way anymore, I kept avoiding you. Probably because deep down I knew your voice mattered more than most. And if I listened to you, I'd have to face shit I wasn't ready to face."

The cracks in my heart widen, and I can't take it anymore. Closing the distance between us, I wrap my arms around her. She stiffens at first, but then a miracle happens. Her weight drops against me, forehead thudding on my chest. And while her arms stay between us, the extra space is a good thing—my stupid cock doesn't care that this is an intense and tenuous moment.

"I'll never judge you," I whisper.

A tremor wracks her body. I hold her as close as I dare, rubbing circles on her back with one hand and cupping her head with the other.

"I'm jealous of you," she mumbles. "You've got it all figured out while I... well, I don't. Not even close. I don't know what I'm doing anymore. Nothing makes sense. Nothing feels right."

This feels right.

I keep the thought to myself and rest my chin on her soft hair. "I definitely don't have it all figured out. Believe me, I've felt the same way you do more times than I can count. In my case, it's usually expectations that trip me up, specifically the ones my younger self had. I get stuck comparing how I thought my life would look to how it really does, and I lose sight of what matters."

Her breath waterfalls against my chest, warming the skin over my heart. She says tartly, "It's really weirding me out how mature and wise you suddenly are."

I shake with a soundless laugh. "I have my moments, I guess. Catch me on a different day, and I'll be the same immature freak you've always known."

"Somehow I doubt that."

I hum a low, soothing note, gratified when she relaxes even more. "There's one thing my younger and current self agree on, though. A truth I accepted in childhood that has never been challenged."

"What?" she whispers.

"You," I say just as softly. "The truth of Evangeline Marie Sullivan. From birth, you've been a force to be reckoned with. I know you feel lost right now. That's okay. Feel what you feel. But someday soon you're going to remember how powerful you truly are."

She trembles, and I pretend I don't notice as her tears soak through my T-shirt.

"Damn you," she croaks.

I can't help grinning. "I know," I say, my voice thick. "I'm still the worst."

Her answering laugh is strangled.

Movement across the room brings my gaze to the hallway connecting to the front of the house. Rye and Lily take us in, their expressions a mix of pain and relief.

When Rye's gaze moves to my face, I widen my eyes, hoping to communicate that I desperately need his help. My arms don't want to let go of Evangeline, and I'm seconds from ruining the moment with an inappropriate confession of my feelings.

He leans down to whisper in Lily's ear. She nods and backs up until she's out of sight.

I hold my breath.

"Hey, Lily!" Rye throws the jovial words over his shoulder. "You're not gonna believe this, but it looks like grandma and grandpa are friends again."

I groan.

Evangeline giggles and rubs her snotty nose on my chest.

Thank fucking God for Rye.

evangeline

Rye's obnoxious comment comes at the perfect time, interrupting the equally unbearable and euphoric experience of being in Wilder's arms again.

I'm likewise grateful when not five minutes later, Anita, Sandra, and the team of stylists arrive. Despite coming straight from the airport, our publicist and PA barely stop to greet us. Anita herds everyone to the master suite while Sandra runs through our timeline for the day, including where we'll change after the event and the afterparties we're expected to attend.

My last glimpse of Wilder is of him talking quietly to Rye near the windows. I shouldn't be surprised when he turns his head, but I am. Our eyes meet, his crinkling in a subtle smile. Then Sandra's arm steers me around a corner.

As chaos cyclones around Lily and me, I don't miss the disgruntled looks she throws me. But there are too many strangers in the room for her to grill me about Wilder—a gift I'm glad to accept. I'm not sure I'd have the fortitude to deflect her questions or downplay the gravity of what happened.

Wilder holding me.

Me, voluntarily being held.

Soon enough, the mayhem settles into a well-oiled machine. Anita and Sandra come and go, phones glued to either their hands or ears. Lily takes pity on me, drawing me into a familiar rhythm of lighthearted banter as the stylists have their ways with us.

As we chat and laugh, more walls fall inside me, and I remember what having a best friend feels like. What having *Lily* feels like. And I don't know how I survived the last six months without her.

There's only one serious moment between us. We're sitting on a couch with curlers in our hair and sheet masks on our faces. During a lull in conversation, she catches my eye and whispers, "I've missed you."

Emotion floods me and I'm forced to blink rapidly at the ceiling to keep tears from spilling over. The facialist rushes over in a tizzy, worried that product has dripped in my eye. It takes me a while to convince her I'm fine, which Lily finds hysterical. She then laughs so hard she somehow gets product in *her* eye.

It isn't until the makeup artist goes to work on my face and I'm forced to stay still and silent that thoughts of Wilder intrude.

For the next forty minutes, I relive every second of this morning on a loop. From my first sight of him at the window against a backdrop of blue, to my overwhelming impulse to see his face and talk to him. His clear eyes, the compassion and tenderness in them. His shockingly insightful replies to my questions and confessions.

When he hugged me, in the moment all I felt was the comfort and rightness of his embrace. I felt sheltered. Safe. Only now, in hindsight, does dangerous awareness bloom.

Sitting motionless becomes increasingly difficult as I experience a delayed physical response to his touch linked to older, still potent memories. His bare, sweat-slick chest against mine. The flex of his hips between my thighs. Fingers clenched in my hair. A hot palm on my throat.

Low, rasping whispers in my ear.

"That's my girl. Such a good little slut, dripping all over my

cock. Fuck, baby. You're the most beautiful mess I've ever seen."

Memories spiral out of control, turning my face and chest red and blotchy. My makeup artist has a silent panic attack.

"Can we turn the A/C on?" I ask weakly.

Seated a few feet away, Lily takes one look at me and her eyebrows disappear beneath her bangs. I avoid her laughing eyes and narrow my focus on the movement of brushes on my face. Then on the stylist showing me options for shoes and purses. On the cheerful woman who steps forward to style my hair. On Lily as she shares the woes of sleep regression with everyone in the room. On Anita when she reappears to prep us for questions on the red carpet.

But no matter how hard I try to stay present, Wilder is everywhere inside me. Waiting behind every blink, in every silent moment. He's smoke seeping through all my cracks. A skeleton key opening all of my locked doors.

"I know you feel lost right now. That's okay. Feel what you feel. But someday soon you're going to remember how powerful you truly are."

After all this time, he still believes in me. And I can't for the life of me understand why.

Justified or not, I abandoned him at the lowest point in his life. And when he graduated from rehab and came to my parents' house? When he tried to make amends to me? I had no compassion at all. I couldn't *see* him. I could barely hear him.

In the three months he was gone, beyond shaping my pain into songs that would become Glow's most acclaimed album, I didn't process my heartbreak. I chewed on it. Magnified it. *Drowned* in it. Outwardly, I put on a brave face. Acted like I was coping. Internally, I was digging and laying the foundational bricks of my first, highest wall, behind which I hoarded my misery.

I became fixated on my nyctophobia, convinced that overcoming my lifelong fear of the dark was somehow synonymous with healing. Every night, I'd crawl into my closet and sit in catatonic terror until dawn. Eventually, I grew desensitized to the phobia. But there was no healing. I hadn't liberated myself—I'd saturated myself with darkness.

When I saw Wilder again, it was the morning after a particularly bad night. Mentally, I was still in my dark closet. So when he took accountability for his actions and asked me what he could do to make it right, I laughed in his face. I said heinous, unforgivable things

—things that make me cringe to think about now, that stunned my parents so badly they barely spoke to me for days afterward.

But Wilder just stood there and accepted my hostility. He didn't defend himself, not even from my worst, wildest accusations. When I ran out of steam, he said only, "I hear you," and walked away from me like I had from him.

Or I thought he had.

As impossible as it seems, he stayed my friend from afar. My faithful shadow, even when it was so dark I couldn't see him.

"You didn't take your allergy medicine, did you?"

Lily's overly bright voice brings me back to the present as I'm being zipped into my dress. I frown, about to ask what she's talking about, then realize my eyes are burning with tears.

I sniff them back and groan. "Damn. I forgot."

Within a minute, four people have produced antihistamines. As Lily holds in laughter, I thank them and quickly fabricate a story about the medicated eyedrops waiting for me in the limo.

The topic is quickly forgotten when someone else points out the time. There's a flurry of finishing touches to our hair and makeup. We step into our shoes. Transfer our phones and mini-cosmetics into clutches.

A smiling woman who arrived twenty minutes ago unlocks a case of fine jewelry for us. Lily and I choose a few pieces to wear, giggling because playing dress-up still hasn't gotten old.

Anita gives us air kisses and leaves to meet us on the red carpet. Sandra oversees the room being packed up.

In the living room, Rye waits in a charcoal suit to match Lily's dress. She admonishes him for looking so good while she's ovulating. He gushes over her ethereal beauty. I laugh at their antics, feeling joyful by proximity. But when they start playfully groping each other and whispering, the brightness inside me dims.

Looking away, I stare toward the windows, the space before them now empty.

"Did Wilder already leave?"

As the question slips out, my face heats. The shocked silence behind me magnifies not only the disappointment in my voice, but the incongruity of me asking in the first place.

With a sigh, I turn to face my friends in time to see Lily land a solid punch to Rye's stomach. He winces and attempts a neutral expression. But his blue eyes are too bright.

"Never mind," I say quickly. "Stupid question."

Obviously Wilder left to meet his bandmates. It's not

like he could have ridden with us, arrived at the event with us.

The sense of loss I feel is completely irrational. So is the fact it lingers until Clay arrives. Then shame takes centerstage inside me, followed swiftly by a dance of irritation and hurt when he says, "I thought we agreed on the cream chiffon dress, not this Morticia Addams shit."

I pull away from him, glad Lily and Rye are saying goodbye to Emma down the hall.

"For fuck's sake, Clay. This is vintage Versace."

His eyes flash and narrow, but before he can say anything, Lily and Rye return. He's immediately all gracious words and smiles. My irritation simmers as we file out to the limo. When Lily heads for the bench behind the driver, I take the seat beside her. Clay's reaction is brief—a clenched jaw and searing glance—before he starts talking sports with Rye.

What happens next is my fault.

I'm not paying enough attention to the conversation, focused mostly on quelling my internal chaos as I gaze out my window at passing scenery.

Then Rye says, "I had no idea you were into baseball, man. We should catch a few Mariners games this summer."

"This summer?" echoes Clay.

I whip my head around, but it's too late.

Rye smiles and nods. "You'll be coming up with Eva, right? God knows we'll barely see them the first few weeks they're in the studio. Plenty of time for us to catch a game or two."

My body flashes cold, every muscle locking, my mind blanking.

Clay's laugh is a harsh, truncated burst. "What are you talking about? They're not recording this summer."

Lily sucks in a shocked breath.

Rye's eyes dart to me. He blanches, then coughs. "I mean, I, uh—just some wishful thinking on my part. Wouldn't that be cool?" No one acknowledges the obvious lie.

If I were braver, if I had a voice at all right now, I'd tell Rye this isn't his fault. I'd take accountability. Come clean to Clay, to my friends, all three of whom I've wronged.

For weeks, I've offered and omitted pieces of myself as needed. All to maintain a laughable facsimile of control over my life. Now Clay knows I've been lying to him, and my friends are probably confused as hell.

"Explain yourself, Eva. Right. Fucking. *Now.*"

Scratch that—now they know something is seriously wrong with my relationship. For the first time in front of them, Clay has dropped all pretense. His voice oozes so much menace that I flinch, Lily gasps, and Rye turns toward him with a furious glare.

Before they can come to my defense and make everything a thousand times worse, I force my numb lips to move.

"Later." I gesture weakly to his window.

Clay glances outside to see that we're nearing the arena. For the rest of the short drive, he stares at me and seethes.

No one says a word.

CHAPTER SIXTEEN

I made a mistake

Tasting you

Before I knew

What starving was

Fifteen feet away, on the other side of Chateau Fontaine's upscale bar, Evangeline sits with five other famous faces in a horseshoe booth. The lighting is dim, the music loud, and it's close to two in the morning.

Besides the waitstaff, I'm the only sober person in the place.

The luxury hotel in West Hollywood is the last stop on Glow's afterparty tour, and thank fuck for that. I'm exhausted, my senses overloaded to the extreme, and Zander is at the end of his rope from me dragging him all over the city. Or he was until a few minutes ago. Now he's flirting with a nerdy-looking dude I vaguely recognize from television.

Evangeline throws her head back in a laugh. I can't hear it, but I don't need to in order to know it's fake.

The bad feeling I had earlier is back with a vengeance.

Something happened after I left the house. I have no idea what, since Lily and Rye have avoided me like the plague all night. But they've also avoided Eva. Or maybe it's Eva who's been avoiding them.

My gaze narrows on what I can see of Clay's face. He's currently at the bar, his back to Eva's booth. He's chatting with two men—one of them a recognizable music producer—and sipping a bright green martini like a dumbass. He looks even more smug than usual. Not surprising, since Glow took home two more Grammys tonight and Clay's deluded enough to think they're his by proximity.

But I haven't missed the fact that besides arriving and leaving together, he's kept his distance from Evangeline all night, too.

"You good if I head out?" asks Zander. A quick glance behind him reveals the blushing actor.

Smirking, I nod. "I'm not going to stay much longer. Thanks for hanging." Leaning toward him, I lower my voice. "Have fun polishing your new Grammy."

Zander laugh-groans. "You're such a loser. Speaking of, have fun with your stalking."

I roll my eyes and wave him off. When they're gone, I look back across the room just as a scowling Lily walks in from the other side. I don't see Rye, but he's probably not far behind.

I straighten from my slouched position against a wall. Before I can decide whether or not to approach Lily, she beelines for Evangeline's booth. Leaning down, she whispers something to Evangeline, who rears back, shaking her head and laughing. Lily tries again. This time, she's able to tug Eva to standing.

It's immediately apparent that Evangeline is wasted. She stumbles in her high heels. Lily reaches out to help her, but she jerks away and almost falls again. When she finally balances, she does a little bow that makes everyone in the booth laugh.

Lily steps forward again, urgency and worry clear in her expression. She says something that causes Evangeline to frown, and I watch her lips shape the words, "I can't, Lily."

After a pause fraught with enough tension that I feel it across the room, Lily spins on a heel and stalks away. Evangeline stares blankly after her, swaying on her feet.

A quick glance toward the bar tells me that Clay hasn't noticed the drama. But others have.

I'm walking before I've processed the thought. Just as Evangeline turns to sit back down, I curl my fingers around her bicep. Startled, she looks up at me with wide eyes.

"Can I talk to you for a sec?"

She nods, her gaze lowering to my mouth. I tell myself I'm only imagining the heat in her eyes, that the increased glassiness is from booze and not lust. My body, of course, decides differently.

Ignoring my suddenly tight pants, I slide my hand down to her elbow and guide her into a nearby hallway. She's so out of it, she doesn't comment when I pull her into a family bathroom.

Given the luxury of the attached hotel, it's no shock the space is huge and spa-like, with a separate seating area, high-end finishes, and mood lighting. On the double-sink vanity, there are baskets of toiletries and a pitcher of ice water next to a stack of sparkling glasses. The toilet is off to the right, the partially open door confirming that we're alone.

I flip the deadbolt on the main door, then steer Evangeline to a leather couch. She sits—or rather, falls

—then topples to the side until her cheek is smooshed on a cushion.

Her eyes flutter closed. "Mmm cold. Feels good."

Swallowing a sigh, I head for the water dispenser and fill a glass. Then I crouch next to her head.

"Can you sit up for me?"

"Nopity nope."

Despite my frustration, my lips quirk. "Evangeline, come on."

"Pfft." Eyes still closed, she squirms, bare legs scissoring until her high heels thunk to the floor. "Thas better."

She rolls onto her back and stretches with a hum of pleasure, completely oblivious to the fact her silver-beaded minidress isn't stretching with her. The hem rides so low over her chest, I can see the small mole above her right nipple and a hint of pink areola.

My cock, already stiff against my thigh, pulses in agonized want.

Out of desperation, I snap, "Fairy."

Her eyes pop open. Glazed, they roam my face before stalling on my mouth. "I thought I dreamed you."

Jesus fucking Christ, I'm not strong enough for this.

I'm still reeling from the longing in her voice when her eyes suddenly widen. She laughs, the sound soft, throaty, and designed to torture me.

"Remember asking me if I'd ever pierce my nipples?"

The water glass almost slips from my hand. Setting it down quickly on the end table, I look up at the ceiling and start counting down from a hundred. When I get to seventy-three, my balls stop throbbing. At sixty, I find the willpower to lower my gaze back to her.

"Evangeline, I—"

"Do you remember?"

She's not laughing anymore. Her eyes are more lucid, the look in them brave but resigned. Like she's expecting disappointment. Like she's used to it.

It fucking hurts. Even if I understand why. Even if it's my own damn fault she's ever doubted that our time together was as real for me as it was for her.

I've never had a chance to explain that by the end of my using—which she had a front-row seat to—I was lucky if I managed to stave off the full brunt of withdrawals every day. Actually *feeling* loaded was rare. As weird as it sounds to most people, it hadn't even been a priority. If it had been, I would have stuck to drinking.

I have no doubt alcohol would have taken me to rock bottom eventually, just like it did my dad. Opiates got me there first because they did what alcohol couldn't. They turned down the volume on my anxiety and—most importantly—helped me function like a somewhat normal person. Initially, at least. Until my addiction progressed. Until I was walking a fraying tightrope of lies, avoidance, and denial.

Until I lost her.

I was a junkie, no question. Enslaved to my physical craving and mental dependence. But the times I was impaired enough to forget a single moment from that month of my life?

Zero.

Maybe someday I'll be able to tell Evangeline everything. Maybe it will matter to her, or maybe it won't.

But at least I can fix one misconception right now.

"I remember asking more than once. You finally told me that if I shut up about it, you'd let me take you to get pierced on your twenty-fifth birthday."

She looks away, flushing and blinking fast. Probably remembering the other part of the deal, just like I am—that if she went through with it, I'd owe her twenty-five orgasms. And ice cream.

My thoughts are sluggish, bloated with memory and desire and regret. When she grabs my hand, I don't understand what's happening at first. And when I finally do, I'm incapable of resisting as she guides my fingers to the peak of her breast.

Fuck me sideways.

Even with all the beads on her dress, I can feel the metal beneath. Adjusting her grip, she guides the tip of my index finger from one side of the petite barbell to the other.

I'm concentrating so hard on not nutting in my pants that when she speaks, I barely register her soft, forlorn voice.

"Everyone's mad at me. You should be, too. I'm... I'm not a good person. I used to be one, I think. Was I, Wilder? A good person? I've been trying to remember, but all I can really remember is you. What we were. What we did to each other."

There's a delay while my bloodless brain processes the words. Then I'm suddenly, acutely clearheaded. Slipping my hand from beneath hers, I sit back on my heels and heave air into my lungs.

Evangeline turns her face toward the back of the couch. A thick section of her pale hair falls off the edge and lands on my thigh, light as a feather and heavier than lead. I clench my hands to keep from touching it.

"S' okay," she whispers. "I wouldn't want me anymore, either."

"You have no idea—" I clench my teeth to hold back the rest. Nothing I say is going to land right now. Chances are she won't even remember this conversation tomorrow.

I reach for the water glass, determined to at least have her drink some before I decide what to do. I don't want to send her home with Clay, especially without knowing whether or not it's safe for her. But Lily and Rye are ignoring me, and I can't exactly carry her out of here myself. Not without serious consequences.

A sudden vibration in my back pocket threatens my grip on the water again. I put it down for the second time and yank my phone out, sighing in relief when I see a text from Rye.

RYE

Not avoiding u on purpose. Shit went off the rails after u left. Been trying to keep Lily calm all day. Headed back to house now

WILDER

Wtf happened?

He types, and types some more. In the interim, I lean forward to peek at Evangeline's face. She's passed out and drooling.

Finally, Rye's texts come through.

I stuck my foot in my mouth in the limo. Said something about Eva being in Seattle this summer to record. Clay was like "haha what? No, she's not."

> Eva got so pale I thought she was gonna pass out. Clay told her to explain herself in this super psycho voice. I almost put his face through the window. I can't explain it. My skin was legit crawling from the look he gave her

> We tried all night to get her to talk about it and come home with us but she wouldn't. Lily finally lost it. I had to get her out of there before she went postal

My adrenaline skyrockets, my muscles quivering with the desire to break Clay's bones. When I look down at Evangeline, a different need rises. One just as implausible, just as reckless. But far more appealing.

I want to carry her out of here and straight to the airport. Fly her home. Lock her in my house. Never let her out of my sight again.

"Fuck," I whisper. "Fuck. Fuck."

Clenching a hand in my hair, I look wildly around the bathroom.

Three things I can see. Three I can touch. Three I can hear.

Inhale. Hold. Release.

My phone buzzes again.

> U there? Pls tell me you haven't left the party

I haven't. With Eva in a bathroom. She's trashed and passed out on a couch

Thank god. Don't let her leave with Clay ok? I'll drop off Lily and come back. We'll figure something out

K. No way in hell she's leaving with him

I toss my phone to the floor.

Eva stirs. "Wilder?"

"I'm here."

Unable to help myself, I stroke the hair off her forehead and temple. Her eyes are still closed, but tightly, as though she's in pain.

"Need you to know something…"

I lean closer to hear her faint voice. "Yeah?"

"You weren't a footnote. You were the title of my favorite book."

Her whole body tenses.

Then she lurches toward me and vomits all over my lap.

evangeline

The second I wake up, I remember how much I hate alcohol. My mouth tastes like a trashcan, my stomach is on a boat, and my heartbeat thuds in my eyelids.

Rolling away from sunlight that burns my face like a chemical peel, I search blindly for a pillow to put over my head. After a few seconds, I give up with a groan of defeat. Even if by some miracle I was suddenly the type of person who could fall back asleep easily, the ache in my bladder would negate the option.

Nevertheless, opening my eyes is a mistake. For several reasons.

First, my eyelashes have glued themselves together in retribution for me not taking off the eight pounds of mascara I wore yesterday. By the time I force them to part, my eyes are stinging and watering.

Second, I can no longer ignore the fact my bedroom is south-facing and doesn't get direct sunlight—the kind blasting on my back right now.

And lastly, the man sleeping in an oversized armchair beside the bed, clearly having kept an eye on me all night, is *not* Clay.

Wilder's arms are crossed over his bare chest, his head propped awkwardly on what looks like a bunched up T-shirt. His long legs, encased in plaid pajama pants, are crossed at the ankle on an overturned luggage case. Dark hair falls artlessly over his brow. His lips are slightly parted, his breathing deep and even.

My physical misery now has a challenger—absolute panic. They go to war as I sit up too fast and almost hurl. Cold sweat breaks out on my body. Swallowing bile, I look around and recognize the style of the room. I'm back in the Santa Monica house.

What the hell happened last night?

As if waiting for the mental cue, flashbacks unfurl like a row of middle fingers eager to extend a *fuck you* to what's left of my mental stability.

What happened in the limo. Surviving the red carpet and Clay's touches through sheer willpower. The cool satisfaction in his eyes when I sat down after Glow's final win. Changing in a hotel room and dodging Lily's attempts to talk. Avoiding her and Rye the rest of the night. Laughing and pretending everything was fine. Drowning my despair with alcohol.

My memories melt somewhere between Lily's final attempt to speak with me and Wilder's hand on my arm as we walked somewhere.

My panic reaches new heights, manifesting as a high-pitched note in my ears. I scramble off the bed, almost eating floor when my feet are momentarily caught in the comforter. My tangled, product-encrusted hair whips around my face as I dart erratically around the room. In the attached bathroom, I locate my dress—damp for some reason—hanging over a towel rack. But my clutch is nowhere to be found.

I run back into the bedroom.

"Wilder, wake up! Where's my phone?"

He jerks upright with a grunt, then winces and grabs his neck. "Shit. Why are you yelling?"

His sleep-roughened voice arrows right between my legs. Before I can recover, he stands, visually punching me with the mouthwatering sight of his bare upper half.

No one should have that many abs. It's not natural.

Wilder's rapidly clearing eyes scan my face, drop down my body, then snap back up. He drags a palm over his mouth, his brow pinched. Air leaves his nose in a short burst.

That's when I realize I'm wearing a thong under one of his T-shirts, which just so happens to be soft, thin, and white, and that the sun is behind me. Not only can he see how tightly my thighs are squeezed together, he can see everything else, too.

Another flashback hits. Mortified, I slap my hands over my face and shake my head, not caring that the violent movement magnifies the pounding in my skull.

"Please, please tell me I didn't make you touch my nipple."

He coughs over a sound suspiciously close to a laugh. "You totally did."

"Why didn't you lie?" I wail.

Now he's for sure laughing. "I make an effort not to these days. Besides, you were shitfaced. It's not like I took it as an invitation." He pauses. "Do you remember anything from after that?"

I slowly lower my hands, turning my back to him at the same time so I can stay sane. "Not at the moment, no. Why? What else do I need to be humiliated about?"

"Absolutely nothing," he says, quick and firm. "I just wondered if you knew how you got here."

I shake my head. Panic creeps back in. "Do you know where my phone is? I really need it."

I listen to the familiar sound of him pulling on a shirt, then his soft footsteps approaching me. They pause a few feet away.

"Your phone is in the kitchen, but before you bolt, listen for a sec. Everything is okay. After you passed out, Rye and Lily came back to the party. Lily stayed with you while I went outside to meet my driver. Rye found Clay and told him they were bringing you here. He was fine with it."

Too relieved to acknowledge the edge in his voice, I whisper, "Thank God."

His following sigh is weighted with intent. A whole different level of anxiety ripples through me, shortening my breath.

"Evangeline..."

Turning fast, I dart around him toward the bathroom. "About to pee my pants, sorry!"

After closing the door and locking it, I brace my hands on the vanity and try to catch my breath. My body shakes intermittently, cramping with so much tension that my bladder has gone into hiding. The mirror tells me I look as bad as I feel. My bloodshot eyes are ringed by melted makeup. A section of my hair sticks up in defiance of gravity, the rest flattened and tangled in chunks. My skin is grayish-white, my lips bloodless.

There's a soft thud on the door that I instinctively

know is from Wilder's forehead meeting the wood. Sure enough, his low voice slips around the frame and curls into my ears.

"I know about what happened in the limo. Why you got so drunk."

Another thud.

"This might make you hate me again, but I have to say it. Juggling lies, partitioning off parts of yourself, avoiding the truth screaming in your gut... it's no way to live. I should know. I also know how scary it is to break free of the bullshit and let it all go. Feels kind of like jumping without a parachute. But you *can* take your life back."

There's a long pause. My stomach churns, and it's not from the hangover this time. I can feel what's coming, sense it in the same way you smell ozone between lightning strikes.

Because no matter how drastically storms have altered our topography as adults, the structure of us as children still stands. Within those unassailable walls, Wilder remains my silent protector and reluctant hero. Challenging me to be brave even as he tries to shelter me from pain. And always, always finding me when I'm lost.

"I've broken promises to you, Evangeline. I broke *us*. I'll never forgive myself for it. I don't expect you to forgive me, either. But you have to know… even if you don't want me to be, I'm in your corner. Forever. That's one promise I will never, ever break."

There's a final thud of his forehead on the door before his footsteps move away.

I don't know how long I stand there unmoving, covered in goosebumps and staring blankly at the door. It could be a minute or ten before Lily knocks and tells me she's leaving a change of clothes on the bed, and that I'll find toiletries, including ibuprofen, under the sink.

Her calm voice cracks the plaster on my limbs. I open the door, stalling her retreat from the room.

"I'm sorry, Lily. For so much. The Indigo meeting and what I said to you after. Shutting you out. Being a shit friend and godmother. I've never wanted to leave Glow. I'm *not* leaving Glow. I just…"

My voice hits an emotional blockage in my throat.

Her chin quivers before firming. "I'm sorry, too. I haven't been a good friend to you, either. I was too wrapped up in my own life to see what was going on, and I wasn't there when you needed me."

"W-what are you talking about?"

But I already know. I fucking know because like Wilder said, it's the truth screaming in my gut. The one I've been terrified to face for longer than I can admit to myself.

"I'm talking about Clay. He's abusive. Some part of you must know that."

My chest tightens, burning. More pieces of the walls I've been dismantling rip free, falling and shattering. Tears fill my eyes. Suddenly dizzy, I grab the doorframe.

Then I force out probably the hardest words I've ever had to speak.

"I know."

Lily's expression softens, the sympathy in her eyes half balm, half acid on my heart.

"Leave him, Eva. You can do it. We'll help you. Anything you need."

Panic rises again. I break out in a sweat. "I-I want to. I... I've tried. I'm trying. Please believe me. I'm sorry."

She closes the space between us and wraps her arms tightly around my waist. "It's okay. I understand. I love you, and when you're ready to talk about it, I'll be here." Stepping back, she wipes tears from her cheeks. "Right now the only thing you have to do is shower. Please. Between your pits and your breath, I'm about to pass out."

I laugh, sniffing back tears. "Ugh, you're right. It's so bad." Another memory abruptly appears, and I groan in embarassment. "I puked on Wilder, didn't I?"

She nods, failing to hide her amusement. "A few

times. I cleaned you up and got you out of your dress, though. In case you were worried."

I nod, wincing. "I'm remembering now. Thanks for doing that."

"Sure. I would have stayed up with you, too, but I literally couldn't keep my eyes open, and Emma…"

"No, no. I completely understand." I laugh weakly. "I can't believe Wilder babysat me all night. What alternate dimension is this?"

She smirks. "A good one, trust me. Just wait until you try his French toast."

evangeline

Four ibuprofen and washing my hair three times in the world's longest, hottest shower bring me most of the way back to the land of the living. Fresh clothes and minty breath do the rest. I'm still hungover, my eyes aching and limbs weak, but at least I'm clean.

Dressed in a pair of stretchy black leggings and a baggy, faded T-shirt from Glow's first tour, I venture out of the bedroom. I make my way through the quiet house to the kitchen, where I find Rye sipping coffee. When he sees me, he stands and gestures to a stool at the island, then moves to the oven.

I sit, murmuring thanks as he sets a warm plate of thick, browned brioche slices in front of me and slides three small bowls my way. Powdered sugar, maple syrup, and fresh blueberries and raspberries. Despite lingering queasiness, my stomach growls.

I pop a berry in my mouth. "Where is everyone?"

"My mom took Emma down to the beach for a bit, and Lily's showering. Coffee?"

"God, yes. Thank you."

He pours me a cup, topping it with half and half before sliding it my way. I take an eager gulp as he hops back onto his stool.

"And where's... the chef?"

Rye's smile doesn't reach his exhausted eyes. "He went to see some friends."

I glance at the clock on the oven. "Before nine on a Monday?"

He takes a sip of his coffee, avoiding my eyes. "Wilder went to a meeting, Eva. The sober kind. He should be back soon."

Realizing I'm drowning my plate in syrup, I hastily set the bowl down. "Oh. Well, it was nice of him to cook breakfast." We both wince at my too-cheerful tone. Thankfully, he doesn't comment.

I distractedly cut into my French toast. Did Wilder go to a meeting because of me? I hadn't considered that dealing with me drunk might have been triggering for him.

Of course it was, idiot.

My appetite fades, but I make myself take a bite.

"Holy shit," I mumble.

Rye snorts. "Right?"

I chew and swallow. "Are you guys still going to Disney today?"

"As much as it pains me to say it, yes. Leaving in thirty if you want to join."

"I'd rather stab myself."

He smirks. "Wilder said the same thing."

I swallow another mouthful. "Did he seem okay? When he left?"

There's a flash of something on Rye's face. Something I've never seen there before, at least not directed at me. A mix of disappointment and resentment. My heart pangs.

"He's fine."

I manage a few more bites. Even oven-warmed, the French toast is hands down the best I've ever tasted. I have no idea whether it's because I'm hungover or it's actually that good, but I suspect the latter.

Setting down my fork, I reach for my coffee and courage. "I'm sorry, Rye. For what I put you through yesterday. And for... everything."

Eyes on his mug, he shakes his head. "We're not doing this right now," he says tightly.

My stomach drops, my eyes instantly on fire. I blink fast. "O-okay. Sorry."

I make to push back from the island, but Rye quickly turns toward me. His blue eyes are beseeching. "I'm not mad at *you*, Eva. I'm mad at... all of it. Mostly, though, I'm mad at your—" His lips seal, but the word *boyfriend* floats between us.

Lily must have told him about our conversation. How when I tried to talk about Clay, I could barely form a sentence. I lower my eyes to my plate, my neck heating as I imagine them talking about me. Their *pity*.

I try to stay calm, but it's no use. An ugly trifecta of humiliation, emotional nakedness, and defensive anger swallows me. My spine stiffens, fingers curling until my nails bite my palms.

"I bet you both think I'm some hapless victim, huh? Poor Eva, too weak and clueless to know her boyfriend is a raging asshole. How long has this been going on?" I lift my gaze to Rye, whose freckles turn stark as he pales.

"Eva—"

I cut him off with a low, bitter laugh. "I should have known something was off with how you guys were acting. Like nothing has changed between us. Like I haven't been ignoring your calls for months and didn't completely fuck over Lily at the Indigo meeting." Thinking back over the last couple of months, I land on an explosive conversation with my dad when I told him I wasn't visiting for Christmas. "My parents are behind this, aren't they?"

They've never liked Clay. My dad especially. The first time I brought him to meet them was a disaster. When I confronted my dad afterward, he justified his borderline rudeness by telling me a bunch of old rumors about Clay's father.

I was stunned and instantly defensive. Clay had swept me off my feet a few months prior, at a point in my life when I'd been battling listlessness and rapidly worsening depression. Suddenly I had a mature, confident, supportive man in my life. Someone who wasn't threatened by my career or schedule, who had his own life in Los Angeles. We talked daily and saw each other once a month, spending long weekends together. He was the brightest spot in my dim world.

I accused my dad of condemning the son for the actions of the father, callously adding I would've thought he'd be the last person to do that.

Hindsight is a real bitch.

My dad *was* wrong to judge Clay based on rumors of his father, but his concern was justified all the same. I just didn't know it for another few months. By then, however, I'd already begun distancing myself from my family. Not seeing or calling them as often to avoid talking about my relationship.

The first few times I cried myself to sleep over something Clay said to me, I wanted to call my mom badly but talked myself out of it. She has PTSD from a relationship in her early twenties, and I convinced myself I'd only be triggering her trauma. My situation wasn't nearly as bad—Clay was mean sometimes, and controlling, but he wasn't physically abusive. Plus, if I told my mom, she'd tell my dad, and I didn't want to deal with his militant, overprotective mode.

But what really kept my mouth shut was pride and its shadow, shame. I couldn't bring myself to admit that despite being raised to recognize red flags, I'd missed them all. *Again.* And that my second serious relationship was somehow even more toxic than the first.

By the time Clay and I celebrated our one-year anniversary, I was already numb to the cycle. The slow build of tension. Scattered, tiny hurts escalating into a deeper betrayal. Confrontation and misery. Apologies and a period of repair and comfort, which invariably degraded as tension built again.

My oldest friend stares at me, eyes wide and searching like he can see the emotional sewage leaking out of me.

"It's a simple question, Rye. Did my parents put you up to this?"

He swallows thickly. "They're concerned. We all are."

Something in his tone connects more dots in my mind. When I see the line that forms and understand what it means, the pain I feel is indescribable. A thousand savage cuts.

I jolt to my feet, my nerves on fire.

"They went to *him*," I choke out. "That's why he showed up at the party on New Year's Eve. It wasn't a coincidence at all. It was manipulation. Wasn't it?"

The answer comes from behind me.

"Yes."

Before I can turn, Rye stands and snaps, "Your parents wouldn't have gone to Wilder if you hadn't turned into someone none of us recognize!"

I gasp, swaying against the edge of the island.

Wilder says quellingly, "Enough."

"I'm sorry, Eva." Rye's voice is muted, his following steps swift as he leaves the room.

Then it's just us. Wilder and me. But there's none of the sparkling warmth I felt yesterday or this morning. No connection or comfort in his presence. No childhood bond or tentative new friendship.

I'm still alone.

evangeline

"Don't bother trying to explain, Wilder. Just leave me alone."

I load the condiment bowls onto my plate, then grab my mug and carry everything to the sink.

Wilder, *being fucking Wilder*, ignores my demand, following and leaning a hip against the counter a few feet away. Refusing to look at him, I turn on the hot water, then grab a sponge and squirt too much soap on it.

I hate that he doesn't tell me not to wash the dishes.

I hate that the last two years have proven to me, over and over again, that he and Clay could not be more different.

Yes, Wilder hurt me when we were younger. Both with his words and actions. In the months before I left

Night Theory, he was a total dick, and his behavior afterward was atrocious. Then, after ignoring me for three years, he seduced me on a false premise of honesty. Overwhelmed me with mind-blowing sex, intimacy, and promises of forever. All while he lied about his drug use, a fracture of trust that shattered my heart and tainted every second of our time together.

But in spite of being an asshole intermittently from nineteen to twenty-five, Wilder has never, *not fucking once,* made me feel as small, empty, and worthless as Clay.

"Will you look at me?" he asks softly.

I shake my head and keep scrubbing. The dishes are clean, but I can't make myself stop.

"I'm sure this won't be a surprise to you, but I've always felt different, even as a little kid."

His voice is just loud enough to be heard over the faucet. I pour more soap on the sponge and keep scrubbing.

"In some ways, it was probably natural for me to compare myself to others. To look for a place I fit. But my units of measurement were wrong. I was comparing my insides to everyone else's outsides. They never matched, so I invariably felt less than."

I still don't look at him, but my hands stop moving. Against my will, every part of me is listening.

"I have so many memories of watching you, Rye, and the other kids playing, laughing... I wanted to be a part of your joy, but my own conviction that I wasn't good enough held me back. It happened in school. With Night Theory, too. In focusing on how different, how alone I was, I suffocated myself with shadows of jealousy, self-loathing, and fear."

I didn't notice him move, but he's suddenly so close his chest brushes my shoulder. Heat spreads from the contact, radiating down my right side. I suck in a breath on reflex, inadvertently saturating myself with his scent. A hint of coffee beneath mint. A whisper of soap over his natural scent, that improbable fusion of dark forest, rain, and lightning.

A muscled, tattooed arm reaches into the sink. His fingers close around mine, squeezing them and the sponge I'm still holding. Suds explode, thick and silky.

His lips graze my temple. "I think it's easy to forget we're all just human. Inherently fallible. We think admitting weakness makes us weak, but it's the opposite. Only the strong admit their failings and confront the deeply uncomfortable work of growing."

A thumb wedges itself against my palm, rubbing slow circles. Gasoline hits the fires inside me, detonating in my chest, my face. Between my legs. My head empties, overwhelmed by the sensation.

I stop breathing as he shifts to stand behind me, then gasp as his other arm slips beneath mine to cage me between his body and the sink. His second hand joins the first, both of them now spreading slick bubbles over my hands and up my wrists. Strong thumbs knead tiny pressure points. Calloused fingertips enclose and twist around mine.

My breaths are staccato, my heart galloping, my pussy throbbing.

"Wilder?"

"Yes, Evangeline?" His teasing tone is so unexpected that it takes me a few seconds to answer.

"W-what are you doing?"

"Am I not being obvious enough? Here, let me fix that."

He erases the space between our bodies. The counter digs into my stomach, but I don't notice. All I feel is his hands, still moving over mine, and the heat of his chest down my spine. Ninety-nine percent of my awareness, though, is now on my lower half. Specifically my ass, against which presses undeniable evidence that he's still attracted to me. Thick, rock-hard, searing evidence.

Deep inside me, behind a rattling door, is relief so sudden and potent that if I dared to feel it, I'd probably sob for hours.

He murmurs, "The second part of my answer to your question is that I'm turning off the noise in your head so you actually hear me. Ready for the hard part?"

My mind blank, I nod.

"First and foremost, have you even met me? No one can *make* me do anything. Yes, your parents showed up at my house a few days after Christmas. Completely blindsided me. First your dad apologized for being a jerk to me years ago. I told him I'd deserved it. We had a bromance moment—it was great."

My lips twitch, then compress as he continues, "Then they dropped a bomb on me. They told me you were in trouble and asked me to try to help you."

When I immediately stiffen, he pulses his hips. Caught on the rougher fabric of his jeans, my leggings drag upward, pulling the seam tighter between my legs. A small, choked whimper leaves me.

"Listening ears back on?"

Annoyance pierces my sensory overwhelm. "Asshole," I hiss.

My back vibrates with his low chuckle, but there's more threat than humor in it. "You're right. I'm such an asshole. Only an asshole would be sick with worry for a woman who told him he might as well have overdosed because he was as good as dead to her."

A hammer hits my heart. "I didn't mean that."

He counters calmly, "I never held it against you. Honestly, I felt like I deserved worse for what I did." A sigh ruffles my hair. "Regardless, you're not wrong. I'm still an asshole. I've decided to disregard your request to leave you alone. It's been almost seven years. I'm done playing dead. Done pretending my heart will ever stop belonging to you."

A different hammer hits my chest, this one spiked.

Catastrophic.

"No. You can't say that. You don't mean that. Let me go."

Water and soap fly over the counter and backsplash as I struggle against him. But he only holds me closer, tighter, as he speaks in a voice of gravel and iron.

"Right now you have two choices. One, you shut your beautiful mouth and listen because I haven't finished. Or two, I take you to the nearest bed and fuck the stubbornness out of you."

My whole body shudders, my clit pulsing so incessantly I know a purposeful touch would send me over the edge. A moan rockets up my throat. I manage to catch it before it escapes, but I'm powerless to stop my hips from searching for friction.

Wilder muffles a groan on my shoulder. "Stop that. This is hard enough without coming in my pants." He pauses, then chuckles. "Punny."

With a breathless note of hysteria, I sag against the counter. Wilder nuzzles my neck, inhaling deeply and humming when I tremble.

"Option one it is."

I stare into the sink, musing that my sanity is draining away with the last of the soap. At the thought, guilt pricks me for wasting so much water.

He slaps the faucet off.

My mouth drops open. "What, are you psychic now?"

"Runs in the family," he replies lightly, like he didn't just threaten to fuck me, laugh at his own pun, then read my mind. "Suffice to say, when your parents left my house, I was pretty freaked out. They were vague about why you needed help. Lily and Rye didn't have answers, either, at least not ones that were good enough.

"I needed to see you in person, to draw my own conclusions. So I found out where you'd be on New Year's Eve and yes, I ambushed you. But you ambushed me, too. Because instead of finding the indomitable Evangeline-fucking-Sullivan, I found one of those wooden dolls that hide a bunch of smaller dolls inside it."

"A Matryoshka doll," I say in spite of myself.

"Exactly. You'd covered yourself with a dozen protective layers, thinking no one would notice." His voice lowers to a rasp. "Did you think for one fucking second I wouldn't see all the way to the center of you?"

Closing my eyes, I shake my head helplessly. "Why are you doing this? What do you want from me?"

"You know what I want."

The undisguised need in his voice sends a wave of blistering heat beneath my skin. I'm seized by longing so intense it scalds, so bright it spears into the deepest shadows of my psyche.

For a single moment, I imagine it. *Us.* Then what lives in those shadows—complex knots of memory and pain—rears up in defense of itself.

"I can't." My voice is reedy, naked with fear. My heart whispers the rest: *I won't survive you twice.*

Wilder tenses, his exhale harsh on my neck, then straightens and steps back. My body immediately protests the loss. Locking my knees, I transfer my pruned hands to the lip of the sink.

I don't have the courage to face him, a weakness I'm grateful for when he says the same thing, in the same empty tone, that he did when I told him I wished he were dead.

"I hear you."

I flinch. "I-I'm sorry."

"Evangeline, no." Dry amusement and self-deprecation tangle in the soft words. "As far as I'm concerned, you're exempt from apologizing to me for anything, for all time. I shouldn't have said that. And it doesn't matter, anyway. It doesn't change anything. I'm not going anywhere." After a moment, he adds, "As your friend."

"What if I hit you with a car? Should I apologize then?"

There's a beat of silence, then his smiling reply, "Just say 'oops' or something."

I bite my cheek to keep from laughing, knowing the sound won't resemble anything sane. There's also a chance I'll sob, risking the delicate boundary just restored by inviting his physical comfort. And while my skin hums at the prospect, muscles deep within me clenching in agreement, I breathe through the sensations.

What I feel now merely confirms what I've always known. Nothing will ever diminish my desire for Wilder. Not pain, time, or distance. My ears will always long for his voice, my eyes for his face, my body for his.

He's like the eczema on the back of my knees—even when it's dormant for long periods, it's still there, just waiting for the right conditions to flare up.

I reach for a nearby hand towel and start wiping up the small puddles around the sink.

"Is the hard part over?" I ask, attempting levity.

There's a pause, then I hear the familiar, whispery

swish of his fingers dragging through his hair. And I know what he's going to say before he says it.

"Not quite."

"Then just say what you want to say. I have to get going soon."

The water is gone, the sink clean. But I keep wiping, my movements rote but necessary, providing a tiny buffer between my body and mind.

"Your parents came to me as a last resort, probably because they knew I had nothing left to lose. What was the worst thing that could happen? You tell me you hate me, to fuck off? Been there, done that."

His amused tone lessens the sting of his words, but I still stiffen.

"If it makes you more comfortable to believe I'm here because your parents guilted me, go right ahead. But it was only a matter of time before I showed up. You think I didn't notice your light dimming over the last two years? You think I didn't know why? I wish I'd come sooner. I *should* have. I should have let go of my stupid attachment to the idea that staying away from you was the only way I could make amends."

I turn before I can stop myself. "This hero-complex shit is getting old. I don't need you or anyone else to save me."

His jaw works. "I'm not trying to save you," he grinds

out. "I'm trying to give you a weapon that will help you save yourself."

I toss the towel down and cross my arms. "And what's that?"

The forest of his eyes turns dark. "Clay has a history of preying on young, vulnerable women. Once they're seduced, he begins slowly undermining their self-worth. Forcing them into smaller and smaller versions of themselves. Gaslighting them until eventually they start thinking *they're* the crazy ones. Sound familiar?"

I swallow thickly.

"Ask me how I know, Evangeline."

CHAPTER TWENTY

evangeline

Been breathing underwater

Waiting on a slaughter

Shaping sand like it was clay

Hoping it would stay

Forgot how to be honest

(even though I promised)

Forgot how to be strong

(somewhere I don't belong)

But I remember now

Wilder's driver, a giant and kind-faced man named Sam, takes me home an hour later. Besides asking me if I'd like air conditioning, he leaves me alone with my thoughts.

The world outside the tinted windows is a blur of faded greens, grays, and browns. I watch it streak past, feeling surprisingly serene. Or I could be numb. Overloaded and shutting down. But regardless, I feel lighter. As though despite not speaking a word of my own experience, hearing Kendra's history with Clay somehow unburdened me.

"He was twenty-three when he seduced Kendra, who'd just turned sixteen. He played the perfect prince and made her fall in love with him. Then it started. Insults wrapped in justifications about how much he cared, withholding affection like food until she starved. Manipulating her emotions until she felt crazy, then turning her reactions around on her as proof that she was the problem.

"He dumped her the day she turned eighteen, then continued toying with her off and on for the next five years whenever he was single. She was so fucked up over the whole thing, by the time I met her she was hooked on speed and painkillers. When we dated—if you can even call it that—she was just starting to face the abuse."

As Wilder spoke, each word precise and ringing with truth, it was like a crooked painting was being slowly straightened and brought into focus.

On some level, I must have always known Clay was lying about him being responsible for Kendra's drug use. About him being the reason she disappeared and shunned her family.

"It's a game to him, one his father taught him how to play. Kendra even overheard them laughing about it once. Conrad was congratulating Clay for doing to her what he'd done to her mother. Clay joked that it had been too easy. He said he was going to stick to women over twenty-five from then on because a 'fully developed brain' would be more of a challenge.

"All he cares about is power and control. In Clay's mind, you're the ultimate catch. Someone strong enough to provide a long-term challenge while also giving him access to circles of higher influence.

"These are Kendra's words, by the way. I'm merely the messenger. She suspected he'd be drawn to you years ago based on your potential alone. It's why she brought him to your showcase—something she deeply regrets and hopes to apologize for someday.

"He hunted you, Evangeline, probably from that first

night. Watched and waited for the right time to lead you into his carefully laid trap. And if you need even more confirmation, hear it from his own mouth."

He played the recording he made of Clay at lunch last month. When it stopped, I calmly asked him to play it again. I didn't cry or shout or deny. Instead, the oddest thing happened.

My entire body relaxed.

Wilder noticed. With a small, soft smile, he said, "It's cathartic, isn't it? When you finally realize you're not crazy."

He told me he felt the same way the first time his sponsor, Frank, shared the story of his own youth, struggles with addiction, and eventual recovery. On the outside, his and Wilder's life experiences were starkly different. But their emotional experiences growing up were eerily similar.

I may never have warm and fuzzy feelings toward Kendra, but Wilder was right. I feel a kinship with her now. Her experience validated mine. Because of her, I know I'm not crazy.

I'm glad she's safe now. Sober and healing far away from those responsible for her abuse.

I'm even glad she and Wilder reconnected and were able to resolve the toxicity of their shared past to become friends—a sentiment I'll never admit has far more to do with Kendra being happily married to a woman than my emotional maturity.

♪

AS WE PROGRESS up a long driveway bordered by skinny palm trees, the last of my fluttering thoughts fade away.

There's no confusion left.

Only resolution.

The car stops. I thank Sam and step out. He tips an imaginary hat to me, then does a U-turn and heads back down the drive. I watch him go, allowing myself a moment to think about how his next journey will be taking Wilder to the airport.

When the car turns onto the street, disappearing behind a hedge, I face the house.

The sun-warmed concrete soothes my bare, aching feet as I walk toward the front door. The air smells of freshly mowed grass; beneath it, the dry earthiness of the desert and a touch of alkaline from the smog layer.

I'm not surprised when the door opens before I reach it. Given the event yesterday, I knew Clay would be working from home. And given what happened in the limo and last night, I knew he'd have his eye on the exterior cameras.

He doesn't say anything as he holds the door open for me to pass. I walk across the foyer into the living room I've never liked, with its dark walls, overpriced art, and empty glass shelves framing the television.

Not bothering to sit, I turn and lean on the back of one of the boxy leather couches.

"We need to talk."

Clay stops a few feet away. Murky eyes take me in from messy hair to bare feet. There's a flicker of disapproval, but that's it.

There was a time I thought his ability to appear supernaturally calm was a defense mechanism leftover from an emotionally neglectful childhood. But that was me trying to humanize him. The skill is merely another weapon in his arsenal, one he exchanges as needed for anger, humor, disappointment, affection, et cetera.

I'm not sure he *has* real feelings.

Wilder's face flashes in my mind. His mood-ring eyes with their shifting greens, golds, and browns. The way even his micro-expressions are easy for me to decipher. How even when he looks perfectly calm or happy, I've always been able to tell when he's actually sad, or over-stimulated, or annoyed—

"I don't have all day, Eva. Go ahead and talk."

I inhale slowly, then meet Clay's frosty stare. "I'm moving out."

His features rearrange into a facade of exhaustion. "I was hoping for an apology, but I can't say I'm surprised. You're clearly hungover and emotional right now. I'll set up a massage and an aromatherapy treatment."

"I'm only here to pack a few things. I'll arrange for a moving company to come this week."

His aggravated groan sets my teeth on edge. "Jesus Christ, do we have to go through this again? Let's just skip the part where you throw a fit and issue empty threats. If you want some space, fine. I'm due for a golfing trip to Palm Springs, anyway. I'll leave tomorrow and come back Friday. How's that sound?"

I almost laugh. What comes out instead is, "The night we ran into each other two years ago, did you really not remember me from the first time we met?"

His brow furrows. "What?"

"We met at Glow's first showcase."

"Why are we talking about this again? I told you I vaguely recall being there but not meeting you."

I tilt my head to the side. "I don't remember much of that night, either. But I have the strangest memory— funny, really—of you telling me that you only dated women with fully developed frontal lobes. That if I was single at twenty-five, I should call you."

Apprehension flickers in his eyes, along with a touch of what looks like fear. If I didn't know better.

I'm no longer relieved, resolute, or even resigned. I'm a category five hurricane of disgust and rage. The impulse to scream at him is so powerful I have to bite my cheek. I want to expose him. Tell him I heard the recording, that I know what he did to Kendra. I want to make him crack, unravel, and admit it all.

But he won't.

There will be no restitution. No consolation prize for my awakening. Only a truth so bitter it burns.

I let this happen to me.

Clay takes a step forward, his face a mask of concern, hands lifted like I'm a wild animal.

I feel like one.

"Eva," he says in a placating tone. "We've been through this before. You're not leaving me. Think about it. Think about everything I do for you. Who else is going to put up with your moods? I'm the only one who understands what you need. I take care of you, remember?"

A wave of lethargy hits me.

I feel myself sinking, water closing over my head. I'm powerless to fight it, incapable of swimming a second longer.

The doorbell rings.

Clay stares at me another moment, then stalks from

the room. The front door opens. I hear voices, the words muffled by the white noise in my ears.

Movement in my peripheral vision turns my head toward the nearest doorway. I blink in surprise at the sight of Paul, a hand towel twisting between his hands.

Features set in worried lines, he whispers, "Leave him, Eva," then backs away as Clay's footsteps pound toward me.

Another set of footsteps follows his. Lighter and faster. And suddenly, I remember how to swim.

"Eva, what the hell is—"

"Shut the fuck up, Claybee," trills Martin, skirting around him to plaster himself to my side. Arm around my waist, he pulls me up until my knees lock. "Get it? Claybee like baby, because you're a whiny little bitch."

I snort.

Clay flushes, his features twisting with rage. His mouth opens.

"By all means," Martin says, lifting his phone to show he's recording video. "Show the world exactly who you are."

Air hisses through Clay's teeth. He gives me a long look that should probably scare me but doesn't. Then he spins on a heel and leaves.

Martin exhales noisily.

"Thank you," I whisper.

"Honey, thank *you*. I've wanted to call him that for years." He palms the side of my face, his dark eyes glistening. "I'm so fucking proud of you. Let's pack a bag and get out of here, okay? You and me and margaritas on the beach."

I blink away tears and nod.

wilder

TWO MONTHS LATER

Soft music floats amidst the voices and laughter at my dining room table, cutlery and glasses clinking in an irregular but melodious percussion line.

I never thought I'd be someone who hosts and enjoys dinner parties, but here we are.

"That was phenomenal, Wilder."

I raise my water glass toward Jax's wife. "Thank you, Shannon." Then I give my bandmate a pointed look.

He rolls his eyes. "Yeah, yeah. The student has surpassed the teacher. Great lasagna."

"Pastitsio," I say with a smirk.

"Just accept it, bro," chides Eddie. "He's been in another league for years. Do you even know what a béchamel sauce is?"

After a beat of silence, Eddie's girlfriend, Holly, asks what we're all thinking. "How do *you* know what a béchamel sauce is?"

Laughter rings out. After some good-natured grumbling, Eddie admits he has no idea how to make béchamel. He points at me. "Blame him. He made me watch cooking shows almost every night of our tour last year."

I chuckle. "I made you, huh?"

He grins. "Okay, maybe I got sucked in by how cutthroat they are with all the challenges and shit."

"Damn," says Holly with an exaggerated sigh. "I was really hoping you were dropping a hint about cooking me dinner for our anniversary next month."

Eddie gulps. "Oh shoot, I ruined the surprise."

More laughter fills the air. Over Holly's head, Eddie sends me a beseeching look. I make him sweat for a few seconds, then nod. He relaxes and slings an arm around a smugly grinning Holly.

As the merriment fades and everyone finishes eating, the back of my neck begins to tingle and tighten —the first warning sign that I'm nearing my limit on socializing. Before long, my mind will start losing clarity, my skin will grow sensitive, and the assorted sounds around me will grate.

Glancing discreetly at my watch, I'm surprised and gratified to see it's nearing ten o'clock. I made it almost four hours—a new personal record.

I push back my chair. "Who's ready for dessert?"

Soft fingertips land on my forearm, and Aubrey's blue eyes sparkle up at me. "No way. You're not allowed to do anything else."

I relax back into my chair, hoping she doesn't notice that my smile is a little forced. When I told Jax that Zander and his date couldn't make it, he took it upon himself to invite Shannon's sister. Despite suspecting ulterior motives, I didn't have a good reason to say no.

As far as Jax knows, Aubrey and I are friendly acquaintances. It's not like I could tell him we hooked up at his and Shannon's wedding last year or that I regretted it almost immediately.

"I concur," says Shannon with overly bright enthusiasm. "The chef should relax."

Jax stands. "Eddie and Holly, if you guys want to grab dessert, we'll clear the table." A second of silent but painfully obvious communication passes between the couples, then they're all moving.

I swallow a sigh. "Thanks, guys."

When Aubrey makes a weak attempt at helping, Shannon chirps, "Stay, sis. Keep Wilder company."

The moment we're alone—or as alone as we can be with the kitchen ten feet away—Aubrey whispers, "She failed out of afterschool theater club."

My lips quirk. "I think they all did."

Her laugh dances nervously. "You're probably right. I'm glad we have a second, though, so I can thank you privately for being so... not awkward with me tonight. You're a good guy, Wilder."

I shrug, smiling vaguely. "No reason for awkwardness."

Mentally, I'm chanting, *Shitshitshit.*

With a deep breath, she pivots further in her seat. Her shoulder grazes mine while her knee taps my thigh. There's no way I can pull away without being super obvious about it, and my head is already too fuzzy to think of some way to defuse the intent I see in her eyes.

I try not to grit my teeth as she leans even closer to me. "This is me shooting my shot. Any chance you're ready to reconsider the no-dating rule?"

This—*this* is why sleeping with Audrey was a giant mistake. She's kind, genuine, and charming. At the wedding last year, we talked for hours before she invited me to her hotel room. But when I woke up the next morning and saw her sleeping face, all I felt was a mix of regret and disappointment.

Through no fault of her own, the seed of connection I'd felt the night prior was gone. Shriveled before I could even consider planting it.

She sees the truth in my eyes, her hopeful expression falling. I open my mouth to fumble through an *it's not you, it's me* explanation, but the chime of the doorbell cuts me off. The sound is so unexpected, I startle and recoil from Aubrey. She looks away, her face flushing.

Jax asks, "Are you expecting someone?"

Already halfway to standing, I sense rather than see Aubrey shrinking in her chair.

"No," I say quickly. I grab my phone off a nearby shelf and frown at the screen. "They're supposed to text me before letting people through the gate after dark."

"Ohhh, someone's getting fired," Eddie sings.

Holly giggles. "Stop. It's probably that weird neighbor. He saw our cars and wants to party."

Shannon chimes in, "The guy who showed up at the barbecue last summer?"

Eddie laughs loudly. "I forgot about him! Didn't he just walk right into the backyard and help himself to food?"

"Yes! Then he talked Zander's ear off for an hour about aliens until Jax finally got him to leave."

Between one moment and the next, I cross the line into overstimulation, the chorus of voices melding into an abrasive buzz. In lieu of telling everyone to shut the fuck up so I can think, I clutch my phone and walk swiftly toward the hallway.

"I can answer it," offers Jax as I pass the kitchen.

"I've got it," I force out.

Halfway down the hallway, the chatter fades enough to no longer feel like the sensory equivalent of nails on a chalkboard. I stop beside a window and lay my palm on the glass.

Inhale. Feel the cold. Exhale. You're fine. Just tired. Breathe.

My heartbeat eventually retreats from my temples, the tightness in my lungs releasing. Leaning my shoulder on a wall, I pull up the app for my doorbell camera. If Holly's correct—and she probably is—I have no intention of opening the door. My neighbor, Herman, is a single retiree with a habit of showing up uninvited and ignoring cues to leave. He's also an absolute wacko obsessed with conspiracy theories, who occasionally forgoes pants and underwear because they *chafe.*

The video feed is slow to load. I wince in anticipation of Herman's cold-shriveled dick and balls. But when the image clears, it's not Herman.

An unfamiliar woman stands at the bottom of the porch steps, her back to the camera. Shoulder-length light brown hair, a winter coat, shapeless cargo pants, and sneakers.

Torn between curiosity and apprehension, I keep staring. Ten seconds later, she seems to pull herself straighter. Then she walks into the darkness.

On her third step, my breath stalls in my chest.

Then I'm running.

wilder

I tear open the front door and make it across the porch before realizing I'm barefoot and wearing a T-shirt. The wind off the water doesn't care that it's technically spring, immediately diving beneath my clothes and inducing a shiver.

Not that a blizzard would stop me.

Her retreat halted when I opened the door, but she doesn't turn around as I jog down the brick path. Stopping a few feet from her back, I tuck my hands into my armpits.

"Evangeline?"

I'm aiming for calm, maybe even amusement, but I miss the mark by a mile. My chest heaves like my ten-second sprint was a triathlon. I sound angry.

I *am* angry.

It's been two months since the Grammys. Two months since she disappeared from the public eye. Eight *long as fuck* weeks in which I've wondered and worried about her, my only comfort the texts she sent Lily, Rye, and her parents before vanishing. She told them she'd left Clay, was somewhere safe with Martin Page, and needed time to think.

Evangeline slowly turns around. Her head stays lowered, eyes on the ground between us and hands tucked in her coat pockets.

"I guess you're wondering where I've been and what I'm doing here."

I choke on a thousand replies, all of them too emotional.

She glances at the house, then at the two other cars parked in my driveway. "You have company. I'm sor—I mean, oops. I'll just... go."

I jerk forward, grabbing her arm before I even finish the thought of stopping her. "Don't."

She startles, chin and eyes lifting, her face finally visible in the ambient glow of the house lights. My brain absorbs new information so fast the steam from my breath might as well be leaving my ears.

I can hardly believe it, but she's not wearing a wig like I thought. She actually chopped off and dyed her signature white-blond locks. The color, a shade darker than her lashes and brows, looks ridiculously sexy. She's put on some much-needed weight, too, her cheekbones not as stark and her jawline a touch softer. And she's tan —or as tan as she can get, her face and neck the light bronze, freckle-sprinkled hue I saw each summer as a kid. The final difference is the only one that bothers me: she's covered her pale gray iris with a contact lens color-matched to her hazel eye.

A gust of wind slaps me out of my stunned silence. "Are you okay? Where have you been?"

Her gaze slides off my face toward the water, visible only as winks of moonlight through the trees.

"I'm fine. I was in Baja." She sighs. "I'd still be there if a local hadn't recognized me at the market. Lazy mistake on my part—I was wearing a hat but forgot my contact lens. Honestly, I don't blame her for following me and taking photos. Hopefully she holds out for a lot of zeroes."

Given the ongoing media buzz around her disap-pearance, I have no doubt a few clear shots will earn the fan a life-changing payday.

I'm glad she understood the implications and left, but I still have to swallow the urge to lecture her. The mere thought of her wandering around for weeks without protection makes me feel sick. There's a reason women in her position have bodyguards.

Between stalkers and obsessive fans, it's fucking dangerous.

"I've been at my parents' since I got back." She grimaces, then grumbles, "Three nights was all I could handle."

I smother a huff of laughter. Matt wouldn't have held back on telling her exactly how irresponsible it was to play tourist, and it's not hard to envision Evangeline's reaction.

"And now?"

"I'm not sure." She glances at the cars again. "I shouldn't have bothered you."

"You're not bothering me." Only when she trembles at my low tone do I realize I'm still holding her arm. My fingers loosen, but I can't bring myself to let go entirely. "Why are you here, Evangeline?"

Her tongue peeks out to curl over an incisor. Despite my balls currently impersonating ice cubes, arousal stirs in my gut. It joins lingering anger and general over-whelm, creating a mess inside me. Half of me wants to rip her pants off and fuck her against the closest tree, while the other half wishes I hadn't answered the damn door.

Wind tries to steal her next words, but I catch them.

"I didn't have anywhere else to go."

Shock forces air from my lungs in a burst of vapor.

I have no idea why she feels like she can't go to Lily and Rye, or her grandparents, or one of her aunts or uncles...

But I don't fucking care.

She came to *me*.

Mistaking my silence for confusion, she explains hurriedly, "You gave me your address that day at lunch, remember? I should have texted or called, I know, but I..." She trails off with a shake of her head. "Anyway, I'm sorry for dropping in like this."

"Try again."

She frowns for a moment, then gets it. Her lips curve. "*Oops.*"

I grin. "Much better."

Her gaze flickers between my dimples, then strokes across my mouth. When she swallows thickly, my mind cartwheels into the gutter. That elegant neck under my hand. Feeding my cock past those lips. Feeling her swallow from the inside.

"It's okay if you've changed your mind. I completely understand."

I blink away the fantasy. "I haven't changed my mind. You're always welcome here."

She sucks in a breath. "Oh."

The sight of her pursed lips sends another zap of desire down my spine. For my own sanity, I release her arm and take a half-step backward. My teeth immediately start to chatter.

"Do you have a bag? I can grab it for you."

Relief softens her features. "Yes, but I'll get it. You're obviously freezing." She turns, then pauses to grin at me over her shoulder. "Thank you, Wilder. So, so much. I won't stay longer than a few weeks."

She walks quickly toward her car, parked near the end of the drive ahead of Jax's and Eddie's. I gape after her, certain I must have misheard her final words. Because if I didn't, and she's staying a few *weeks*?

I'm seriously fucked.

Evangeline in my house, in my kitchen, on my furniture...

I won't survive it. More accurately, my dominant hand won't survive it.

A shiver so violent I almost bite through my tongue sends me hustling toward the house. Halfway up the porch steps, a bolt of fear halts me. I spin around and search the darkness.

Light flares at the end of the driveway, highlighting Evangeline as she leans into the back seat of her car.

I start breathing again.

A creak of wood behind me precedes Jax's soft, surprised voice. "Is that who I think it is?"

I nod and join him on the porch, sighing as the heat escaping the open front door laps against my body.

"She's on a list at the gate."

What I don't say is that the list she's on is different from the main one with approved guests. Only one person has no restrictions, can show up whenever, without notice, even if I'm not here.

Jax's sigh makes me think he can deduce as much. "Okay. I'll round everyone up and we'll get out of here. Kitchen's mostly sorted, and we already demolished the cannoli. Eddie's fault, naturally."

I chuckle. "Naturally. Thanks, man." I hesitate, then blurt, "About Aubrey, I—"

He quickly lifts a hand. "Dude, no. That was my bad. I warned Shannon it probably wouldn't go the way she wanted. I'm guessing I was right?"

Grimacing, I rub the heels of my hands into my eyes. "Pretty much. Aubrey asked me out, but the doorbell rang before I could answer. She's super cool, I'm just... I guess it was bad timing."

Lowering my hands, I see Jax's too-wide smile a second before a throat clears softly behind me.

"Hey, Jax," says Evangeline. "How's it going?"

evangeline

Staring at a curtained window in Wilder's guest bedroom, I rub a towel over my hair and try not to focus on how fucking nervous I am.

So far nothing has gone the way I hoped it would. Most of the drive here, I felt good. Confident and full of purpose. Both feelings drained away on the ferry from Seattle to Madrone Island, which I spent hiding in a corner with my hood pulled low.

By the time I navigated off the ferry, my stomach was in knots. I ended up driving the main loop on the south side of the island for an hour in hopes my nerves would settle. Instead, I grew more and more paranoid that I was going to be pulled over for suspicious activity.

Finally, after checking to see when the last ferry of the day was leaving, I made it to the northern tip of the island. Then I almost turned right back around when I saw the manned security booth outside of Wilder's gated community.

I stammered out my name and who I was visiting. The guard asked for my driver's license and looked between it and me so many times I half expected him to citizen's arrest me for impersonating a celebrity.

But then he smiled and gave me a small envelope with a key and a slip of paper inside. He explained that the key was for Wilder's front door and the code on the paper would disarm his security system. Before I could muster a response, the thick gate rolled open.

A minute later, I was here, crashing a dinner party with Jax and Eddie, their significant others, and a woman who glared at me like I'd shit in her cereal. Which, given what I overheard Wilder tell Jax on the porch, I kind of did.

Bad timing, like Wilder said.

Or maybe perfect timing.

Who knows what might have happened if I'd waited a few more days, or even a few more weeks? Maybe he wanted to say yes to that date—would have, if I hadn't shown up. From my ten-second glimpse of the woman, Aubrey, as everyone left, on looks alone I can't blame him.

As much as I want to slap myself for comparing

myself to her, I can't help it. She was beautiful. Pacific blue eyes, bright and sparkly. Long, thick, shiny brown hair. Peaches and cream, freckle-free skin. Curvier hips. Much bigger boobs. The sweetest smile—when she aimed it at him.

She's basically animated princess material. Probably does yoga and meditates. Doesn't need therapy because she's spiritually and mentally stable. Oh, and let's not forget she's *super cool.*

"Stop it," I hiss at myself.

Giving up on my hair, I walk into the en suite to hang my damp towel on a rack.

The bathroom, like the guest bedroom and the glimpses I had of the rest of the house, is gorgeous. I feel like I'm standing in one of those architectural magazine feature homes. The ones that look so inviting, even whimsical, but also impossibly elegant. Soft white walls, rich wood floors, warm metallic accents. Tons of plants. Color and texture everywhere from rugs, throws, and art.

The style actually reminds me of the house I bought not far from my parents, which I sold before moving to Los Angeles. Or rather, it reminds me of the stylistic vision I had for that house before *someone* talked me out of finding a designer.

Before my brain decides to meander down Traumatic Memory Lane, I splash my face with cold water. Then I brush my teeth, moisturize, and finger comb my hair until I stop looking like I was drowned before being electrocuted.

Wilder still cares about me. I know he does. If he didn't, he wouldn't have run after me. Nor would he have stopped me from leaving.

That his relief manifested as anger was no surprise. Everyone who loves me is acting the same way right now. I know they're not angry *at* me—even Lily, who has every reason to be. Beneath their anger is helplessness, and beneath that is their fear for me. For my safety, my mental health, my future.

The way I unplugged and disappeared certainly didn't help. It scared the hell out of everyone. But I don't regret going. It was necessary.

Regardless of my tan, my time in Baja was anything but a vacation. With Martin's unfailing support, I started deconstructing and processing the last two years. It was fucking exhausting. A nonstop emotional spin cycle of sadness, rage, numbness, hilarity, confusion, manic hope, and sluggish depression. It took a week for me to actually break down and let it all out. I cried for three days straight.

When I woke up on the fourth day, I felt it for the first time—the reason I'm here. Another crossroads.

One that was always inside me, hidden behind the bricks I'd routinely stacked in front of it. I did my best to ignore it, but as weeks passed, it only grew clearer. Larger. *Louder.* Until I could no longer resist its call.

It doesn't matter what I interrupted tonight or what might have happened. Nor does it matter that Martin might be right and this is too much, too soon.

What matters is that time is running out.

To forgive.

To repair.

To remember.

♫

I'M PULLING BACK the covers on the bed, about to surrender myself to the lengthy process of falling asleep, when there's a soft knock on the door.

My heart yaps, adrenaline flooding my body.

"Evangeline?"

With no denial buffering me anymore, the sound of my full name on his lips weakens my knees and shortens my breath.

I glance down at myself and wince at what I'm wearing: a pair of my brother's old sweatpants and a Breaking Giants T-shirt I stole from my dad. But looking like a slob is what I get for leaving Baja for the Pacific Northwest's version of spring. Somewhere in Seattle, there's a storage unit with all my stuff, but the details are buried among the thousand other emails I've ignored for the last two months.

Running my hands through my hair one more time, I move to the door and open it. I'm still not ready for the impact of him standing right in front of me, close enough to touch in flannel pajama pants and a soft gray T-shirt. His hair is brushed back, wet from his own shower. Dark bristles shadow his jaw and neck.

A magical forest lives in his eyes.

A midnight rainstorm brews in the air around him.

My, "Hi," is embarrassingly breathy.

Wilder's gaze travels around the room, pausing on my guitar case before returning to me. He smiles softly.

"Hi back. I wanted to make sure you were settling in okay. Do you have everything you need? Enough blankets? Towels?"

"Yes. I'm perfect. Super great. Your water pressure is godlike. Towels were fluffy. Ten out of ten."

His eyes flare with amusement. I mentally slap myself and pray my tan hides the heat crawling up my neck.

"Sure you're not hungry? I have leftovers I can heat up. It's no problem at all."

"Positive, thanks. And thanks again for letting me

invade your space. I'll keep out of your way as much as possible."

"Not necessary." White teeth capture a corner of his lower lip, scraping gently before he clears his throat. "If you're up before me tomorrow, feel free to eat and drink whatever. Or if you want to wait, I usually make breakfast around nine."

I blink fast, my eyes burning. "Thank you."

A dimple deepens on his cheek. "Please stop saying thank you. Just treat the house like it's yours. There's a studio out back, too. Used to be a guesthouse. You can get in with the key the guard gave you. There's a piano out there and... stuff."

He shifts on his feet. Scratches his jaw. Looks down the hallway and all around me but not *at* me. And even though I can hardly believe it, it finally sinks in.

He's nervous, too.

Another surge of adrenaline lifts my heart to the base of my throat. I can hear my own breathing, steady if fast, but I'm suddenly not getting enough oxygen. My hands and feet tingle. My armpits, too.

I open my mouth.

Wilder says, "Okay. Um, goodnight. I'm just down the hall if you need me—*something*, I mean. If you need something."

Our eyes meet for half a second before he pivots and walks toward his room. One step, two steps, three...

"Wait!"

My plea is far too loud and high-pitched. Basically a screech.

Wilder freezes in place, then spins back around. "Holy shit, I thought I was about to fall down the stairs."

We both look at the stairs—that are at least five feet away in the opposite direction—then look at each other.

"Oops?"

He pinches the bridge of his nose, then chuckles. "Oops, she says." Lowering his hand, he squints at me. "Were you trying to give me a heart attack or did you think of something you needed?"

Butterflies thwack against my ribcage and dive-bomb my centerline. I lick my lips. Take a stuttering breath.

Fuck it.

"You."

His brows pinch. "You need..." Understanding dawns, lifting his chest on a sharp breath. His eyes darken. So does his voice. "Tell me what you mean by that."

My toes curl against hardwood. "I need—or want, I should say—what I mean is I'm offering, if *you* wanted to, you know—"

"Evangeline," he says in a pained voice. "Please stop."

My teeth click as I close them. Before I can decide whether to throw myself in the bedroom and slam the door or run down the stairs and out of the house, Wilder takes a step toward me. The intensity in his expression pins me to the floor.

"So I don't misunderstand, are you asking for my company? Like you want to talk or hang out? Or are you asking me if I want to fuck?"

I choke on my next breath but manage to force out, "Second one."

A muscle on his jawline jumps. His stare penetrates me but not in a fun way. The longer he looks at me, the tighter vines of fear wrap around my chest.

When he sighs heavily, my heart dehydrates.

I'm too late.

Whatever he sees on my face makes his lips thin. "How are you one of the most observant people I've ever known and still so blind? If you'd so much as glanced down once in the last few minutes, you'd already know the answer."

My gaze drops right as his tattooed hand strokes across the outline of his erection. A bomb explodes at the base of my spine, instantly drenching my underwear.

"I jacked off twice in the shower. *Twice.* And all you had to do was say 'hi' to me for this to happen." He grunts. "Enough. Eyes up."

My gaze lifts to his face. But instead of the anticipation I'm expecting, I find frustration.

"Me wanting to fuck you is like taxes and gravity. Immutable."

I whisper, "Why do you sound angry about it?"

Hands sinking into his hair, his head drops back. I have no idea what he's looking at on the ceiling, but ten seconds pass before his shoulders and face lower.

The frustration is gone. Now he wears a patchwork mask over sadness.

"No matter how much I want to have sex with you, it wouldn't be right. Not after what you've just been through." He takes another step toward me, eyes imploring. "Let me be here for you in every other way while you heal. And I swear to God, if you still want me down the line, I'm all yours."

wilder

When the bedroom door closes behind her, I fold forward and release a silent scream into my fists.

I don't know if that was the best, most selfless thing I've ever done in my life, or a decision I'll regret until the day I die. Either way, it seriously fucking sucked.

Silently cursing myself and the universe at large, I retreat into my bedroom and close the door. The room is dim, only a small bedside light on. Before I'd given in to impulse and knocked on her door, I'd been reading some dry-as-hell philosophy book my dad gave me for Christmas, hoping to bore myself to sleep. And that was after back-to-back orgasms in the shower failed to exhaust me.

My body vibrates with frenetic energy as I sit on the

bed and lower my head into my hands. Thumbs on my temples, I massage as I count my inhales and exhales.

It doesn't fucking help.

All I see is her endearing, stammering nervousness. Her fear and courage. The lascivious gleam in her mismatched eyes when she finally let herself look below my waist.

Mostly, though, I see the last, stricken look she gave me before she closed the door. She thinks I rejected her. I *did* reject her.

"What have I done?" I mumble.

She's probably going to leave, might be packing right now.

The thought brings me to my feet right as my bedroom door swings open and slams against the wall. Flash frozen, I stare at Evangeline as she strides toward me.

When she's a few feet away and still moving like she's on a warpath, I open my mouth to say fuck-knows-what.

"No," she snaps, jabbing her index finger into my chest. "You said your piece, now I get to say mine. Two months ago, you told me I was powerful. A 'force to be reckoned with.' Was that a lie?"

I croak, "Of course not."

She waves a paper in my face until I take it. Angling

it toward the light, I see what looks like a letter from a doctor's office. But it's in Spanish.

"What is this?" I ask, but then I turn it over and see a series of familiar-looking words, all of which have *Negativo* in bold next to them.

"That's my clean bill of health because I don't want to use a condom. As long as you can produce a similar report. Can you?"

"Yes, but—"

"Good. I'm still on birth control."

She pulls the paper out of my hand, folds it into a square, and shoves it in a pocket of her sweatpants.

Then she pulls her shirt off.

And she's not wearing a bra.

Pressure instantly engulfs my cock. I'm so hard there's a notable pulse in my shaft, and the soft flannel of my pants has turned to sandpaper.

Evangeline's breasts are every bit as perfect as I remember, teardrop-shaped and fuller on the bottom. Her nipples sit high like offerings of dusty pink hard candy. Now they're even more delicious-looking, each framed by two small, silver balls begging to be flicked, licked, and sucked.

I close my eyes. Open them.

Nope. Not dreaming.

"I want you to prove it, Wilder," she says sharply.

I have no idea what she's talking about, but thankfully she keeps going.

"Prove to me that I'm powerful. Don't treat me like everyone else right now, like I'm fragile and I'll fall apart if you tell me how angry you are with me. I can take it. I want it. Show me."

I drag my gaze from her chest and up her throat. Over her defiantly lifted chin. Along the lines of her silky, succulent, stubborn mouth. Her small, flared nostrils. The freckles on the bridge of her nose.

Finally, I study the mismatched eyes that fucking haunt me. The hazel one with its ring of green flecked with blue that blends into golden brown. And the other —her fairy eye. *My* fairy eye. Icy blue-gray with a thin border of steel, it pierces me like it always has. Cracks me in half and exposes my most feral self.

I grab the back of her neck and yank her forward. She stumbles and gasps, her hands flying to my chest to brace herself. But I already can't remember why I wasn't supposed to do this.

"I *am* fucking mad at you," I growl.

Closing my fingers around a fistful of hair, I pull her head back and bite her chin, her jaw. I scrape my teeth over her mouth but don't kiss her. Nip her lower lip, then upper. Hard enough to sting, not hard enough to hurt. *Yet.* With every bite, she jerks and produces a breathy, needy note.

Her hands climb to my shoulders, nails digging. When she tries to kiss me, I tug her hair to remind her who's in control. She surrenders with a sigh, looking up at me with lust-drunk eyes.

She's so stunning I almost wish I could be gentle. *Almost.*

Keeping her head still, I drag my mouth toward her ear. I take my time, enjoying the subtle rasp of my unshaven cheek against her smooth, warmer skin.

"Do you remember what I feel like? You told me it's close to overwhelming at first. That I stretch you so good it burns. Did you miss my cock? Did you miss all that pressure in your sweet little cunt?"

She whimpers.

"Answer me."

"Yes, I missed your cock." She writhes helplessly against my chest. "*Fuck.* Stop torturing me. I'm begging you."

I shake my head, smiling against her temple. "I've waited seven years for this. Beg all you want, Fairy. I'm taking my time."

The rhythm of her breath vanishes, then resumes even faster. Her neck tenses under my hand. A shudder runs down her body. Alarmed, I lean back to see her face.

The second our eyes meet, I realize what I said.

"Fairy," I repeat, transfixed by the lifecycle of a tear on her lower lash line. The shimmering sphere grows until it drops, splashing against her cheek.

"Again," she breathes.

"Fairy." I trail a fingertip down her nose. "You're a perfect song. Even though I know every note, I'll never be able to replicate it. It's simply too exquisite to exist outside of you."

Her lips quiver. "My God."

"Not yet, but I'm about to be."

Transferring my hands to her waist, I lift and throw her onto the bed. She squeaks when she hits, her bouncing tits an irresistible lure. A moment later, my mouth captures a nipple, and her moan slides down my throat like honey.

By the time I'm done reacquainting myself with every inch of her chest and have teased her nipples and piercings to my satisfaction, she's crying again. The kind of tears I love. *My* tears. Her head tosses, hips jerking toward my hovering body, hands fisted in the comforter.

"Such a needy mess. So overwhelmed, aren't you?"

She sobs my name. "Please."

My thumb sinks past her lips, capturing her lower

teeth and pressing down until her jaw opens. I spit into her mouth. She makes a sound that's half lust, half outrage.

I grin.

She glares.

"You've been so good, Fairy. Keeping your hands to yourself. Letting me play with your gorgeous tits. Do you want a reward?"

She nods fast.

I push my thumb deeper into her mouth. "Suck."

Eyes flaring, her lips seal around my finger. She sucks hard, her tongue swirling. I grunt, the sensation echoing around my cock.

"Do you want more?"

Another eager nod.

I give her my first and middle fingers and she goes to town on them. Teeth and tongue, sloppy and ravenous. Then she grabs my wrist and lifts her head, sinking my fingers to the back of her throat. Eyes on mine and glittering with challenge, she sucks and swallows. When she gags a little, then moans, it's game over.

In seconds, I have her sweatpants off, her legs around my head, and my face buried in her pussy. One arm over her stomach to hold her down, I lick everywhere except her clit, reveling in the return of her taste on my tongue.

When her thighs start to shake and the tone of her cries changes from pleasure to torment, I find her hands and put them on my head. They immediately sink into my hair and clench. Her shoulders lift, upper body curving. Panting, she stares down at me like I'm more devil than god.

I wink.

She pulls my hair roughly, guiding my mouth to her clit.

"Suck," she snarls.

I happily comply.

Her grip is merciless as she rides my smothered face, too far gone to care about whether or not I can breathe. I can't, but it doesn't matter because in less than thirty seconds she comes with a gloriously profane cry.

I kiss her swollen clit, then devote myself to the task of licking up every drop of tart cum. Legs splayed and arms over her face, she's too blissed out to notice my exploration further south until my finger joins the party.

She whacks my head. "No way."

I chuckle against the crease of her thigh. But I don't move my finger. "What? I'm not even pushing."

An arm lifts off her face. Her eyes narrow, but amusement dilutes the effect of her glare. Watching her face carefully, I massage with a bit more pressure. Not breaching the ring of muscle yet, just reintroducing myself. Her breath hitches, pupils flaring.

"Mmm, that's what I thought. You remember how good it feels to take me here while I work a vibrator in your pussy, don't you?"

"Yes." She licks her lips. "Is, uh, that what you want? Tonight?"

I shake my head, almost smiling when she can't hide her relief. Then I do smile. "Maybe tomorrow."

Her eyes round in panic, but I don't give her time to think about it. Lifting onto my knees, I slide forward, forcing her legs wider with mine. With my free hand, I stroke her arms and thighs. Slow, heavy pressure that makes her eyes glaze. Then I palm each of her breasts, tapping and lightly pinching her nipples until she's panting again. All the while, I slowly increase the pressure of my other finger.

"Left foot on my shoulder. Good girl."

I kiss her ankle in thanks, then look down and bite my cheek at how she's spread open for me. How well she remembers. How naturally we still move together.

"Fucking perfect." I make her aware of my finger again, circling and pulsing it. "You're already nice and slippery. Just one finger for now. I've never hurt you before, have I?"

"No." She takes a deep breath. "Okay, I'm ready."

Her bravery, her trust, make my heart hot and my head light.

She's still better than any drug.

"That's my girl," I say, my voice gravel. "Inhale nice and slow. Now exhale and relax. *Fuck*. There you go."

Her body swallows my finger to the second knuckle before clamping down in resistance. I keep my hand still, letting her adjust at her own pace.

She winces. "I'm sorry, I—"

"Stop it. You're fucking flawless. Look at what you do to me."

I yank my pants off my hips, wincing as fabric scrapes hypersensitive skin. As intended, she immediately forgets about my finger in her ass, her eyes fixed on where I'm flushed, pierced, and leaking.

She licks her lips. When my cock jerks in response, her eyes widen in shocked delight. I take a mental snapshot so I can laugh about it later. Right now, I'm fast approaching my limit. There's edging myself, and then there's torture.

"Touch me, Fairy."

She doesn't hesitate, grabbing me in a fist and jacking her hand roughly—just how I fucking like it. I groan, battling the urge to match her rhythm with my hips. If I do, I won't stop until I come all over her stomach. And there's no fucking way I'm spilling anywhere but inside her.

Maybe she senses how close I am because she shifts tactics. One hand strokes me loosely, dipping to cup my sack on the downstroke, while the other plays over my head. She's so entranced, I don't think she realizes that my finger is all the way in or that she's been fucking my hand this whole time.

I haven't moved my arm once.

She swipes a fingertip over my slit, gathering fluid, then circles it around the balls of my piercing. Her nail grazes where I'm most sensitive, and I wince in spite of myself. Catching it, she blinks up at me with false concern.

"Oops. Did that hurt?"

I smirk. "You know one of my kinks is when your claws come out. Playtime's over, though. Can you let go of my finger? I need to fuck you and I want to look at you while I do it."

Another mental snapshot: her face as she stops using my finger as a dildo in the same instant she realizes she was. I can't stop my laugh this time.

Thankfully, before she can decide to be hurt or embarrassed, she peers up at me. Whatever she sees on my face—probably my utter joy—makes her smile sheepishly.

"You have nice fingers. Very skilled."

"Oh, do I?" I ask, chuckling anew as I gently slip out of her body.

She nods, then squeezes my cock so hard I choke. "But I want this now, please and thank you."

My laughter evaporates, single-minded intent pooling at the base of my spine. "Say it."

Her breath hitches. "I need you inside me. Fuck me. Please."

I kick off my pants and finally lower onto her. The first full contact of our naked bodies pulls moans from us both. Her hands glide down my back, legs hooking around my thighs. My cock notches right where it needs to be. Where it's supposed to be.

Home. I'm home.

Short nails dig into my ass, beckoning me closer, deeper. My body starts to shake.

"Wait. I need a second—"

"No," she says, voice firm against my jaw. "I want it. I deserve it. Make it hurt, Wilder."

I don't want to.

God, I don't want to.

But I snap anyway.

My hips work in rough thrusts, forcing her body to yield to mine one devastating inch at a time. On some level, I recognize familiar cues and sounds. Her moans and pleas. How wet she is, how she doesn't push at me but clings. But none of it is enough to change the fact I'm hurting her.

Or that I like it.

"Goddammit," I snarl, mindless and suddenly so angry I can't see. "Damn you, Evangeline. God fucking damn you."

Her arms and legs tighten around me. "I know. I can take it. It's okay."

I lift onto my hands, the movement forcing my cock deeper. *Not deep enough.* In a burst of unwanted clarity, I realize I'll never be as deep inside her as I want to be.

Evangeline's hands rise, framing my face tentatively. Tears leak from her eyes in continuous streams. Her thumbs stroke my clenched jaw.

"I'm sorry," she whispers. "I'm so sorry."

Not enough.

"You're not forgiven."

Her eyes close, then flutter back open. The gray one catches all the light in the room, sparkling like a star.

"Show me."

My laugh is madness as I clasp the delicate column of her throat in one hand. My other curls around her hip, fingers digging into the lush globe of her ass. I lift and tilt her hips to exactly where I want her.

Then I fucking show her.

I pound into her viciously until I bottom out, but I don't stop. There's no relief, no return of tenderness. No music, either—just a cacophony of my grunts, her whimpers, our gasps. The slap of our flesh is obscene and arrhythmic.

Sweat drips until we're slick with it. Her pussy is a molten sheath, swelling more with every thrust. But I'm still shocked when I feel the first flutters.

"You're actually going to come again. You little sl—" By some miracle, I manage to swallow the rest of the word.

"Don't hold back," she pleads, her eyes frenzied and desperate. "It's true. Only with you."

Instead of her admittance pleasing me, it only makes me angrier.

"You're such a greedy slut. Pushing me past my limits, making me fuck this cunt harder than I want to. You love this, don't you? Are you going to come all over my cock, Evangeline?"

"Yes, yes."

I bark a mirthless laugh. "Then fucking come."

Rearing back, I reach between us and pinch her clit. Once, twice, before she wails like a banshee. Her eyes roll back in her head, her body lifting like a bowstring, every muscle straining. Then her pussy clamps down and pulses so hard I know what's coming. Sure enough, her release soaks my balls and the comforter beneath us.

"I bet that felt good," I remark, slowing my pace as her contractions ease and fade. Her moans could be sobs, but it's hard to say and I'm not sure I care. She melts back onto the mattress, gasping for air, trembling all over.

Not. Fucking. Enough.

I stop moving. Anchored in her body, I lean down until my mouth hovers so close to hers that I'm swallowing the weight of our shared breath. When she tries to kiss me, I jerk my head back.

"No," I snarl. "You walked away from me like we were nothing. *Nothing.* Just like that, you wiped me out of your heart and life. And believe me, I know how messed up that sounds. How wrong it is. I'm well aware that I'm the villain in this story. But you *left me.* You fucking left me when you were supposed to forgive me."

Her chin trembles. "I know."

Unable to help myself, I grind against her. It doesn't matter that my broken heart is currently clawing its way out of my chest, or that my tears join the sweat already dripping off my chin.

My body sings for hers whether I want it to or not.

"My Fairy. My perfect song. I remade myself for you, but you still threw me away. All these years, I've been waiting for my missing piece to come home. But you aren't home, are you? You're not here to love me. You're not here to keep me."

Her eyes shift between mine, sorrowful and searching. Maybe finally seeing.

I hit an angle that makes her breath catch. Lightning zips down my spine, gathering and building.

"You *are* powerful," I bite out. "So powerful I almost killed myself for you. Because I thought if you wanted me to die, I didn't have anything to live for."

Horror slackens her mouth. "No."

Unable to look at her another second, I drop to my forearms and lower my head to the bed beside hers. My voice thickens with my cock, my hips pumping faster as release barrels toward me.

Sick, twisted release.

"I loved you so much, but you didn't feel it. How could you not feel it? How could you forget me like that? We were supposed to be more. We were supposed to be everything."

"Wilder, please. Oh God. No, no..."

She can't help it any more than I can.

Her body sings for mine.

She weeps through her third orgasm. My release slams into me between one breath and the next.

Shattering me.

When I come back together, I have even fewer pieces than before.

But it's enough.

"I know it's not your fault," I whisper, nuzzling her ear as she cries silently beneath me. "I forgive you, and I forgive myself. For all of it. And I'll be your friend always. I'll give you this, too—whatever you want for as long as you need. But please, Evangeline, please don't ask for what's left of my heart unless you plan to keep it forever."

evangeline

I didn't mean to fall here

Bringing all my broken pieces

But I just couldn't help it—

You're the only consequence I want

When Wilder told me his studio used to be a guesthouse, I was expecting something small, maybe a thousand square feet. Cabin-sized. What I wasn't expecting was a whole-ass, two-story house hidden behind trees about a minute's walk down a path from the main house.

Granted, in terms of size for the neighborhood, it's a

shack. But it's also twice the size of my first home, the little bungalow I still miss.

Downstairs is almost entirely studio space, a wide-open floor plan with a modest kitchen toward the back and half-bath tucked under stairs. The second story boasts two small bedrooms, a bathroom, and a closet stacked with linens.

The studio is a literal dream. Bright and airy, it has the same cozy vibe as the main house. There's a lounging area with a fireplace and inviting couches and armchairs. Rugs are strewn liberally over the hardwood floors. The walls showcase professional concert photographs, framed posters from Night Theory's tours, and floating shelves with all their awards.

It's clear the whole band spends time here. Pristine guitars hang along one wall: multiple acoustic and electric, as well as Jax's favorite Fender bass. There's a drum set for Eddie, a standing keyboard for Zander, and a massive workstation with multiple screens, extensive audio interfaces, and top-of-the-line studio monitors. Literally everything you could possibly need for recording, editing, and mixing. There's even a partially enclosed vocal booth with panels to tame sound reflections.

For me, though, the unquestionable centerpiece of the studio is the grand piano, a stunning, nine-foot-long vintage Steinway. I've been sitting at it for close to twenty minutes, my fingers ghosting over silky keys as I listen to phantom notes of memory.

I saw this exact piano nearly every weekend of my life growing up. It sat in the front room of the Ashburn home, a gift from Julian to Rose shortly after Wilder's birth. It's the piano he learned to play on. The piano I spent hours lying beneath as a child, dozing and dreaming and listening to him tinker through his first compositions. I still remember the first time he let me play it, the pride I felt when he realized how good I was.

A messy stack of sheet music sits on the shelf, the topmost page half-covered in penciled notes. I finally give in to temptation and read the first few lines. My fingers ache to descend and hear the melody aloud.

Lost in imagined music, I don't think anything of a draft of cool air against my back.

"My mom gave it to me as a housewarming gift."

I spin on the bench to find Wilder standing near the open front door. His soft smile doesn't entirely capture his eyes. In them, I easily read what he's feeling: surprise, wariness, and cautious hope.

I'm sure when he woke up, he thought I'd run. He was so exhausted last night, I doubt he even remembers falling asleep still inside me. He barely stirred when I slipped out of bed to use the bathroom or when I covered him in blankets. And he definitely doesn't know I lay awake beside him all night, watching him sleep like a total creep.

"Lucky you. I love this piano."

He nods toward it. "Go on. You know you want to."

Turning back around, I set my fingers on the keys and find the pedals. I start with scales, my pressure tentative at first, then more confident as the incredible resonance of the piano surrounds me. My eyes close in pleasure. A few seconds later, the fine hairs on my neck lift in awareness.

"Quit teasing," Wilder murmurs behind me.

Smiling, I launch into something he'll recognize, a piece he played a lot in his early teens. When I reach the final note of "In Flight" by Michael Harrison, he sighs.

"Such a show-off."

Craning my neck, I smile up at him. "Come on. I had fourth graders who could play that with their eyes closed."

He moves around the bench to sit beside me. Our arms brush, triggering a cascade of goosebumps from my shoulder to my wrist. His right hand dances over the upper register, coaxing a tinkling melody.

"Piano never came as easily to me as guitar," he says softly. "It took me months to learn that song."

I frown. "No, I vividly remember you playing it the

same day you got the sheet music. It was winter—I was nine, maybe ten? We'd just eaten grilled cheeses for lunch. You snuck out of the kitchen and I followed you to the piano room. I was nine or ten? You glared at me and said you wanted to be alone, but then you let me stay."

He shakes his head, a dimple deepening on his downturned face. "Actually, you stuck your chin out and said, 'Duh, we *are* alone,' then crawled under the piano. The last time I'd tried to pull you out of there, you'd screamed like I was sawing your leg off. I decided to spare my ears the pain."

Unduly pleased he remembers, I laugh. "That does sound more accurate."

He glances at me with teasing eyes. "You were a brat."

"Nah, I was just obsessed with you."

When his gaze narrows, I flush and look down, tapping a few keys before saying, "In any case, you told me your mom had given you the sheet music that morning."

"I lied."

My head whips up. "Shut up, you did not! Why?"

He chuckles and shrugs. "I was an adolescent boy trying to impress a girl. A few days before that was the first time I'd played the song without fucking it up."

I study his profile, struggling not to laugh. "You knew I wouldn't leave?"

"I was pretty sure, yeah." He looks up, scanning my face. "You're not mad? That I manipulated you?"

My chest tightens at the real worry in his eyes. "Wilder, I crawled under the piano knowing you wouldn't pull me out. We were kids. I think that kind of manipulation was probably developmentally appropriate."

When he just keeps staring at me, I gently close the lid over the keys and turn toward him. My knee comes to rest against his. His eyes flicker with more wariness, but he doesn't pull back—he pushes closer instead, taking my hands and holding them over our thighs. The contact makes me forget what I was about to say, allowing him to speak first.

"I wasn't my best self last night. Cooking all day, having guests... I was already feeling dysregulated before you even got here. I said things I didn't mean. I *don't* resent you for the choice you made back then. It was absolutely the right decision. I was an addict who lied to you and betrayed your trust. And to be real with you, newly sober me didn't deserve you, either. I was a wreck and just beginning to deal with my issues. Last night, my anger... it wasn't about that. Not really."

Having spent all night thinking about and preparing

for this conversation, I nod. "I know. It was super fucked up of me to push you like that. It definitely wasn't the plan, just so you know."

His brows lift. "You had a plan?"

Holding his gaze feels a bit like looking at the sun, but I manage it. "I figured that was obvious when I shoved my test results in your face."

His lips quirk. "So you did come here to get laid."

I want to tell him the whole truth about why I'm here, but the last words he spoke before falling asleep play in my head for the millionth time. I know in my gut that they were the source of his anger. His underlying fear.

We broke each other's hearts, and there's not a damn thing either of us can do to change that. Two months ago, he confessed he still had feelings for me, and last night he asked me not to take advantage of that. He's willing to be my friend, even my lover, but nothing else. Not right now. Not until I'm ready to recommit to him, to *keep him*. And while I want to be with him so fucking badly, I'm also sane enough to know I'm kind of insane at the moment. An erratic, sensitive mess—as my actions last night clearly demonstrated.

Until I can untangle the chaos inside me, the least I can do is respect his wishes.

As much as I don't want to.

"I came here foremost because I trust you, Wilder. I feel safe with you, with the man you are today. And yes, I wanted to have sex with you. But my headspace wasn't the greatest last night, either." I look down at our entwined hands. "As completely out of character as it sounds, I've been pretty emotionally volatile lately."

His fingers tickle my palms lightly. "To me, you've always been emotionally volatile."

I snort. "Yeah, well, it's kind of new to me. Generally speaking. I *was* planning on spending a few days hanging out before propositioning you, but I overreacted to, um, Aubrey."

"What the hell does... Oh, shit. Were you *jealous*?"

"Ha-ha, so funny. Laugh it up."

I try to tug my hands free, but he merely tightens his grip. The mirth on his face fades to earnestness.

"I'm not interested in Aubrey or dating anyone. Even if I was, it wouldn't have factored. Your body is my Roman Empire, Evangeline. I'd have dumped anyone for the chance to be inside you again."

Air leaves me in an unattractive *whoosh*. Wilder smirks and taps a knuckle to my chin, closing my mouth. That knuckle then grazes over my hot cheek. His eyes follow the path of his hand before he lowers it back to his lap. With a sigh, his expression turns grave.

"If you're staying, if we're doing this, we should set

some boundaries. What happened last night—*how* it happened—can't happen again. I told you I'd never hurt you, and then I did. I'm so sorry."

I immediately shake my head. "I'm fine, really—"

"You're not," he growls. "The whole time we've been sitting here, you haven't been able to stay in one position for more than ten seconds. I was beyond rough with you. Fuck, I—" He shakes his head. "I can't believe you didn't leave in the middle of the night after what I did."

I stay composed with effort, rolling my eyes and shrugging. "So I'm a little sore. Have you seen your dick? It takes some getting used to. But if you think I regret coming so hard I squirted, you're out of your mind. I forgot how awesome it feels. By the way, is your washer big enough for the comforter on your bed? If not, I can soak it in a tub."

He blinks rapidly, clearly trying to juggle the pieces of his exploded brain.

"Um, yes. It'll fit in the washer."

I reach up and palm the side of his face. His eyes sharpen.

"I regret pushing you last night, but only because it caused you pain." I smile as much as I can. "Also, despite my historical difficulty with them, I promise to respect whatever boundaries you set. Can we talk about them over breakfast? I'm starving."

He scans my face, eyes full of tenderness and wonder. "Of course."

Taking my hand in his, he presses a kiss to my palm. An answering pulse in my core makes me hiss and snatch my hand back.

"Don't turn me on right now. I need another twelve hours of recovery time and at least three magnesium baths."

His smile begins in his eyes—my favorite sunrise.

Standing, he offers me a hand. "In the mood for a burned bagel?"

I want to sob.

I laugh instead.

wilder

I can't believe Evangeline is finally eating my food —not the horrible first attempts she was sweet enough to pretend to like years ago, but good, seasoned food. When I set the plate down, her first words were, "This is too pretty to eat." One bite changed her mind.

I was pretty confident she'd enjoy my Eggs Benedict. What I hadn't anticipated—and probably should have —was that she'd make eating it look borderline pornographic. I've been taking distracted bites off my own plate, barely tasting them, while staring at her like a perv. She's so into the food she hasn't noticed.

In the last ten minutes, I've entertained a hundred depraved fantasies, all of them centered on stuffing something else in her mouth. Hearing what sounds she makes. Replacing the hollandaise she licks off her lips with cum.

When her plate is clean—and I mean *clean*—she seems to finally realize I'm sitting across from her. Her cheeks turn a delicious, apple red shade.

"That was really good, thank you," she mumbles from behind a napkin.

My grin has a life of its own. By the way her eyes narrow, she can glean its source.

The napkin drops. "Are you seriously hard right now?"

I bark a laugh; God, I've missed her. The *real* her. The beautiful contrasts in her personality that only those closest to her ever see. Easily embarrassed yet crass. Deeply sensual but reserved. Sensitive and compassionate, but as stubborn as a bulldozer with cut brakes. Ambitious to the point she's a workaholic, while simultaneously a homebody who'd rather take a bath and read a romance novel than endure an awards ceremony.

"I don't know why you're surprised." I stand to collect our plates, shaking my head when she starts to rise. "Don't even think about it. Do you want more coffee?"

"Yes, please."

Her ass hits the chair—padded, but she still winces.

It makes *me* wince. I drop off the plates in the sink and grab the carafe of coffee, then return to the table.

"You should take a bath. We can talk later. I have magnesium salts in my bathroom—"

"Don't," she snaps. "Don't fucking do that."

The vehemence in her voice sends my heart rate into overdrive. I recover enough to refill her coffee, hoping she doesn't notice the tremble in my wrist, then return to my seat.

Feeling like my skin is suddenly two sizes too small, I study her profile as she stares blankly out a nearby window. I clearly triggered her trauma, but I'm not sure why or how to fix it.

Then Martin's words from New Year's Eve come back to me. *"Clay is really good at camouflaging control as care."*

Thinking back over what I said, my stomach sinks. I didn't give her a choice. I gave her a command.

"You absolutely don't have to take a bath if you don't want to. If you want one later, the salts are under my sink."

Evangeline draws a shaky breath. As she exhales, life returns to her eyes. She reaches for her coffee, wrapping her hands around it but not drinking.

"You didn't deserve that. I know you're not... that you don't—" She cuts herself off, lips pressing tightly together.

"It's okay," I say, firm enough that her eyes lift to mine. "You never have to dilute yourself with me. Ever. If you're not ready to talk about what you've gone through, that's okay too. But I also won't tiptoe around it. You reacted that way because I didn't ask what *you* wanted, right?"

She blinks fast, fingers whitening around her mug. "I don't know. Probably. It's like my brain just shuts off. I'm suddenly so angry I could scream and have zero control of what comes out of my mouth." Her eyes redden even as she smiles weakly. "Things got pretty tense with my dad because of me freaking out on him for no reason."

"It's not for no reason, Evangeline. You know that, and I'm sure he does too."

She nods distractedly, gaze roaming over the living room. "Between my mom and Martin, I've had a crash course in PTSD. But even that's hard to wrap my head around. Intellectually, I know what I experienced is affecting me, but processing it in real time feels like trying to shape water."

"Give yourself a break," I murmur. "It's only been two months."

In a clear bid to change the subject, she points into the living room. "Why haven't you hung anything there? It's the main focal point of the space."

I study her for another moment, then follow the line

of her finger to the glaringly empty spot above the fireplace.

My long-held commitment to not looking at the painting there broke last month. For days afterward, I stared at it obsessively and even slept on the couch one night so I could see it right upon waking. I finally confessed the unhealthy habit to Frank. He stayed on the phone with me as I pulled it off the wall and stored it in a closet.

As hard as it was to remove the art, I'm glad I did. Otherwise I'd have to explain why I have a painting hanging in my living room of two kids—obviously us—sitting with guitars under a sycamore tree.

"I've been meaning to," I hedge. "Maybe you can pick something out. I have a few of River's paintings that I haven't decided where to hang."

She looks startled. "No way. I mean, I'd love to check out River's stuff, but you should choose what goes there. It's your house."

I capitulate with a nod, ignoring the rebellious urge to tell her that when I built this house, it wasn't just for me. A bad idea on several levels, not the least being she's not mentally or emotionally ready to hear it.

Her wandering gaze returns to me. "This place is amazing, by the way. The design, the flow, the window placements—everything. I love that it feels spacious, but it's not giant, if that makes sense."

"It does, yes. And thank you. I'm proud of it."

"Did you and your dad really tear down the old house and build this by yourselves?"

Grinning, I shake my head. "My dad loves spreading that rumor, but no. I partnered with an architect for the design, then worked with a general contractor and subcontractors for the actual demo and remodel. I wasn't about to let my dad touch electric or plumbing, no matter how confident he was in his YouTube education."

She laughs. "So you didn't hammer in every nail?"

"Only a few thousand of them. But I did lay all the flooring and tile and installed most of the drywall." Far too pleased by the impressed look on her face, I smirk. "I don't know why you're surprised. According to you, I have skilled fingers."

I love that she doesn't hide her blush.

"Stop it."

I feign innocence with raised brows. "Stop what?"

Evangeline rolls her eyes and stands, taking her coffee with her into the living room. "Let's go, Mr. Fancy Fingers. Time to tackle the hard stuff."

At my laugh, she throws a disapproving look over her shoulder.

"What did you expect? I know I've changed a lot, but some things never will. Especially around you."

Adorably flustered, she sits on the couch facing the water and pulls a nearby blanket over her legs. When I approach her, she points to the other couch.

"For my vagina's peace of mind, you're sitting over there."

I veer around the coffee table and sit. "If you're trying to make me stop thinking about sex, it's not working."

She hides a smile behind her mug. "Given the conversation we're about to have, it would be pointless to try."

"I'll show you something *not* pointless."

She groans. "Horrible. Really horrible."

Smirking, I toss my legs onto the coffee table and cross my ankles. To my satisfaction, her gaze drops to my groin—namely, the tent in my sweats.

"Yep, still hard over here."

Her eyes flash up. "Since we're all about honesty these days, why did you never let me give you a blowjob when we were together? Was it because you thought I'd suck at it?"

My lips twitch and she glowers.

"I wasn't trying to be punny."

I sigh, allowing the gravity of her question to settle inside me. "There isn't a simple answer."

"Then give me the complicated one."

Despite literal years of wanting to have this conversation with her, now that the door is open, I can't decide where to start. There's too much I want to say all at once.

When the curiosity in Evangeline's eyes shifts to apprehension, I give up and pick a random thought.

"Do you remember the day I sat in on the music lesson with one of your students?"

"Yes." Her blush conveys that she remembers what happened after the lesson. How she was so turned on she forgot where she was and almost went down on me in the classroom.

"I had every intention of letting you... you know, later that night. But then we had dinner with the guys."

As the words pass my lips, a wave of anxiety crashes over me. My throat closes. Imaginary fire ants march down my arms.

"Shit," I mumble. "Give me a sec." Closing my eyes, I focus on my breath.

"If you don't want to talk about this..."

"No. I'm okay." I force myself to look at her—at the woman I hurt. "I do need to back up a bit, though. Or a lot. I'd like to explain from the beginning."

She nods hesitantly. "Okay."

Dropping my feet to the floor, I rub my face roughly. *Just do it. Tell her.* I take one more deep breath, then prop my elbows on my thighs and begin.

"I learned really young that being around you was like taking medicine for my anxiety. From thirteen on, I lived for the weekends. Making music with you was the only time I felt relief."

"Really?" she whispers.

I nod. "I know now it was because I felt safe to be myself around you, but back then..." I shake my head. "I think I was fifteen when I wanted to kiss you for the first time. By seventeen, I fantasized about you constantly. I didn't know how to handle it, so I made all these rules for myself. For us. But at the same time, I was doing weird shit like deleting texts from boys on your phone."

Her jaw drops. "That was you?"

I offer a wincing smile. "I might have also pretended to accidentally touch you in the pool more than once."

Her eyes flare with laughter. "I was guilty of that too."

"Did you also sneak out of the pool, find my clothes, and steal my boxers to masturbate with?"

Evangeline gapes. "Oh my God, I remember freaking out when I couldn't find my underwear. That's nasty, Wilder!"

"It's like you've never met me."

She considers me for a moment, then nods. "Fair point."

Our shared smile fades from my face first.

"By the time you left the band, my feelings for you had become synonymous with my fear of losing you— or more accurately, my fear of your rejection and this perceived control you had over me. It was a self-fulfilling prophecy. I was abusing substances by then, too, so my self-loathing and denial journeys were well underway."

She frowns, her gaze falling to her lap. "When we started dating, you told me that you'd pushed me away because you were afraid." I'm not sure what she means until she adds, "You were telling the truth. Or as much of it as you could articulate at the time."

I swallow so hard I almost choke. "Yes. The only thing I lied to you about was my using."

She nods to herself. "Go on."

"Fast forward a few years—I met Kendra, who was already strung out on pills. With access to a steady supply through her, I started using Oxy consistently. There were immediate benefits. My drinking slowed down, I finally wrote our sophomore album, and my anxiety was managed for the most part. For the first time in years, I felt like I was in control of my life. I even developed rituals to support the narrative that I wasn't an addict."

Her eyes widen. "Really? Like what?"

"I was obsessed with finding the right dosage to not look high while also shutting off my disorder. I was militant about controlling how much I took and when— even had a hidden calendar on my phone to track everything. And every few months, I'd detox myself. I convinced myself that if I cleared the drugs out of my system periodically, it meant I wasn't addicted."

Evangeline shakes her head in disbelief. "That sounds like a nightmare."

"It absolutely was. But I was so locked in, I couldn't imagine living a different way. When I showed up at your Cathedral show, I was coming off a really rough detox. I'd been sober for ten days. Jax had figured out what was happening, and earlier that night he'd offered to do a dry month with me. For the first time in a long time, I felt hopeful. I didn't agree to it for you, exactly, but I'd be lying if I said you weren't part of the reason. After all, you were my first addiction. My favorite high."

She makes a soft, distressed sound, but my gaze has dropped to the floor and I can't bring myself to look up.

"I made it another four days. Until dinner that night with the guys. When I left the room, I had the worst panic attack I'd had in years. Completely debilitating. And I cracked. I found two pills that I'd hidden in my bathroom and took them. I didn't want to, but the compulsion was overwhelming."

I glance up, catching the tail-end of her pained expression, and add quickly, "My relapse had nothing to do with you. It had to do with me not addressing any of the underlying causes of my addiction. Any substantial stressor would have yielded the same result. It was going to happen sooner or later no matter what."

She blinks a few times. "Thanks for saying that. So from that point on you were using daily again?"

"Yes," I admit hoarsely. "In the following weeks, I learned what true self-loathing was. I'd finally admitted to myself that I was an addict, but I didn't know how to stop or ask for help. I couldn't see a future where I had what I wanted: freedom from anxiety and you. All I knew was that I couldn't lose you. So I lied."

Her mug clanks on the coffee table. Wiping her tearing eyes, she whispers, "I hate that you went through that just as much as I hated you back then for lying to me."

"Losing you was my rock bottom, Evangeline. It's what made me ask for help. You saved my life."

The glassiness in her eyes doubles. "But then I told you I wished you were dead."

I grimace, my entire body clenching with regret for what I said—*how* I said it—last night.

"Just like my relapse, what I did was *not* your fault. I'll put you on the phone with my sponsor right now and he'll tell you the same thing. I was newly sober and barely coherent. I knew fuck-all about how to handle my emotions and was too self-centered to see the situation from your perspective."

She sniffs loudly, then uses her sleeve to wipe her nose. "Tell me. Please?"

Breathe in.

Breathe out.

"I found an old stash, a half-full bottle my parents had missed when they searched my bedroom. I took..." I swallow a few times to coax the words past the resistance in my throat. "I took all of them."

"What the fuck?" She lifts trembling fingers to her mouth.

"It was almost one a.m., but my parents showed up not five minutes later. An ambulance arrived a few minutes after that."

"What? How?"

Blinking back tears, I smile slightly. "It doesn't make sense, does it? It's almost like someone knew what I was going to do before I did it."

She gasps, understanding instantly. "Katherine."

I release a strangled laugh. "Yep. She called my mom, waking her up, and told her I was going to die if she didn't get an ambulance to me. And my mom believed her. My dad, too."

Evangeline's face crumples. Then she folds over her knees and makes the worst sound I've ever heard, a jagged wail like I just ripped her heart out. In seconds, I'm around the coffee table and pulling her into my arms.

"I'm sorry," I say into her hair. "I'm so sorry. It wasn't your fault. You've never once been responsible for my choices."

She fists my shirt, her forehead rolling against my chest.

"I can't believe you almost *died*. I can't—it's too much."

Closing my burning eyes, I allow myself to feel and accept her shock, anger, and pain.

"I'm never going back there, Fairy. I won't make you any promises, but only because actions speak louder than words. I'm going to show you the same way I show myself. One day at a time."

evangeline

I dig my fingers into Wilder's waist, flooded with a confusing mess of anger and imagined grief. I want to punch him repeatedly, then handcuff him to me for the rest of his life.

"How do you know?" I ask against his chest. It's not a fair question, but I can't help my need to hear his answer.

A warm palm cups the back of my neck. "A lot of reasons, but mostly because I'm selfish. I'm not willing to give up the life I've built or the person I am today. Shockingly enough, I kind of like the guy."

Dragging in a steadying breath, I sit up and wipe my wet cheeks. "He's pretty cool, I guess. Makes great music and a mean Eggs Benedict. He does have a weird obsession with sexual puns, though."

Wilder grins. One dimple deeper than the other. Eyes a bright forest, with those unbelievably charming crinkles at the corners.

Although I'm well aware of how much he's matured in the last seven years, it suddenly hits me how different he *feels*. He's still himself—unquestionably the boy I grew up with—but gone is the undercurrent of volatility I remember. Missing, too, is that old feeling that I'll never really know him. Because he's not hiding parts of himself anymore. He faced his demons. Drew all those disparate, dark elements of himself inward and used them to repair his cracks.

"What's that look for?" he murmurs, eyes scanning mine.

"You're like Kintsugi," I blurt.

His brows jump. "The Japanese art?" When I nod, he gives me a questioning smile. "What made you think of that?"

My face warms. "I don't know. You seem so different. At peace with the past and yourself."

He squints doubtfully at me. "I wasn't very peaceful last night."

I shrug, scooting back on the couch and drawing my knees to my chest. "I think what happened last night was a long time coming." I tilt my head. "Speaking of coming... you never answered my question."

He grins, smug as hell. "Look who's the conductor of the Pun Train now."

I roll my eyes but can't resist a laugh. "Whatever. Are you going to tell me why you never let me give you a blowjob? No joke, your refusal gave me a complex."

His eyes widen. "It did?"

Ignoring the prickling heat crawling up my neck, I mumble into my knees, "I've never given one because of you. I was too afraid I'd be bad at it."

Wilder stares at me unblinking for an extended moment, then jerks halfway to his feet before collapsing back to the couch. He covers his face with his hands.

"I can't believe this."

My embarrassment spikes even higher. "What did you expect? You went down on me all the time, but every single time I tried to return the favor, you rejected me."

His hands drop, revealing a stricken expression. "No, Fairy. No, no. My refusal... that was a combination of some weird mental shit and being on opiates."

I frown. "Explain."

"Once I started using again, it wasn't easy for me to come. I didn't want you to think you weren't able to get me there with your mouth. The main reason, though, was that I constantly felt like a piece of shit for lying to you. The idea of you doing that for me, with how vulnerable and selfless the act is... I couldn't stomach putting you in that position."

My left eyelid twitches. I press a finger to it, then glare at him through my other eye.

"Let me get this straight. You thought you were being *noble*?"

He grimaces. "Yes?"

A laugh bubbles out of me. "What the hell, Wilder!"

The glint in his eyes ruins his attempt at a serious expression. "You've seriously never given a blowjob?"

"We can stop talking about this now. Thanks for answering my question, and also, screw you."

He cracks, his rich laughter filling the room. "This is so twisted. I should feel bad—I know I should—but I can't. It's like I accidentally gave myself a gift."

"You're such an asshole."

Sparkling eyes slant my way. "I volunteer as tribute. Anywhere, anytime you want to practice, whether I'm awake, asleep, driving, cooking, doing laundry..."

Fighting a smile, I kick his thigh. "What makes you think I want to give you a blowjob anymore? Maybe I'm perfectly happy with my virgin mouth."

"Liar," he murmurs huskily.

Ignoring the blush that gives me away, I fake a yawn that turns into a real yawn. "I need a nap and a bath." He frowns and I quickly add, "We're not discussing my sleep issues, but if you want to talk about boundaries, now's the time."

He bites his lip. "Have I ever told you how hot it is that you're a boss in the streets but a total slut in the sheets?"

I kick him again. "Focus!"

"Fine, fine." His grin fades as he sits up and drags fingers across his scalp. The action makes *me* sit straighter since it's his nervous tell—that and the fact he's not looking at me but staring out the windows lining the back of the house.

"Wilder?"

"I'm getting there. Just fighting with myself." He glances at me. "I'm not sure how you'll respond to this."

I hug my knees tighter as my stomach flutters. "If you don't want to do this..."

"Nope. Definitely want to." He sighs heavily and faces me. "I want you here, Evangeline. I always have. But I'm also too old and too sober to pretend a friends-with-benefits situation with you is the healthiest choice for me."

I swallow back denials. "I understand. What do you need?"

"If at any point I feel like I can't do this anymore, I'll tell you. I need your commitment that you'll do the same."

"Agreed," I whisper.

He nods and looks away again. "No holding hands, kissing on the mouth, or sleeping in the same bed."

Pain flares in my chest—sharp, pinpointed like a bullet—and spreads down my arms. I want to cry. Applaud him. Slap him. So many feelings flood me all at once that I can't speak or blink or even breathe.

I finally manage enough air to ask, "Really?"

Wilder looks at me and nods. Eyes wary but resolute. The soft lips I suddenly can't imagine not kissing open on a swift inhale.

"Are you okay with those stipulations?" he asks tentatively.

"Sure." The word feels like broken glass on my tongue.

"Is there anything you need? A boundary that will make you feel more safe?" He hesitates. "I could try not to call you Fairy."

I'm the one who looks away this time. A storm is rolling in, darkening the sky and water, but a few stubborn rays of sunlight cling to a sycamore. The branches are still bare, ghostly and glowing against a shadowed backdrop. As the clouds thicken and the branches dim, something inside me dims too.

I would give anything to be able to trust what my heart is telling me—that I love Wilder more in this moment than I ever have before. But I don't know how to trust myself when I feel so tainted. So unworthy.

So small and violent and broken.

I finally turn back to him, meeting his worried eyes. A smile comes with surprising ease.

"Don't you dare stop calling me Fairy. As for boundaries, I can't think of anything right now, but I'll let you know if I do." I stand up, grabbing my mug. "I'm going to pass out for a bit, then I'm commandeering your bathroom. That soaker tub is calling my name."

He stands with me. "Of course. I'll be around—if I'm not in the house, I'm in the studio."

"'Kay."

I rinse the mug, pop it in the dishwasher, and head toward the hallway. As soon as I know he can't see me anymore, my eyes flood with tears.

I'm almost to the stairs when his voice stops me.

"Evangeline?"

I pause but don't turn around. "Yeah?"

"I'm really glad you're here."

"Me too."

I duck around the corner and haul ass upstairs.

We were wasting time

Racing to hold steady

So either leave me here

Or kiss me already

I play a small, morose melody on the piano, then sigh and look at my phone. It's propped on the shelf against sheet music, my mom's face visible on the screen.

"I'm almost positive she was crying when she left the room. What if I royally fucked up?"

She shakes her head, curls swaying around her

shoulders. "You did the right thing, Wild. For both of you."

"I don't know. I can't stop thinking about the look on her face when I told her my limits. She was hurt. What if she actually does want..." I finish the sentence silently.

Me.

Maybe she wants *me.*

The possibility is too big to hold, too close to my longest-held dream to consider as a real possibility.

Gleaning where my head went, my mom says gently, "Maybe she does want more, but you need to remember what she's been through and her mental state right now. I love Eva, and my heart breaks for her, but I won't tell you not to protect yourself."

I nod for her comfort, knowing that my so-called boundaries are performative bullshit. I'm trying to bulletproof myself with Styrofoam.

There's no way to protect myself from this, from Evangeline. I'm in love with her. I always have been and always will be. The only thing I'm really doing is preparing for the pain when she leaves.

My mom continues, "I haven't been exactly where she is, but I do know what it's like to have your foundation cracked and your sense of self turned upside down. She doesn't trust her own feelings right now. Even if she wants to."

Wind lashes rain against the nearby windows. The lights in the studio flicker.

"Shit. I forgot to call someone to fix the generator last week."

"I thought your dad looked at it," she says with a knowing smile.

I roll my eyes. "I stopped him before he took the whole thing apart and started Googling."

From somewhere behind my mom, my dad says, "I totally could have fixed it!"

She laughs. "Sure you could have."

His face appears beside hers, whiskey-colored eyes locking on mine. "For what it's worth, I agree with your mom. I know it wasn't easy setting boundaries with Eva, but it was the right choice. It's the selfishness paradox of recovery—we stay clean and sober by learning how to be of service to others, but we can't show up for anyone unless we're first selfish about our recovery. Unfortunately, sometimes that means going against our own hearts."

He gives my mom a weighted look. She smiles softly, and he kisses her forehead.

"You did something like this?" I ask, stupefied.

His eyes return to me. "In the same wheelhouse."

My mom laughs lightly. "We weren't even technically

together, but he preemptively dumped me because I was in the way of his sobriety."

I gape as my dad grimaces. "Keep in mind I'd just been hit by a car, broken most of my bones, and was on a steady drip of painkillers. And before that, I'd been on the verge of relapsing. I loved your mom, but I knew I couldn't give her what she needed. I had to fix my shit—physically and mentally—before I felt worthy of her."

She strokes his cheek, then turns to me. "He did what he had to do to protect us both, which is what you're doing now. Sometimes you and Eva remind me a lot of your dad and me—it took a while for us to be on the same page."

"At least it wasn't seven years," I mutter, and she winces in sympathy.

The lights flicker again, this time staying off for several seconds. I grab my phone and stand. "I have to go."

"Be careful walking back to the house," she says, big eyes filled with worry. "Love you."

My dad squeezes her shoulder. "We trimmed all the trees around the paths last fall. He'll be fine. Love you, son."

"Love you guys."

After I make sure the computer and lights are all off,

I slip my feet into the dirt-speckled rain boots I left by the door and shrug into a raincoat.

Neither matter much the second I step outside, as nothing short of a hazmat suit will keep me dry in these conditions. We're at the tip of the island and the winds are merciless, driving the heavy rains in gravity-defying directions. I'm forced to hold a hand over my eyes to keep it from blinding me.

Despite it being the middle of the day, the sky is so dark the solar lights along the main path have come on. They're dimmer than usual given the lack of sunlight today, but their glow guides me as I jog toward the house.

Right as I reach the back door, the single light I left on in the kitchen goes out. I let myself into the mudroom and shuck off my jacket and boots. It's almost as loud inside as it is outside, the rain pounding on the glass over the dining area. But there's a stillness, too. A quietude that unnerves me.

My hair drips onto my shoulders and my pants are wet and heavy, but neither sensory irritation registers as I walk quickly toward the stairs and take them two at a time.

Evangeline's bedroom door is open, enough light coming through the windows for me to see it's empty.

The sight of her duffel and guitar case at the foot of the unmade bed should reassure me. Instead, my heart rate triples. I was in the studio for a couple of hours. She said she was going to nap, then take a bath. Did she already wake up, or did she decide on a bath first?

Dear God, please don't let her have fallen asleep in the water.

I tear into my bedroom, the space notably darker due to the thicker tree line on this side of the house. When I see the closed bathroom door, panic destroys any semblance of propriety. I pound on it once before swinging it open, my eyes snapping to the extra-large soaker tub.

Water sloshes as Evangeline jerks upright, a hand slamming against her chest. "Mother of pearl!"

My relief is so heady my knees almost buckle. "Sorry. The power went out, so I wanted to check on you. When you weren't in your room, I freaked out."

Thanks to the abundance of white tile and the massive skylight over the tub, I can clearly see her confused expression—and the moment it clears.

"You thought I fell asleep and drowned."

It's not a question, but I nod anyway. She doesn't sound angry, at least.

"My brain is hardwired to jump to worst-case scenarios," I admit, my voice still shaky from the offload of adrenaline. "You should have seen me the first few times I babysat Emma. I was an absolute wreck. I'm not much better now, honestly."

Her lips tug upward. "Helicopter parent, huh?"

"Probably worse than your dad," I say wryly.

Smiling wider, she sinks back into the water. "Well, as you can see, I'm fine. I had a lovely nap, and now I'm soaking up the ambiance of the storm. Water's still hot if you want to join."

My system resets from anxious to aroused in a second flat. Evangeline giggles as I rip off my clothes.

"Damn," I hiss as I lower into the water. "Are you trying to burn your skin off?"

"Scalding is the only acceptable temperature for a bath," she says primly. "Besides, it's not as hot as you think. You're just cold."

The stinging fades in a matter of moments, encompassing warmth melting tension from my muscles.

"As usual, you're right."

She gives me a smug smile and leans her knees to one side. "There, now you can stretch out."

I take advantage, extending my legs and sliding down to dunk my head under. When I come back up, I make a face. "How much salt did you put in here?"

"Um, the whole bag?"

I laugh, wiping my stinging eyes. "No wonder your

hair is dry. By the way, did you actually say 'mother of pearl' when I came in or did I hallucinate that?"

"Sure did," she says with a smile. "It's a Lily-approved cuss word. I'm actually kind of impressed with myself for using it spur of the moment like that."

"Very impressive," I say drolly.

She whips a foot out, presumably to kick me, but I grab it and start massaging. Revenge instantly forgotten, she offers me the other one as well. Humming happily, she closes her eyes and drops her head back. I'm extra grateful for the extended length of the tub when the position elevates her off the bottom, giving me a mouth-watering view.

"How are you feeling?"

"Right now? Amazing. Don't stop. Oh, right there."

"Are you *trying* to torture me?"

She smirks. "Maybe."

"Brat."

The foot I'm not massaging slips up my thigh. I think the movement is unintentional until her toes brush purposefully along my stiff cock.

Her smile widens. "I hope that's not left over from breakfast."

"A brat *and* a menace." I release a slow breath, my hand tightening reflexively on her foot. "How sore are you?"

Even in the low light, I see her breath quicken and her already flushed skin turn a darker red. Her eyes open, the gray one so dilated it's almost as dark as the other.

"Turns out I'm not nearly as sore as I thought."

wilder

I forget how to speak for a few seconds. When my voice returns, it's sandpaper.

"You touched yourself? Put fingers inside that pretty pussy?"

Evangeline bites her lip and nods. I reach over and flip the drain, then toss her feet off my lap and stand.

She laughs. "We need to wash the salt off first."

I'm already halfway out of the tub. "Way ahead of you."

I crank on the dial in the walk-in shower. Water cascades from the oversized showerhead, steam billowing almost instantly. I say a silent thank you to my dad for convincing me to install a gas water heater with a standing pilot light.

When I turn to help Evangeline out of the tub, she's

already walking toward me. Glistening like Venus from the sea, loose tendrils of hair curling around her determined face, she steps into the shower and points.

"Rinse, please."

I don't bother pretending ignorance—or hesitance. Ducking beneath the water, I rinse as quickly as possible. When I'm done, Evangeline nods at the tiled bench beneath a high window, close enough to be within reach of the steam and mist.

"Sit."

I'm so fucking turned on I don't even make a quip about her bossiness. Nor do I feel the cold tile as it meets my ass. I do, however, have enough functioning brain cells to say, "Please get a towel for your knees."

Her eyes narrow like she's considering arguing for the sake of it, but then she looks down at the tile and sees the wisdom in my statement. After a quick detour to the towel rack, she drops the twice-folded material between my spread feet. Delicate hands grip my knees, and then she's lowering to hers.

My breathing turns harsh as her eyes meet mine, then meander down my tense body. Chest. Arms. Abs and thighs. When they land and narrow on my cock, she licks her lips. It's too fucking much. I hiss and grab myself to keep from erupting.

Evangeline's head tilts, a tiny, devious smile on her face. "But I haven't even touched it."

As soon as I'm under control, I croon, "You're so beautiful on your knees for me. I can't wait to see my cum dripping off those lips."

Her composure cracks, then shatters. She pulls my hand away and replaces it with both of hers, then bends forward and licks my tip like a lollipop, humming at the taste of me.

Every nerve ending in my body singing, I hang on to the bench and let her explore. Her tongue swirls all over my shaft and piercing before she takes me slowly into her mouth. Shallow the first time, then a little deeper. When she draws back completely, a thin ribbon of saliva follows. Her tongue flicks out, capturing it, and I make the world's most pathetic sound.

She pauses, her eyes jerking up to mine. The haze of lust in them falters, hesitance and self-consciousness taking its place.

Oh, fuck no.

I sink my fingers beneath the loose bun at the back of her head. "You're perfect. I guarantee I'm going to come really hard and really soon. I also don't care where. Neck, chest, face, mouth, tile—it's all the same to me, all perfect because it's you. Do absolutely whatever the fuck you want."

She chews her lips, frowning. "I want to make you lose it. Tell me how?"

I gaze reverently down at her, my heart on fire. "Stop thinking so hard and eat my cock like you've always wanted to. I'm not an appetizer, baby. I'm your favorite main course."

Her eyes glaze again, thick lashes fluttering as her breath quickens. Knowing she's close to letting go, I give her hair a little tug.

"And rub that needy clit for me while you're at it."

With an eager whimper, she sneaks a hand between her thighs as she lowers her head.

This time she doesn't hold back. And now that I know what she needs, I don't hold back either. I give her my unrestricted moans and praise. My hand stays on the back of her head, my fingers tight in her hair, but I don't guide her. She doesn't need me to.

Evangeline devours my cock like she's starving for it. Zero finesse. Sloppy as hell.

Abso-fucking-lutely perfect.

It's beyond a doubt the best blowjob of my life, and my body knows it. Telling pressure builds fast in my spine. My fingers and toes tingle in warning.

"Fuuuck," I grit out. "Make a choice, baby."

Her eyes roll up to mine, fierce despite the tears leaking from the corners. She squeezes her hand around my base and takes me to the back of her throat. When she swallows around me, I'm *done*.

The first pulse of euphoria is followed closely by a second, third, fouth. I come so hard, for so long, that my soul leaves my fucking body. My head snaps back, hitting the wall with enough force I see stars. The pain compounds the pleasure, making it unbearable, and my vision spirals into blissful white.

"Wilder? Wilder! Are you okay?"

I blink at Evangeline. Her worried face is sideways and right in front of mine, which makes zero sense until I realize I'm lying on the bench. Mist from the shower tickles my forehead and nose.

"Yeah," I croak. "You have a little something..." My thumb swipes her chin, then her cheek.

As more brain function returns, I realize how pointless my efforts are. There's cum in her hair. On the tip of her nose. In her eyebrows.

My stomach contracts. My cheeks tighten. I try—I really, really try—not to laugh. But it's another wasted effort.

Evangeline's worry makes way for rage. She punches my shoulder. "Goddammit! You cracked your skull on the wall and keeled over. I was about to call a fucking ambulance."

I can barely breathe I'm laughing so hard. "I can't... your eyebrows—it's all over you."

"Obviously," she hisses. "You convulsed right out of my mouth and Jackson Pollack'd me as I was trying to grab you. Ugh. Whatever. I'm done playing nurse."

She stands and turns toward the water. I sit up fast and grab her arm before she can escape.

"Fairy," I cajole, tugging her between my knees. She sighs as I draw a pert nipple into my smiling mouth, flicking it with my tongue until it hardens before giving the same treatment to the other.

Her hands come to rest on my shoulders. "You scared me," she whispers.

"I'm sorry." Sliding my hands to her ass, I squeeze. Her back arches, fingers clenching. "I have a hard head —I'm perfectly fine. That was the best blowjob of my life."

"Liar," she says breathily.

My mouth is full, so I shake my head as I slip a hand between her legs. I tease with my tongue and fingers until she's panting and circling her hips.

"Wilder," she whines.

I release her nipple with a pop and look up at her flushed, beautiful, cum-speckled face. "You did so good," I purr as I sink a finger inside her. Her body clenches around me, her breath hitching. "How much did you swallow?"

Her eyes flash. "Quite a fucking lot, thank you very much."

I grin and give her another finger, curling both toward me and pulsing them against her G-spot. Her head cants back, a low moan saturating the air.

"Give me those fairy eyes." I wait until she complies, her gaze focusing when she registers my serious expression. "I'm so proud of you. Thank you for trusting yourself and letting go for me. You were an absolute savage, and I fucking loved watching you swallow my cock. That *was* the best blowjob of my life."

My praise princess melts in my arms, her entire body shuddering.

I swirl my tongue around a nipple piercing. "Do you want to get off on my fingers, my mouth, or my cock?"

Her eyes flicker downward. Swollen lips part in surprise, and a small, pleased smile follows.

"Always hard for you, Evangeline," I murmur.

When she sways toward me, I immediately read her intent and lift her by the thighs, spreading them over mine. Her arms come around my shoulders, breasts mashing against my chest. She wiggles around until she finds what she wants, then rocks her way slowly down my cock. By the time she's seated on my thighs, we're both panting.

Her wide, awed eyes roam my face. "Nothing feels as good as this."

I manage to nod before my thoughts scatter as she starts to grind. Her heavy-lidded gaze falls to my mouth, and it takes every last drop of my willpower to resist the lure. Tightening my arms around her, I tuck my face against her neck and mirror the rhythm of her hips with mine.

The prettiest whimpers fill my ears.

"More," she says on a gasp. "I want you everywhere."

Her admission triggers another wave of building pressure inside me. "Fuck. Just like that, you're gonna make me come again."

I draw back enough to feed two fingers into her mouth. She moans, sucking and coating them with saliva, then bites down when I try to pull them out.

I slap her ass. "Bad toy."

Her teeth sink deeper into my knuckles, so I slap her ass harder. A gasp frees my fingers to find her ass. The second I start applying pressure, she pushes back and swallows them both. With a guttural cry, she picks up the pace, fucking my cock and fingers with abandon. Hell-bent on taking what she needs from me.

I've never seen anything more beautiful.

"Yes, yes, ah—"

Her breath stalls, body arching. I bite the juncture of her shoulder and neck as she falls over the edge, pussy and ass clamping down and throbbing, her cries echoing around us. Free and safe in her pleasure, without thought or reservation. Messy, loud, and mine.

Exactly as she should be.

As my own release races toward me, I take over from below, bucking my hips hard and fast. And when I go rigid, she bites me in the exact same spot I bit her.

Because we're a perfect song.

Matched note for note.

evangeline

Wilder builds a fire in the living room fireplace as I light candles on the mantel and make a nest on the floor out of pillows and blankets. He digs out a deck of cards. We play Go Fish, Hearts, and Crazy Eights.

I win every round for twenty straight minutes, and I'm smug about it until I remember I always won whenever we played card games as kids too. Annoyed, I tell him to stop losing on purpose. He complies and wipes the floor with me until I throw the cards at him.

When my stomach growls, he puts together a massive charcuterie board that looks like it belongs on a food blogger's Instagram. I eat like I'm feral, moaning and licking my fingers, which has the intended effect of him tackling me to the ground and yanking off my sweatpants. After, we doze on the blankets, my head on his chest and his fingers twirling in my hair. With the soft snap and crackle of logs and the steady patter of rain on the roof, I float in sensory heaven.

The power comes back on midafternoon, but we don't bother turning on any lights. Wilder makes us tea and disappears upstairs, then reappears with my guitar. When he asks me to play some of my new material for him, I do. He listens the same way he always has, with a rapt expression that makes me feel like the center of the universe. Like I'm precious and worthy and magical.

I have to stop to wipe away tears. He doesn't ask me what's wrong, simply holds me until I'm calm again. I reward him with another blowjob, thankfully less traumatic than the first. Then I make the mistake of confessing that I thought swallowing cum would be grosser.

He laughs so hard, for so long, that I attempt to smother him with a pillow. My punishment is his mouth on my pussy, two fingers in my ass, and a husky warning that soon it'll be something a lot bigger than his fingers inside me. The so-called threat triggers an immediate, shattering orgasm.

I'm still buzzing and relearning how to breathe when he whispers in my ear, "The reason my cum tastes good is because I'm made for you." He leaves right after to wash his face and hands, sparing me the embarrassment of a witness as I dazedly wonder if he's right.

When he returns, he has his own acoustic, a custom Gibson slightly larger than mine. I cozy up in blankets, grinning like a fangirl because I haven't heard him play in far too long.

He stands dramatically before the fire. Makes a show of tuning the guitar with a frown of concentration and nervous glances. Right when I'm convinced he's about to break my heart, he launches into a ridiculous, ad hoc song about a storm cloud that contains no less than five sexual puns.

We spend the rest of the afternoon playing an old game where we give the other person a color, emotion, and a setting, and five minutes to come up with a jingle.

Just before sunset, the rain lets up and the sky partly clears. We bundle up and go outside, presumably to see if any tree branches have fallen, but end up walking down to the water on a path clogged by yellow and white daffodils. The blooms are a little beat up from the storm but glow like fallen stars in the fading sunlight.

I crouch beside a section of flowers near the small beach and gently lift bent stalks. "I planted these same colors once. Did you ever see them? At my first place?"

Wilder's gaze lifts from the flowers. "I saw them."

I almost ask whether these were here when he

bought the property or if he planted them, but something stops me. Maybe how presumptuous the question is, but more likely his lack of smile.

A cloud covers the sun, the temperature instantly dropping, and a gust off the water makes me shiver.

"Let's head in," he says softly. "I'll get started on dinner."

He pulls me up, warm fingers around mine for two seconds before he releases me and tucks his hand in a pocket.

Those two seconds—and the loss of them—stay with me as he reheats leftover pastitsio. As I fold the blankets and clean up the mess we left on the coffee table.

Lights are turned back on. Candles are blown out. The fire is covered by a grate and left to die.

Over dinner, we try to get it back—the peaceful, joyful bubble we floated in most of the day—and we almost do a few times. But as we finish eating, Wilder's phone starts vibrating on the mantel and doesn't stop. He ignores the first two calls, but on the third, he leaves the table to grab it.

He frowns down at the screen.

"Everything okay?" I ask.

His eyes meet mine for a moment. "Fine, but I need to return a call. Be back in a sec."

He walks from the room before I can decide whether or not I have the right to ask who's calling.

By the time he returns, the kitchen is clean and the dishwasher is running.

"Don't tell me I didn't have to," I say as he opens his mouth. "I might throw a chair at your face."

He chuckles. "I was going to say 'thank you,' you maniac. Want to watch a movie?"

I stare at him, waiting for more before realizing he's setting another boundary. He's not going to tell me who was on the phone, and he doesn't want me to ask.

Because he's not mine.

The silence vibrates, a rubber band stretched to snap. I can already feel the impending sting.

I summon a weak smile. "I'm actually pretty tired."

Concern, regret, acceptance—they cross his face like fast moving clouds before he nods. "Absolutely, sure. Sleep well, okay? I'll see you in the morning."

I'm smiling as I thank him for dinner and say goodnight. Smiling as I grab the two blankets I brought down from the guest room. *Smiling, smiling* as I say goodnight again and leave him standing in the kitchen with a lost expression on his face.

Upstairs in my room, I close the door, flip on the light, and faceplant on the bed. The sting in my chest intensifies. When it migrates to the backs of my eyes, I growl and haul myself into the bathroom.

Wilder's doing what's right for him, and the only thing I can do is respect that and hope that within the next few weeks, I'll find the fortitude to lay it all out for him. How I'm scared of the future but equally certain I want to spend it with him. How I want to keep him, keep *us*.

I just need a little more time to get a handle on myself. To remember who I am and resuscitate my confidence. To learn how to tune out the voice in the back of my mind that's so intent on undermining every moment of peace with parroted, poisonous words.

Helpless.

Lazy.

Crazy.

Too much, too much, too much...

Showering brings me back to the present via the unavoidable evidence of the last twenty-four hours. I relive every touch. Find and press every tender spot. Stretch to feel the burn of muscles and sigh into the phantom warmth and fullness.

Wilder and I may be in another limbo—this one a strange inversion of our vow as teens—but I take comfort in what my body tells me. What *he* told me. What my soul has always known.

We're made for each other.

Somehow, someway, I'm going to fix what's wrong with me. Course correct our past. Because I'm not letting him go.

Not ever again.

♫

A FEW HOURS LATER, the soft creak of the door opening wakes me from a light sleep. Footsteps cross the room. I hold my breath as the covers lift, as the mattress dips and the sheets rustle. His arm slides over my waist. He fits himself against my back, tucking his knees beneath mine.

Relief pours from my lungs in a sigh. I find his hand and draw it to my face, pressing a kiss to his warm palm.

"I can't do it," he whispers. My stomach drops, but then he continues, "I can't sleep knowing you're right across the hall and I could have you in my arms."

Guilt and elation war inside me. "I'm sorry."

His exhale is thick with humor. "Liar."

I kiss his palm again before cradling it to my chest. Looking over my shoulder, I find his eyes in the shadows. "You're right, I'm not sorry. Sleeping beside you was at least twenty percent of why I came."

His brows lift. "That so?"

I nod. "You're the only nightlight that's ever worked. I haven't slept for seven years. Not really. Not like I did with you."

He exhales my name, eyes dropping to my mouth. My lips tingle. His features tighten, head tilting slightly with intent.

I don't know where I get the strength, but I turn away before he can break another one of his rules. His forehead drops to the back of my head, a long sigh warming my neck.

"I suck at this," he murmurs.

I hug his arm tighter. "I think we both do."

"The phone call—that was stupid, not telling you. It was just band shit I forgot about. Our manager needed a confirmation for a festival headliner slot next summer. Eddie took it upon himself to call me over and over until I picked up."

"Are you taking the slot?"

He rubs his face against my hair. "Mmhm. The booking agent has hounded us for years, but our schedule never lined up before now."

"Bullshit. You hate festivals."

He chuckles. "Truth. They're chaotic as fuck and hell on my nerves. At least this one is local, and the lineup is pretty killer. Horizon Fest at the Gorge. Heard of it?"

I gasp and slap his arm, then twist to see his grin. "Glow is headlining Saturday night. Are you Friday?"

Wilder nods, chewing his lip. "We could write a song. You and me, I mean. No pressure or anything, obviously." He pauses, taking in my shocked expression. "Sorry. *Shit*. I shouldn't have—mmfph."

His eyes widen above the hand I've pressed to his mouth.

"Yes," I say emphatically. "I'd love to write a song with you."

NIGHT ★ THEORY
BABY THIS IS DESTINY
I'LL FOLLOW YOU INTO THE SEA
I'LL COME FOR YOU, YOU'LL SEE
SET US FREE → YOU AND ME
DEAD OR ALIVE

bridge

bridge : *a section of a song that provides contrast,
variety, or tension.*

CHAPTER THIRTY-ONE

Your fingertips left marks

Living bruises I didn't feel

Until I heard them like a heartbeat

Reminding me you were real

I open my parents' front door and wave Evangeline inside ahead of me. The hallway is empty, but the sound of a large gathering floats to our ears from the back of the house.

"I'm starting to think this is a bad idea," she mutters.

"A little late for second thoughts, Fairy. Besides, we've been cooped up for almost two weeks. It was either this or an ambush—and trust me, one was coming. This way we can leave whenever we want. And it's a party. There will be cake. You love cake."

"Ugh, stop it. I'm fine. This is fine. Everything's fine."

When she still doesn't move, I give her a nudge between the shoulder blades. She snarls at me. I smile back until she sighs and trudges inside.

Hiding my relief, I follow.

The last two weeks have been incredible. They've also been super fucking intense. We haven't written one song—we've written an album's worth. We've talked and laughed and fought and fucked until our bodies literally stopped working. There have been countless moments of solace, softness, and peace.

But despite the intimacy of our renewed *friendship*, she still won't talk about Clay or her trauma. Not when she wakes me up thrashing in her sleep in the throes of a nightmare. Not when she comes back from what I call her Empty Place, where she shuts down and withdraws with a thousand-yard stare.

Even worse than the Empty Place, and happening with increasing frequency, are the times she erupts out of nowhere. Her tears, guilt, and negative self-talk afterward are slowly killing me, as is the fact nothing I say seems to make it any better.

I've never felt so close to her before. Or so far.

The emotional strain is affecting me. Not kissing her.

Not telling her I love her. Not knowing whether I'm a stop on her journey or the destination. Not knowing what she needs but suspecting more and more that it isn't me...

We both need a distraction.

Halfway down the hallway, Evangeline glances aside at a mirror. She makes a face and halts, pulling the tie from her hair and fussing with the strands.

"You look beautiful."

I brace for an angry denial, but when she meets my stare in the mirror, her eyes are soft and sad. "I should have washed it again this morning."

I slip my hand up her back and curl my fingers around the nape of her neck. Her hair is soft on my skin —and a lot lighter than it was two weeks ago. It's now more of a honeyed blonde. She hates it. If it weren't for me, she'd be in the shower twice or more a day, trying to speed along the fading process of something called toner.

"I washed it for you yesterday," I murmur, dragging my lips over the back of her head and inhaling. "And I have hair-washing rights for the rest of the week."

Her lips shift into an almost smile. "I still think you cheated."

"Nope. You just suck at Gin Rummy."

She snorts.

"There you two are!"

We turn to see our moms walking toward us, both of them beaming. I gently squeeze the back of Evangeline's neck, bending to whisper, "If you get overwhelmed, hide in my bedroom."

She nods subtly. The moment my touch leaves her neck, a practiced smile slides over her face, her eyes lighting up. She rushes forward to hug both women, then she and Sophie walk arm in arm down the hallway and vanish around the corner.

A pointed throat clearing brings my attention to my mom. Before she can voice the concern I see brewing in her eyes, I pull her into my side.

"I'm okay, Mom. I've honestly never been this happy."

She makes a soft, sympathetic sound. "Or this sad."

I grunt as the words land. "That too." I give her a squeeze, then let her go. "Thanks for putting this together."

She smiles. "Of course. We're missing a lot of the crew, but that's what you get with a bunch of twenty-somethings in the mix. All the old folks are here, though."

Emma's distinctive screech carries down the hall before tapering into a high-pitched giggle. A chorus of adult laughter follows, including Evangeline's. A knot inside me releases.

My mom adds with a grin, "And the star of the show. Come on, let's go see everyone."

My phone vibrates. Glad for the excuse to have a few seconds alone, I pull it from my pocket. "Go ahead. I'll be right behind you."

With a squeeze of my arm and a soft smile, she walks away. I lift my phone to my ear as I turn and veer into what used to be the piano room.

"Shelley? What's up?"

My publicist's voice is sharp as ice and freezes me mid-step.

"I just got off the phone with one of my media contacts. You were right."

I sag against a bookshelf. "Fuck. How much time do I have?"

"Monday morning." She pauses. "Most major entertainment outlets."

Frissons of anxiety skitter up my legs, wrapping spiked tendrils around my chest.

Two days.

Since that lunch in Los Angeles four months ago, I've known this was coming. Clay was never going to go down without a fight. His ego is too big, his pockets too deep, and he hates me almost as much as I hate him.

But I thought I'd have more warning. More time to prepare.

As panic roars in my ears, I realize he must have found out Evangeline was with me. There's no way the leak came from the security guard who let her through the gate, so she must have picked up a tail somewhere in Seattle. Maybe when she landed or at her parents' house. Hell, for all I know, there was a telephoto lens on the speedboat we saw when we were on the beach last week. I remember thinking it was strange when it slowed as it passed.

Chances are I'll never know. This is Clay's hometown. Between his shady contacts and his father's, it was only a matter of time.

It doesn't matter, anyway. He's calling my bluff.

The reckoning is here.

"Wilder?" Shelley's tone tells me it's not the first time she's said my name.

"I'm here. What's the angle?"

"What you thought it would be." For the first time since meeting Shelley eight years ago, I hear a tremble in her voice.

The first zings of anger heat my blood. "Is fact-checking not a thing anymore? Everyone's willing to publish whatever stupid rumor will sell more ad space?"

She hesitates. "He went to the press himself. It's an

interview. My source is trying to get her hands on it, but I'm not hopeful."

I clench my teeth so hard pain blooms in my temples. "Fucking figures. He's made a career off convincing people of lies."

"I promise you, Wilder, we'll fight this with everything we have. The second we get off the phone, I'm sounding the alarm. Cease and desist letters will be sent within the hour. It might stop them."

We both know it won't stop them all, or even most. Especially if the story was juicy enough to be grabbed by multiple outlets. That means whatever is coming was deemed as having enough merit to risk defamation suits. It means he's already convinced people.

Shelley knows as well as I do that no matter what she does, no matter how good my lawyers are or how aggressive our defense is, I won't escape unscathed. And that means Evangeline won't, either.

I look across the room at where the Steinway used to sit, now occupied by cozy armchairs. My vision blurs. In the distortion, I see two kids huddled on the piano bench arguing about a song bridge.

The fire in my blood flares hotter.

"Call Anita Allman and make sure she knows what's coming. Tell her what I told you last month."

"Wilder—"

"No," I interject firmly. "Her job is to protect her client, not me."

She huffs in frustration. "Fine, but we both know it won't be up to her. And from everything you've told me about Eva, she's not going to let you take a fall to save her own face. Neither will Lily Aoki—you're her kid's godfather, for Christ's sake."

"I know," I assure her. "All I need Anita to do is stall them from making any statements for a few days."

In the following pause, I imagine her eyes narrowing to slits behind her glasses. "Is this about the hint you dropped last month? If you have ammunition up your sleeve, now's the fucking time to share it!"

I pinch the bridge of my nose. "It's not my information to share. I'll be asking someone else to put their neck on the line. I'll talk to them today, but I need you to proceed like we don't have a smoking gun."

Shelley's exhale crackles in my ear. "Fine. Sorry for snapping. Keep your head up, okay? A lot of people have your back. In fact, I think you're going to realize just how loved you are."

My throat thick, I say, "Thanks, Shelley. I'll get back to you soon."

As I end the call, movement snaps my head toward the hallway. My dad's eyes lift from the phone to my face. He frowns in concern.

"I only heard the end. Is it happening?"

I nod. The tiny movement is an earthquake, cracking my control. My next breath is a strangled gasp. He rushes forward right as my legs give out, catching me and lowering me to my knees. He guides my head down, a warm hand on my back.

"Breathe, Wild."

He counts for me, breathes with me, until the worst of the dizziness passes. I lift my head, still shaky and slightly nauseous.

"It's over for me, Dad."

"You don't know that," he says gruffly.

"What I know is to not underestimate Clay Eaton." I shake my head with a resigned sigh. "As fucked up as it sounds, I don't even care about losing my career. Not for my sake, at least. And as hard as it will be for all of us, the guys will recover. They'll move on. All I really care about is how it will affect Evangeline. Whatever Clay is about to throw at me will follow me no matter what. I can't protect her from it—from me. Once again, I'm going to fuck up her life."

My dad's eyes burn with intensity. "I had a similar mindset once. Martyrdom with a side of victimhood. You know what it got me? Almost dying in a car accident and losing your mother."

I stare at him in shock; he smiles grimly. "Trust me,

Wilder, women don't want our protection—at least not the kind where we decide what they can and can't handle. What they want is to be invited to fight our battles beside us." He clasps my shoulder, placing his other hand over my heart. "Who you shouldn't be underestimating is *Evangeline.* Stop treating her like she's fragile when she's always been your greatest source of strength."

The words resonate, sending chills down my body. Whatever expression I'm wearing lifts my dad's eyebrows.

"What? Did I say something profound?"

My laugh is closer to a wheeze. "Something like that."

"Good. Oh, one more thing." He reaches into his pocket and pulls out what I call his talisman: a vintage pocket watch that was a gift from his first sponsor before he died. He grabs my hand and puts it in my palm. "I want you to have this."

I look down at the watch, my fingers tingling. I've never seen him without it, and holding it feels surreal. Like I'm staring at a vital piece of who he is.

"I can't take this. No way."

"Then consider it a loan. You can return it when you don't need it anymore."

My thumb grazes the surface his own has worn

smooth over time. A painful memory floats forward of him sitting beside my hospital bed, head down, thumb moving in circles over the metal.

"How am I supposed to know when I don't need it anymore?"

He smiles serenely. "Sounds like a you problem."

With a rough laugh, I press the catch at the base near the silver chain. The case pops open, revealing the familiar off-white face with thin, black Roman numerals, the hour and minute hands forever stuck.

"Thanks for the broken watch." The emotion in my voice outweighs the sarcasm.

"That's the point," he says with a squeeze of my shoulder. "Nothing's perfect, Wild. All of us are a little broken. If we let go of trying so hard to make everything work the way we want it to, we get to see how beautiful that brokenness is."

I smirk. "Twice a day, at least."

"Smart-ass."

He stands and offers me a hand. I let him pull me to my feet, then close the watch and tuck it in my pocket.

"I'm going to find somewhere more private to call Kendra."

He nods, pulling me in for another tight hug. "We're with you, son. Don't forget that."

"Thanks, Dad."

CHAPTER THIRTY-TWO

evangeline

Find her tomorrow

Where the river begins

Listen for mayhem

A storm in the wind

There's a protrusion of bark digging into my spine and a sharp rock under my thigh, but I can't muster the energy to remedy either discomfort. Full-body goosebumps periodically burst along my skin beneath my jeans and sweater—not from the cold, but from the woman I'm watching walk toward the glow of the Ashburn's house.

Katherine moves slowly and gracefully. Long hair,

mostly gray now, spirals down her back. A green velvet and lace duster whispers lightly over dirt and grass behind her.

"It was never the darkness outside of you that needed to be embraced, but the darkness within."

Her voice stays long after she's gone, twirling on the breeze, airy and ageless. As does the challenge that lay within her eyes alongside a kind of detached compassion. Like she expected I already knew what she was telling me. Like the words themselves weren't all that important.

I tilt my head back against the tree. A peel of bark snags my hair, but the tug and tiny flare of pain don't register. Overhead, stripes of shadow paint the giant sycamore. Its curves are sensual, distinctly feminine, the lowest branches resembling arms reaching for what they crave most. Space, oxygen, sunlight. The promise of life. Of love.

"The dam was always meant to break, Evangeline. Let the last barriers fall away. Trust the current and the light you see ahead. He's waiting for you. He will not falter—he will not dim. But hurry. A storm approaches, and only together can you keep the light safe."

The shadows around me have deepened by the time I hear footsteps approaching. Awareness curls through me, opening my eyes as Wilder crouches before me. A warm palm cups my cheek. I turn my face to kiss his palm.

The air stills and thickens with unspoken words. I don't ask him why he disappeared for an hour right after we got here or why he seemed so distracted when he returned. He doesn't ask why I'm here instead of in his room or what Katherine said to me when she followed me outside.

He glances up at the tree, inhales shortly, then rocks back to his feet and extends a hand.

"Let's go home."

Home.

My smile hurts, but it's a stretching pain, like blood circulating to sleeping muscles. Weightless like imaginary barriers falling one by one. Freeing like water rushing forth, finally on its destined path.

I follow the light.

♫

AN HOUR LATER, curled against Wilder on a couch with his fingers in my hair, the final barrier inside me silently crashes down.

My words are fumbling at first. Serrated sentences and stutters. Like spitting rocks from my lungs. But as I go on, they begin to flow. Not easily or smoothly, but unstoppable. Downhill river rapids.

I purge it all. How I buried my pain seven years ago instead of facing it, numbed myself from the inside out until I forgot who I was. How much of my mid-twenties is a blur of brittle effort and flagging self-esteem. Planes, buses, hotels. Stadiums and stages. Roars and flashing lights. The voices of the many becoming louder and louder as I closed myself off to the voice of my own heart.

My pride, turning ever more toxic. My growing fears and personal failures. My insides and outsides becoming as mismatched as my eyes. How my music—the only pure thing left inside me—faded away and took my last flicker of identity with it.

The numbness. Emptiness. The silence and the dark.

I can't look at him when I tell him about Clay, but I feel his subtle flinch when I admit what a relief it was at first. How I was in a downward spiral and Clay's control felt like landing on solid ground.

"Maybe that's where my anger comes from."

Wilder brushes my hair back from the side of my face. "What do you mean?"

"I did this to myself," I murmur. "I ignored all the warning signs, dismissed the concerns of my closest friends, my parents... As angry as I am at Clay, I'm ten times angrier at myself. So maybe when I lash out, I'm really lashing out at myself for being so fucking weak."

He tugs my chin until I lift my eyes to his. "I'm no expert, but I think those are probably normal feelings given what you've been through. But you're not weak—far from it. It's not your fault Clay took advantage of you. He's an experienced manipulator. How the hell were you supposed to know?"

"Logically, I know that. But I can't help feeling like it's my fault."

He nods, sighing. "I'm intimately familiar with guilt, so I get it. Imagine how many times I've wondered if you ending up with Clay is *my* fault."

I stiffen. "What? How can you even say that?"

His eyes squeeze shut. "The night you first met him, at your showcase, I should have told you what he did to Kendra. If I had, maybe—"

I palm his face, silencing him. He opens agonized eyes. "No. I prohibit you from feeling guilty."

Some of his misery fades, a smile lifting one corner of his mouth. "You *prohibit* me?"

"Yes. Besides, you did warn me about Clay. I was the one who didn't listen—or didn't let myself remember." I blink against the sting of tears, my voice dropping to a whisper. "Deep down, I knew he was a bad person. Maybe I felt like I deserved him. Or I was punishing myself. I don't know."

He makes a soft, sad sound and draws me against his chest. I listen to his heartbeat, slow and steady beneath my ear, and pull his scent into my lungs. Glowing warmth spreads through me, burning away the taint of my memories. In their absence, the truth resonates. Katherine's words, my salvation.

He will not falter—he will not dim.

"You saved me, Wilder. Even though I turned my back on you, you still came for me when I needed you most. I couldn't hear music anymore, but I heard you. Your voice led me out of the darkness, just like it did when I got lost on that camping trip. So yes, you're prohibited from feeling guilty about the choices I made in the past."

A tremble moves through his arms. He sighs into my hair, and there's a smile in his next words. "Maybe we should stick together from now on. Seems safer."

"I think that's a good idea." Gratitude and hope shine painfully bright inside me. "I talked to my mom today—she's going to help me find a therapist. I... I'm sorry for what I've put you through the last two weeks. All my mood swings. I know I've been a lot."

He shifts against me, lifting me off his chest so we're face-to-face. Warm hands cup my cheeks. His eyes are almost unnaturally radiant in the dimly lit room, shimmering brown and gold flecks on a rich emerald canvas.

"I'm so proud of you for asking for help." His tongue runs subtly along his teeth. "But I want to redden your ass for that bullshit about mood swings."

My face heats beneath his hands. Fighting the flames of arousal, I shake my head. "It's not bullshit. I literally screamed at you yesterday for putting my underwear in the dryer, then locked myself in the bathroom and cried for an hour."

His brows jump. "So what? Shit, you should have seen me in my first year of sobriety—actually, I'm glad you didn't." The brief flash of humor in his eyes fades. "With what you're processing right now, emotional anarchy is a given. You think I care that you pop off on me sometimes? You think I can't take it? Fairy, I'd face a thousand times worse for the privilege of sharing the same air as you."

That air thins, leaving me breathless. "Then maybe you're as crazy as I am."

A thumb slides across my hot cheek. "Call yourself crazy again and I'll punish your ass with more than my hand."

The throb between my legs intensifies so suddenly I squirm. "Is that a promise?"

A slow, wicked grin spreads on his face. "How pissed are you that I haven't taken that beautiful ass?"

I bare my teeth, more challenge than smile. "The toys and lube you ordered came over a week ago. You haven't even opened the box. I'm starting to think you're trying to give me another complex."

His grin sharpens for a moment before falling. Eyes darkening, he wraps hot fingers around my throat. I swallow against his palm and his gaze drops to my mouth. Parting my lips, I drag the tip of my tongue between them. Wilder grunts, his eyes narrowing in censure.

Being denied his lips on mine has been torture. I hate that he's been strong enough to resist temptation, but I'd be lying if I said I didn't also love him for that strength. For his unfailing commitment to what he feels is right. His never-faltering light.

"Sweet Fairy," he murmurs. "Never doubt that I want all of you all the time. Every inch of your body. Every mood, every scream, every tear and laugh. Thank you for opening up to me tonight. You're so brave, and I'm so fucking proud of you." He pauses, regret flashing in his eyes. "As much as it pains me to say this, tonight probably isn't the time to open that box. It's been a long day.

We should get some sleep. Unless you want me to run you a bath first?"

His fingers loosen on my throat. Before he can fully release me, I grab his hand with both of mine and hold it to my skin. I almost smile at the surprise in his eyes, but the moment is too massive, ringing in my body and soul like a mighty bell.

"I'm not using you as a distraction, Wilder. Not right now, and not once since I got here."

I know I've hit the mark when his expression shutters. An ache spreads through my chest as the full scope of our lives unfolds in my mind's eye. Who we are and have been. How we match and mirror each other now and across the pages of the past.

My first steps as a child were to follow him. The first time I sang was to sing with him. The first poem I wrote and every song I've written since—every single one—all belong to him.

We've been each other's light and darkness. We've broken each other. Saved each other. We've stretched our souls' tether to the point of fraying. But it will never, ever snap. Nothing can destroy the bond between us.

He was right all those years ago, the day we sat beneath the sycamore and promised each other forever.

We *are* more.

We're everything.

My heart flutters, heavy and impossibly light.

"I've been trying to be the girl you loved before, to get back to that version of myself. I thought that was who you wanted, who you deserved."

Frowning, he opens his mouth, but I press a finger to his lips.

"I've realized it wasn't about you at all. *I* wanted to be that person again because I've been struggling to accept who I've become. How my choices have changed me." I trace a fingertip along his lower lip. "But you don't see any of that, do you? You just see me."

He nods. "All I ever see when I look at you is my Fairy—my muse, my reason, my everything. You're the only addiction I'll never give up. My obsession forever."

I blink away a veil of tears. "I see you too. You're *my* perfect song. If the offer is still on the table, I'd like to return your missing piece and come home. Can I keep you forever? Will you keep me?"

His chest convulses and his beautiful eyes shine with tears. "Yes. More yeses than stars in the sky. Always yes."

Shadows swirl around us, the ripples of Katherine's warning: *A storm approaches.* But they can't touch or dim this light.

Wilder's forehead drops to mine. "I love you, Evangeline. So much I burn with it."

"I love you, too." I grip his wrist, straining my face

toward his. "But if you don't kiss me right now, I'm going to smother you in your sleep."

A dimple flashes, then his face lowers. Parted lips meet mine, soft and warm and achingly sweet.

Time stops.

Everything fades away.

And it's just us.

Like it's always been and always will be.

evangeline

I slip out of bed as dawn brightens the crack between curtains. Wilder's arm curls over my absence, a small frown flickering across his brow before smoothing as dreams reclaim him.

Drawing a blanket over his shoulder, I study his peaceful face. Dark lashes twitching against golden skin, chaotic waves of hair fanning his forehead and cheek, lips a little swollen and chapped. My fingers lift to my own lips, still tender from last night, and trace the edges of my smile.

We made out like teenagers until we couldn't keep our eyes open anymore, then stumbled upstairs and fell into bed. I can still hear his whispered, "Love you always," right as we drifted to sleep.

Leaving him to rest, I retreat to the guest bedroom to

dress and brush my teeth, then head downstairs to make a cup of tea. As it steeps, I pull my phone from the charger on the counter and call Lily.

She answers on the second ring, grumbling, "I can't wait for the day I can sleep past six again."

"Aww, you won't miss our morning chats?"

"We'll move to a decent time. Like ten or eleven."

I laugh. "I hate to break it to you, but you have another eighteen years before you can sleep in again."

"More like twenty," she mutters.

Grinning at the reminder of what she whispered to me at the party yesterday, I ask, "Have you told Rye yet?"

"Hold on." A door closes in the background and her voice lowers. "No. I'm going to take another test today. Maybe it was a fluke."

I take my steaming mug to a couch and sit, tucking my legs beneath me.

"Do you want it to be?"

"Not really, but... kind of?" She sighs. "I know it's lame, but I wanted to get married before we had another baby."

Inspiration strikes and I straighten eagerly. "You've seen Wilder's property. The gazebo on the water? And there's a beautiful clearing that would be perfect for a reception. We could plan a wedding in no time at all."

There's a small, shocked pause. "Are you serious?"

"Totally serious. Except for the doing it ourselves part. We'd definitely hire someone."

She laughs shrilly. "And Wilder would be okay with this? You're sure?"

"I'll ask him today, but I'm sure he will be." I smile to myself. "I have ways of sweetening the deal."

Lily squeals, the sound muffled like she's covering her mouth.

"Is that a yes?"

Another squeal. "Yes! Let's do it. Oh my gosh, this is amazing. Can I call you later? I have to tell Rye we might be pregnant again and that we're finally getting married."

"Of course. Say hi to—" I laugh when I realize she's already hung up.

"I love that sound."

I whip my head around, a different smile blooming at the sight of Wilder turning the corner into the living room.

"What are you doing up? It's barely seven."

He shrugs, not answering. I'm not sure I'd hear a reply anyway, my brain fogging as I take in his bare chest and the pajama pants riding low on his hips. My eyes wander greedily, lingering on the dips of muscle cradling his ink-littered abs before dropping lower.

Pajamas beat gray sweatpants any day of the week.

"And I love it when you look at me like that," he purrs.

I hide my smile behind my mug. "Are you flirting with me?"

He pauses to yawn and stretch, the movements slow and intentional, arms lifting, muscles bunching and extending as he rotates and bends from side to side. I ogle him shamelessly until a chuckle lifts my gaze from the music notes wrapping around his hip.

Even his dimples look smug as he sits and pats his lap. I dutifully unfold my legs and give him my feet.

As his thumbs work magic on my soles, he says idly, "Everything, and I mean *everything* I do, is me flirting with you. Case in point—the tattoo you were just staring at." He lifts my feet so I can see it. "Do you recognize the song?"

Leaning forward, I study the notes and my mouth drops open in shock. Not only is it the Night Theory song that put us on the map, it's *my* handwriting.

Wilder snorts. "I don't know whether to be offended or proud that the thought of my dick is so distracting you've never actually read the music."

I trail a finger over the notes, gratified when he shivers. He lowers my feet back to his lap and resumes massaging them.

I can't seem to stop smiling. "What about when we argue? Are you still flirting then?"

"Definitely." He slants a knowing smile my way. "I knew that comment I made on New Year's would piss you off."

I laugh, then lower my voice in a comic impersonation of his. "'You've never even seen me flirt. In any case, I think we can agree that ship has sailed.'" I punch his shoulder playfully. "Asshole."

He grins, lifting my foot to kiss my ankle. "Undeniably *your* asshole."

I arch a brow. "Speaking of..."

Wilder throws his head back and laughs, the sound rich and lovely, his stomach shaking under my feet. I watch him in a lovestruck daze, my ears and heart full. He's still grinning when he plucks my mug from my hands and puts it on the coffee table, then pulls me into his lap. Grabbing his shoulders, I roll my hips and grin as his eyes darken.

Just when I think he's going to crack, his hands tighten on my waist to stop my movements.

"Fairy, wait."

The regret on his face protects me from the sting of rejection, but I still frown. "What's wrong?"

He hesitates, fear flashing in his eyes. And I *know*.

"Already?" I whisper.

Confusion draws his eyebrows together. "Already what?"

I move off his lap and settle beside him, then reach for my tea. A long sip fortifies me.

"Katherine warned me something bad was coming." I glance at him, catching his shocked expression before resignation replaces it.

He leans forward on his elbows, fingers tangling in his hair. "What did she say exactly?"

"'A storm approaches, and only together can you keep the light safe.' She made it clear that you're the light."

Head jerking up, he twists to face me. Reading the wary hope on his face, I belatedly realize his fear wasn't about whatever news he's received but about my reaction to it. He was worried I was going to leave him.

Taking his closest hand, I thread our fingers together. "She basically told me to pull my head out of my ass and trust you. And I do, Wilder. I trust you—and us—implicitly. Whatever it is you need to tell me, I'm not going to run. I'm not leaving you. We're going to face it together."

A moment later his mouth is on mine, the kiss deep, fierce, and all too brief. Cradling my face, he whispers, "You're amazing. I love you. I'm sorry I didn't say anything yesterday."

I nip at his lower lip. "It's okay. I'm used to you withholding crucial information due to misplaced protective instincts."

He huffs a laugh. "I take it I have Katherine to thank for last night?"

I wince. "Pretty much."

"So stubborn," he murmurs, his eyes alight with humor.

"I would have gotten around to confessing my love eventually," I mutter.

He gives me a quick, smiling kiss. "You need to eat before this conversation. Veggie omelet and a smoothie okay?"

I almost protest, but his knowing look stops me. With a sigh, I concede that he's right. My stomach is already grumbling at the mention of food, and it won't be long before I'm officially hangry.

"That sounds good."

Hearing the undertone of irritation, he smirks. "Proud of you, baby."

I grab a throw pillow and chuck it at his head.

wilder

With a scream of rage, Evangeline swings the axe at the giant tree stump I use to chop firewood. She misses the standing log by at least four inches. It topples over as she wrestles the heel of the blade from the stump.

As she heaves and pants, she mutters under her breath. I can't hear every word, but catch "motherfucker" and "fucking kill him."

I'm not sure what it says about me that I'm hard as fuck right now, but I blame it on the sweat glistening on her face, chest, and arms. Then again, I was hard on her first swing, long before she pulled off her sweatshirt to reveal a black sports bra.

I shift against the tree I'm leaning on, adjusting myself discreetly. Evangeline catches the movement, sending a searing glance my way before righting the log and lining up for another swing.

Arms shaking, she lifts the heavy axe. Her form is shit, but I learned my lesson twenty minutes ago and keep my mouth shut.

I can't help a small smile as she bellows her rage into the forest and swings again. I'm not happy about her pain, obviously, but I'm ecstatic that she's expressing it. It means she feels safe to show me the full, messy range of her emotions.

"Wipe that smile off your face," she snaps, hefting the axe and stumbling a little. "There's nothing funny about this."

My smile instantly dies. She's right. There's nothing funny about any of this, especially since Shelley got her hands on a few of the headlines publishing in less than forty-eight hours. Her phone call is what woke me up so early, and I spent five minutes dry heaving over the toilet before I came downstairs.

I knew Clay was going to go for my jugular, but I thought—naively, I guess—that he'd leave Evangeline out of it.

He didn't.

There are the expected, shock-value headlines like, **Sex, Drugs, and Rock 'n' Roll: Wilder Ashburn Exposed,** and an assortment of others all implying I'm back on drugs and a literal monster. Clay apparently found a handful of random industry people to support the narrative, no doubt individuals I've either pissed off or were all too happy to sacrifice morals for money. Shelley even said there are a few publications touting so-called photo evidence. I can only assume they're passing off pictures of me mid-yawn as proof I'm loaded. Either that, or they went straight AI and are hoping the public doesn't notice.

But my literal worst nightmare is the main headline attached to Clay's exclusive interview: **Eva Marie: Mentally Unstable and Back with Abusive Ex-Lover. Estranged Fiancé Asks Public for Help.**

Every word is bullshit, but it's the kind of headline that plays to empathy and will trigger pitchforks. And Clay knows it. He's preemptively pinning his sins on me, attempting to turn me into a straw man the world will light on fire while he stays safe in the smoke.

In his twisted head, I'm sure he believes Evangeline will eventually turn against me and come crawling back to him.

He really doesn't know her at all.

"I'll show him mentally unstable," she snarls.

She swings the axe again and again, each progressively sloppier arc punctuated by insults.

"Saggy-balled—tiny-dicked—hair-plugged—fake-tanned—*psychopath*."

She finally clips the edge of the standing log, sending it flying off the stump. The axe almost flies, too. I push off the tree, but she throws me a look that makes me freeze and lift my hands.

"Just here to make sure you don't lose a hand."

She bares her teeth. "Suck my dick, Wilder."

Maybe I'm experiencing some weirdly euphoric version of shock, but I've never wanted her so badly in my life. "If you had one, baby, I'd drop to my knees right now."

With a groan more amused than annoyed, she lets the axe fall to the ground and sits heavily on the stump.

Panting, she wipes damp hair off her forehead. "There's something seriously wrong with you."

I grin. "You love it."

Sunlight cuts through the clearing, bisecting her flushed face and making her gray eye glow with predatory light. My mouth drops as she spreads her legs and arches an eyebrow.

"Well? What are you waiting for?"

Four strides and I'm dropping, my knees slamming into dirt as I rip my T-shirt over my head. Evangeline's pupils dilate, her breath stuttering, but she still manages a haughty sniff.

"I didn't say anything about returning the favor."

My chuckle is so full of dark promise that goose-bumps lift on her chest and arms. "It's to keep splinters from your ass, you brat. Stand up."

She stands fast, betraying her eagerness. My nose brushes her bare stomach, and I suck in the delicious fragrance of her sweat as I spread my T-shirt over the stump. Then I grab her hips and lick from the waist-band of her sweatpants to the edge of her sports bra. She gasps, grabbing my shoulders to stay upright.

Finding a hard nipple through cotton, I flick it with my tongue before closing my mouth around it and sucking hard. She whimpers, rocking toward me. I take advantage, seizing the fabric under my fingers and yanking her pants down, baring her to the sunlight and fresh air.

"Oh, fuck, we're really doing this?" she asks in a high voice. "Are you sure no one can see us?"

I gaze up at her. "I'd never do this if I wasn't one hundred percent sure it was private. This is the densest part of the property, the farthest from neighbors and the water. I'm also not even close to the most famous person in the neighborhood, hence the giant walls and armed security. But if you feel unsafe at all, we can absolutely go inside."

A smile teases her lips. "Get back to work."

I bite the closest nipple, grinning around her flesh when she smacks my head. There's no power in the blow, probably because her arms are limp noodles from rage-chopping a stump that's so old and hard it barely noticed.

"God, I love you," I murmur, pulling up the band of her sports bra to expose her breasts. I tongue her nipples until she's panting again—for a different, better reason this time. When her hips start moving in needy circles, I guide her down to the stump until she's on her back, splayed out like a wicked offering.

"Fucking look at you." Shadows play over her body, cool air dancing with warm beams of light. I pull her sweats over her sneakers and toss them to her. "For your head."

As she tucks the fabric behind her neck, I shift forward until my knees hit the trunk before lowering to my heels. Sliding my hands up her silky thighs, I spread them up and to the sides. My cock jumps at the beautifully indecent way she's bared to me. Arousal shimmers on her pussy, gravity carrying lubricant exactly where I need it. With a groan of appreciation, I kiss my way up one thigh before blowing over her center.

Her legs stiffen under my hands and I glance up, stilling when I register her closed-off expression. "What's wrong?"

She hesitates, then blurts, "How many women have been on this stump?"

I'm powerless over my slow, satisfied grin. "Why?"

She scowls. "Just answer."

I bite the nearest skin, earning another feeble slap to my head. "You first. Why, Fairy?"

Her chin lifts, jaw set with defiance. "Because it's suspiciously the perfect size and height for this."

The effort of holding back a laugh makes my eyes water and my voice strangled. "You think I had a tree cut down in order to make a sex stump?"

Her face turns red, thighs tensing as she pushes against my hold. "Let me up. I'm not in the mood anymore."

Twenty-four hours ago, I would have obeyed without question. Now, I shake my head. "Too late. You're a sacrifice to the sex stump." Holding her straining thighs, I press a kiss to her clit.

"Wilder," she hisses.

Tracing the tip of my tongue around the flushed, swollen bud, I roll my eyes up to see her livid expression war with equally potent lust. "No one's been on the sex stump but you. No one's been in my bed or shower, bent over furniture or splayed out on my kitchen counter but you. Just you. Only you."

Expression softening, she sighs out her relief. "Suck me," she whispers.

I cover her clit with my mouth. She groans, spine arching. I alternate deep, pulsing suction with taps of my tongue. Her fingers dig into my hair, fisting and yanking me closer so she can grind against my face. Her gasps and moans fill the clearing, making my hips rock and my cock throb and leak.

Content to let her use me for a minute, I pull out the items I stowed in my pocket before we left the house. Focusing isn't easy, especially when her thighs are strangling me and I'm close to coming in my pants, but I manage to squirt lube on the silicone plug and turn on the vibration.

Evangeline's head lifts at the sound, her thighs releasing my neck. I take advantage of the freedom, straightening to show her the toy. Her already blown pupils flare wider, belying her next, irate words.

"You're not fucking my ass in the forest!"

My smile makes her shiver. "We both know you'd let me and love it, but I'm not going to—today. You *are* going to take this plug and wear it as you walk to the studio and find a soft surface."

"But I'm so close," she whines.

"Oh, I know." I drag the slick, vibrating toy over her

clit, enjoying the way her hips jerk. "Do you feel empty, baby?"

She nods and cups her breasts, teasing her nipple piercings. "Please make me come first?"

My smile sharpens. "Nice try. You'll come when I let you. If you're a good little slut for me, I'll put another toy in your cunt while I'm in your ass."

Her eyes glaze, her body shuddering. "Yes, Wilder."

Her submission is an axe to my patience. I drop the toy to her ass and apply pressure. "Let me in. Good girl. Fuck, so pretty. Does it hurt?"

"No. Feels good."

Releasing the base of the toy, I trail two fingers through her folds and tease the hot, silky entrance of her body. She whimpers and undulates in search of penetration.

"Ah-ah." I slap her clit, making her arch with a cry. Her eyes close, breath stalling. "Don't you dare come."

She fights her body's demand for several taut seconds, then relaxes, her chest heaving with the effort.

"Good job, baby. Ready to go?"

She nods, her soft, guileless smile almost undoing me. Before I lose the ability to resist her, I push to my feet and offer a hand. She stands up and gasps, swaying into me.

"You okay?"

"Yes," she says with a soft giggle. "Just feels weird. Kinda heavy."

I smack her ass. She yelps, then groans. Tilting her chin, I give her a soft kiss and a parting nibble.

"I'm going to grab something from the house, then I'm coming for you."

"Ladies first." As soon as the words are out, she cringes.

My delighted laugh startles a pair of squirrels, sending them scampering up a nearby tree.

She glowers at me. "I'm deeply disappointed in myself."

I reach out and gently tweak her nipple. "Get moving, Pun Queen."

She unfurls a middle finger, then turns on a heel and takes a step, only to jerk to a stop. A soft, strained sound rides her heavy exhale.

"You can do it," I say through my grin.

Both middle fingers float up as she begins walking carefully and *very awkwardly* toward the path leading to the studio. Once I'm confident she has the hang of it, I sprint to the house, barely making it inside before I fold over laughing.

evangeline

Hobbling furtively through the woods wearing only sneakers and a sports bra hiked to my armpits is... weird. Almost as weird as the heavy, vibrating plug in my ass.

The latter is a perfect distraction, not allowing for much coherent thought. Every step sends a wave of daunting sensation through my lower half. My thighs are embarrassingly wet, my labia uncomfortably swollen. I focus on putting one foot in front of the other, doing my best to ignore the feeling that something is going to slip out of me any second. From the size of the plug and the initial burn, it's not going anywhere. I still find myself clenching, which only makes the sensations more intense and my steps more wobbly.

Wilder knew exactly what he was doing when he put

the axe in my hands, just like he knew what I'd need after. Sneaky man had the plug and lube in his pocket before we even left the house. If I wasn't so uncomfortably aroused, I might have pretended to be more annoyed by his presumption. In reality, I'm amused. And grateful.

I'm so fucking grateful for him.

When I reach the studio, I waste no time rushing inside. The air is cooler indoors, hushed and still. Without the ever-present breeze, my skin itches with a reminder that I'm coated in drying sweat and a fine layer of dirt from my failed attempt at chopping wood.

Glancing toward the stairs, I briefly consider a quick shower before discarding the idea. Not only does it sound too challenging at the moment, Wilder has a kink for me being sweaty. Biting my lip, I look around the room in search of a soft surface.

My gaze catches on the Steinway. Namely, on the piano's long, padded bench.

I've just made it to the bench when the door opens behind me. My body recognizes his presence with a tingle of familiar energy, so I don't look back as I toe off my shoes and socks and pull off my sports bra. Then I tug the bench out a few more inches and carefully climb on.

His soft groan and rapidly approaching steps are

music to my ears, as are his crooning words, "Better than any fantasy."

Strong, hot hands stroke down my spine and over my hips. I gasp, my skin shockingly sensitive, all my nerves afire so that I feel his touch everywhere. He seems to know it, his strokes exceedingly gentle. When he begins dropping soft kisses down my spine, the pleasure is so consuming I almost fall off the bench. My arms and legs quiver, muscles burning, as I try to stay balanced.

"Wilder—"

"I know, baby, it's okay." He scoops me into his arms and smiles down at me. "We'll try that on a day you didn't spend forty minutes trying to murder a dead tree."

I laugh, then choke on a moan at the unexpected result.

Wilder chuckles. "Hang on for just a few more minutes."

He carries me across the studio, then lays me gently on my back atop an oversized ottoman. A hand clasps my neck possessively, then slides heavily down my chest to my stomach. Eyes bright with love and dark with need meet mine. I squirm, then whimper at the assault on my nerves.

"I need you," I whisper.

"You have me."

He slips out of his shoes and pulls off his track pants. My mouth waters at the sight of his cock, hard and flushed, and I open my mouth in silent demand. With a muffled curse, he kneels beside my head and feeds me what I want.

I lick the salty offering at his slit, then take him into my mouth. He watches with glittering, slitted eyes as I work up and down his length. Between his taste, the rough sounds he makes, and the vibration in my ass, it doesn't take long for me to return to the precipice of orgasm. But when I try to sneak a hand to my clit, he grabs my fingers.

"Not yet," he rumbles as he pulls himself from my mouth.

Thankfully, he's just as worked up as I am and moves quickly, positioning himself between my legs. Lifting and spreading my knees, he guides them toward my chest.

"Hold them right here for me, baby."

I do as he says, my reward his immediate groan. His eyes flash up to mine, jaw clenching and unclenching.

"You ready?"

"Is that a joke? Please, please get on with it."

A small, impish smile flashes before his features tighten with focus. He grabs something from his pants. There's a *snick* as a bottle top opens, then the sound of lube squirting into his hand. As he rubs the liquid over himself, I feel a tug at my ass. The vibration in the plug turns off.

"Deep breath in, Fairy. Relax and exhale."

The toy slips out of me with a faint sting. Before I can process the mingled relief and loss, he presses himself inside me. I tense on instinct, waiting for pain that doesn't come. All I feel is pressure and fullness and a surreal sense of being both inside my body and outside of it.

Wilder moans, low and breathy, his head bowing and hands clenching on my inner thighs. "Don't move for a sec." I stay still and a few deep breaths later, his eyes find mine. "Good?"

"So good." My voice wavers, tears spilling from the corners of my eyes. "I don't know why I'm crying. I'm totally fine. It doesn't hurt at all."

The intensity in his face softens. Leaning forward, he gives me a tender, consuming kiss. "I've edged you super hard. Almost there. Trust me?"

I nod and he grabs something else from the floor. More lube squirts, and then something blunt presses to my pussy. It feels... way too big. I lift my head, focusing with effort. When my eyes finally compute what he's holding, I gape in horror.

"No way is that fitting inside me. It's bigger than

you."

He smirks. "Oh ye of little faith."

The toy comes down on my clit. Sensation explodes, bowing my back. When I fall back to the ottoman, my body is lax with surrender.

"Good girl."

He presses the dildo back to my pussy. It starts to vibrate, sending rippling shocks through my body. As he pushes it inside me, my eyes roll back in my head and all hesitance falls away. The stretch of the toy magnifies the fullness of him in my ass a thousand-fold. Vibrations roll against my G-spot, radiating through my clit and outward. Every inch of my body pulsates, poised on some unfathomable breaking point.

I'm dimly aware of warm, calloused hands stroking me—breasts, stomach, arms, thighs—and of his whispered words, "So perfect. I knew you could take it. Thank you, baby. You can let go now. I've got you."

He draws back slowly, then snaps his hips.

That's all it takes.

I fracture with a sob.

Waves of ecstasy hit one after the other, each bigger than the last. With a guttural groan, Wilder begins fucking me in earnest. Just when I think it's too much, that I need it to stop, I'm carried to another, higher peak.

And as I drop off the ledge, he follows me with a deep, delicious moan.

Floating weightlessly in bliss, I sigh as his body curls over mine. His eyes are all I see. His breath is my breath.

A pure note of rapture sings in my body and soul.

"Forever," he whispers.

Tasting his tears and mine, I echo, "Forever."

evangeline

As Wilder assembles and plates the salad we're having for dinner, I muse that watching him make food is to my eyes what his music is to my ears. His artistry looks effortless, but purpose and passion drive every movement.

Just a few weeks ago, I believed I'd never enjoy salads again. But that was before I watched Wilder make a salad and tasted the result. This one is no exception. Homemade balsamic dressing is tossed with arugula, cucumbers, avocado, and cherry tomatoes, then topped with slices of perfectly grilled steak and a sprinkle of blue cheese. It's nowhere near the most complex meal I've seen him make, but I'm nevertheless awed by the process.

On any other day, I'd be asking for seconds, but

today I can barely taste the incredible flavors. I manage six bites before setting down my fork. Wilder is likewise affected and looks relieved to stop picking at his own meal.

"I know it sucks," he says softly. "But there's nothing we can do right now except wait."

I breathe past the urge to snap at him. "Even if this goes like you hope it does, there's no guarantee it'll stop the articles from being published."

He shrugs a shoulder. "Then we'll deal with the fallout."

My teeth clench. "How can you be so calm about this? He's about to tell the world you're an abusive drug addict and I'm your emotionally unstable victim."

Wilder drags a hand over his face and through his hair. "I'm not calm. My anxiety is through the roof." His eyes meet mine, raw and pleading. "You watched me chop wood for an hour this afternoon when there's already enough for next winter. Was it not obvious I was imagining every log was Clay's face?"

Watching him swing the axe, I hadn't been thinking about anything beyond the beauty and power of his body. While he was processing his anger, I was salivating over the glistening muscles in his back.

I wilt, duly chastised and chagrined. "I don't understand why you don't want me to help. I could be on television tomorrow refuting everything. Why aren't we planning with Anita and Shelley?"

The look in his eyes shatters me—fear and helplessness and stubborn conviction. "Kendra's going to come through."

That now-familiar switch inside me flips again. I shove to my feet and grab both our plates. "Excuse me for not having the same faith in your ex-girlfriend."

I stomp into the kitchen and aggressively rinse our dishes. My arms tremble uncontrollably, sore and weak from the axe. The fear and adrenaline coursing through me aren't helping matters. When the glass container he used to make the salad dressing slips from my hands and shatters against the sink, I scream, "Fuck!"

A second later, my spine warms as Wilder presses against me. Arms cradling my body, he takes my hands and rinses them, making sure I didn't cut myself.

"I'm sorry," I whisper. "I'm just scared. And I'm so angry. I hate this. I hate him."

"Me too, Fairy. All of the above." He shuts off the water and grabs a dishtowel to dry my hands, then turns me around. "Come on, I want to show you something."

He leads me down the hallway and into the office opposite the stairs. Built-in bookshelves cover the wall behind a desk holding a laptop. The rest of the space is devoted to babysitting and entertaining our goddaughter. There's a portable crib, sensory play mats, and a wooden storage unit stuffed with books and baskets of supplies and toys.

Wilder stops at a closet, toeing aside the giant bag of diapers blocking it. He flashes me a small smile as he opens the door. "That was to deter you from looking in here."

Curiosity piqued, I peer around his shoulder as he retrieves something leaning against the wall behind coats. It's obviously a painting. A big one. I shuffle backward, giving him space to turn the canvas around. I'm expecting River's bold, graffiti-inspired style, but although I can immediately tell he's the artist, the subject is nothing like what he's known for.

I stare at the painting so long that Wilder says nervously, "This is what was hanging over the fireplace until about a month ago. Is it too much? We can hang something else."

"No, I love it." I look up at him through tears. "How?"

His smile is giant, so radiant it burns away everything but my love for him.

"My mom snapped this photo of us years ago, and River owed me a favor. Should we put it back up?"

"Absolutely."

I step aside as he hefts the canvas and turns for the

hallway, then almost collide with his back when he stops suddenly. He looks over his shoulder at me.

"I have to confess something. When I told you I'm obsessed with you, I wasn't kidding."

I arch my brows. "I think the painting is proof of that."

He shakes his head, gaze falling to the canvas between us. "It's way more than the painting. I..." He blows out a breath, then says in a rush, "I bought this property because of the sycamore out back and because of all the trees and water. You always said you wanted to live by both. I planted the daffodils for you. Fuck, I designed and built this house and the studio with you in mind. It's all for you—for us. Even though I didn't know if you'd ever see it."

Warmth blossoms in my chest, a crackling expansion that takes my breath away.

He continues before I can speak, "Also, that journalist was right about me. Every one of my songs is a love letter to you. I've never written anything that's not in some way inspired by you. I've never loved anyone but you, never dated anyone seriously in the last seven years. I guess what I'm trying to say is if all that doesn't freak you out, I want you to live here. With me."

"Okay."

His head whips up, eyes wide and shocked. "What?"

I swallow laughter, shrugging. "My master plan showing up here was to never leave, so that works."

Sparkling eyes narrow. "It was?"

I nod. Wilder leans forward to kiss me, but I dance out of reach and dart into the hallway. As I walk away, I throw over my shoulder, "This is perfect timing, actually, because I'm about to be billed for another month of storage. I'll call them right now and arrange delivery. We'll need to pull our cars out of the garage so they can unload all the boxes. Oh, and fair warning, I have a lot of clothes. You should probably just give me the whole walk-in."

The painting thuds on the floor.

"Evangeline," he growls.

Grinning so hard my face hurts, I walk faster. "You're going to need more shelves in the studio, too. Glow has *a lot* of awards. And before I forget—Lily and Rye want to get married on the property. Since I live here now, I'll go ahead and say yes."

His footsteps break into a run.

With a breathless squeal, I sprint for the back door. I don't make it, but I can't say I'm disappointed by the result.

HIGH ★ THEORY

outro

outro : *the ending portion of a song*

evangeline

The call comes at a few minutes past seven that evening. Wilder and I are on the couch, where we've been trying to distract ourselves with a cooking show. The second his phone starts vibrating on the coffee table, I fumble for the remote and mute the television. He sits up, takes a deep breath, and answers.

"Hey, Kendra." He listens for an excruciating thirty seconds, his impassive expression never changing. Then he says, "Yep," and offers me the phone.

My heart skips a beat, my thoughts freezing. I stare blankly at his lifted hand until he lowers it and mutes the call.

"She wants to talk to you, but if you don't want to…"

His gentle tone restarts my brain. "No, no. It's okay." I take the phone and unmute it. "Hello?"

"Hi, Eva. Thanks for speaking with me. I won't keep you long."

Kendra sounds shockingly different, her voice mellow and mature. Thrown, I stammer out, "H-hi. How's it going? I mean, how are you? Besides... everything." I grimace, embarrassment flooding my body. Wilder grunts in amusement, his hand squeezing my knee but retreating before I can slap it.

Kendra's laugh is breathy with relief. "Oh, good. I thought I was the only one with sweaty armpits right now."

My shoulders relax a fraction, a smile twitching my lips. "Definitely not."

"I'll get right to it, then. I know you've been through hell, and this weekend was probably torture because Wilder hasn't told you what my role is in all this. I didn't want him to give you false hope. But now that it's happening, I wanted you to hear it from me first."

I glance at Wilder, confused, but he merely nods encouragingly.

"I'm listening."

"Wilder told you some of what I went through as a teenager, but what he didn't tell you was what happened right before I left Seattle. That day you found me screaming at him in his bedroom? It ended up being rock bottom for me, too. I went straight to my parents' house afterward. I was out of my mind, out of money, and was planning on stealing some of my mom's jewelry. But when I snuck past my stepfather's office, I heard him and Clay talking inside."

She takes a deep breath, and I hear a woman's soft murmur on the other side of the line. Her voice firms. "My stepfather has always had a short fuse. He once threw a paperweight at a wall in his office and put a hole right through the plaster. He never fixed it, just hung a photo of himself and some politician over it. On the other side of that wall, there's a small closet. I don't honestly know what possessed me, but I remembered that hole and hid in the closet to listen to them.

"I'd always known they were shady, but the things they were talking about… it was another level. Blackmail and extortion, exploiting witnesses and minors, the list goes on. They dropped names. Talked about a 'black book.' Basically incriminated the fuck out of themselves and their buddies."

I gasp in understanding. "You recorded them."

"Sure did," she says with grim amusement. "I stayed in that tiny closet for over an hour, listening to them jack each other off over how smart they were. They eventually left to go golfing. When I was positive they were gone, I went into the office and straight to the wall safe. My mom had let the code slip once when she was drunk off her ass. I opened the safe and stole everything in it. Jewelry, a few watches, some serious stacks of cash, and that black book."

Chills drip over my scalp and down my body.

"I went straight to a seedy pawn shop and sold what I could. A few hours later, it finally occurred to me how much shit I was in. But I also felt this sense of freedom and... rightness, I guess. I packed a bag, ditched my car, and caught a bus out of town. By the time I reached Idaho, I was dopesick as hell. I also knew it was only a matter of time before those assholes started looking for me, and I wasn't about to be outsmarted by them. So I holed up in a motel and detoxed, and I've been clean ever since."

She pauses, then continues mutedly, "You're probably wondering why I've kept everything to myself all these years. Honestly, I wouldn't blame you if you hated me for it. If I'd handed the book over to the police, you never would have gone through what you did with my stepbrother. He'd be behind bars where he should be."

My throat tightens, cutting off a protest before I can voice it. Because she's right. Even now, resentment prickles over my skin. But it's also not black and white, my emotions complex. I feel sympathy and sadness for her, too.

When I don't say anything, Kendra adds, "I know it's

a weak excuse, but the simple reason I never came forward is fear."

Compassion for her drowns out everything else. "Of course you were afraid. You'd been abused and traumatized by them for a decade!"

There's a small, teary laugh. "Yeah, that played a role for sure. Plus, their goons almost caught me twice. After the second near miss, it was obvious they just wanted their dirty secrets back. When I realized my actual life was in danger, I stopped making amateur mistakes. After running for close to six months, I landed in a tiny town on the other side of the country. I met my wife, Kelly, at my first job here. We have two kids now, twin four-year-old girls."

She pauses, and the woman in the background murmurs something I can't hear, her tone comforting. Kendra takes another deep breath.

"I guess as time went on, it became easier to convince myself the past was just the past. I had a new life—I just wanted to forget it all, you know? Then I saw a photo of you and Clay online, and I've been wracked with guilt ever since. I wanted to reach out to you, but all that fear came right back and paralyzed me. I'm sorry, Eva. I'm so sorry I didn't stop him. I'm sorry for putting you in his path in the first place and for how I treated you back then." Her following sob is barely muffled by her hand.

Sympathetic tears prick my eyes. "Kendra, listen to me." I wait for her to sniff and go silent, then soften my voice. "As far as I'm concerned, you don't owe me an apology. Not to compare trauma here, but Clay never threatened my life. I'm sickened by what you went through and don't blame you for wanting to keep yourself and your family safe."

"I'm not sure I deserve that, but thank you," she says tremulously. "When Wilder called me on Friday, I knew I couldn't live with myself if I didn't do something. I already had a basic plan—a failsafe I put together when I was on the run in case something happened to me. Kelly helped me fine-tune and execute it."

Hope soars. I instinctively reach for Wilder's hand, letting the strong grip of his fingers anchor me. I stare into his eyes as I ask, "What does that mean exactly?"

Kendra's voice steadies and sharpens. "In the black book, there was a name—a Seattle detective my stepfather tried and failed to bribe. The detective was pissed, arrested him and everything, but Conrad had a judge in his pocket and made it disappear.

"Suffice to say, that detective held a grudge, and I made his day when I sent him everything. Some of the potential charges, like extortion and wire fraud, have passed the statute of limitations, but a judge has issued warrants for the rest. There's also more than enough to open investigations into the last six years of their practices. He's going to tear them both apart."

My eyes widen more on every word, and Wilder's smile grows.

"He made four arrests today, including my stepfather, and the LAPD should be surprising Clay any minute. Thanks to all their hard work making themselves famous, tomorrow every major news network on the West Coast will be covering the story."

There's vicious satisfaction in her voice as she finishes, "A bunch of assholes are about to have the day they deserve."

I slump into Wilder's chest, boneless with relief.

"Thank you, Kendra. *Thank you.*"

She says thickly, "I can't change what either of us went through, but at least the world will be a tiny bit safer for my daughters. Maybe... maybe someday you guys can meet them?"

Wilder's thumb catches a tear on my cheek as I choke out, "I'd like that."

wilder

The following morning, after arguably the best night's sleep of my life, my own moan transports me from an X-rated dream into an X-rated reality.

"Fuucck."

Evangeline's mouth pops off my cock. She swirls her tongue around my piercing before giving me a wicked smile. Her hands, slick with saliva, keep pumping me at a torturously slow pace.

"Good morning," she says huskily. "Is this okay? You said I could practice while you were asleep."

"Yes. Absolutely. Zero complaints."

She smirks, teasing me with barely there swipes of her tongue. I sink my hands into her sleep-tousled hair, my hips straining off the bed.

"Put me back in your mouth, brat."

Her naked chest flushes, eyelids falling to half-mast. With a small moan, she lowers her head and—shocking the fuck out of me—spits on my dick. The visual makes me jerk in her hands and leak pre-cum right onto her tongue. She hums happily as she laps it up, then takes me into her mouth again.

My fingers tighten in her hair as she returns to a rhythm guaranteed to destroy me. I'm already on the edge, and it takes mere seconds for me to lose it. My fingers and toes tingle, pressure gathering.

"You want my cum, baby?" She whimpers and nods. "Relax your throat. Yessss. *Fuck*, just like that. Swallow every drop."

I groan mindlessly, my climax all the more intense as I keep my eyes open to watch her struggle to swallow it all. She finally rears back, panting, red-cheeked, and glowing with accomplishment.

Fucking immaculate.

She squeaks in surprise as I grab her under the arms and flip us. I drop between her legs, throwing her heels over my shoulders.

"My turn."

♫

A few hours and orgasms later, we greet Lily, Rye, and Emma at the front door. It takes less than ten minutes for the women to disappear outside, chatting animatedly about weddings and some famous coordinator who agreed to meet with them next week.

I have a feeling we won't see them for a while; if they end up in the studio, I doubt they'll return before dinner.

"Who's my favorite small human?" I ask the giggling toddler standing on my thighs.

"Me, Whyder! Me!"

I gasp and glare at Rye, who's slouched on the opposite couch scrolling on his phone.

"How dare you teach her how to pronounce my name."

He rolls his eyes, not bothering with a reply. Emma throws her bowl of tiny kid crackers onto the cushion next to us, then squirms off my lap and starts hunting the scattered snacks with her mouth.

"Just like her dad," I note, shifting so I can catch her when she invariably loses balance and tumbles toward the coffee table.

Rye chuckles. "Want to be my best man?"

My head whips toward him at the same time my arm flies out to stop Emma from rolling off the couch. She course corrects, dismissing the crackers in favor of using my arm as a railing to drag herself onto my hunched back.

"Are you serious?" I finally ask.

Rye looks up from his phone with a speculative frown. "You *do* know you're my best friend, right?"

I grin, then let out a grunt as Emma's feet slam into my kidneys. "Hell yes, I'll be your best man." I pause. "Did Evangeline tell you I asked her to move in and she said yes?"

His brows lift in dry amusement. "She did. So did my mom, who heard it from Rose, who heard it from Sophie. At this point, we can assume at least a hundred people know."

"Seriously?" I groan. "Damn, I wanted to surprise my parents."

Rye shakes his head in disbelief. "How have you not learned this lesson? The second Lily finished telling me we were getting married here, I texted my mom, beating Sophie's text by five minutes. Just wait until you have a kid. My mom knew Emma had taken her first steps before I did."

My sympathetic grimace becomes one of pain as Emma yanks my hair. I gently peel her fingers away and swing her around to tickle her. She cackles, swatting at my hands, then abruptly dives off my lap to fish for more crackers.

"How are you feeling about tomorrow?" asks Rye.

My eyes on Emma, I murmur, "Not as nervous as I was. Shelley told me this morning that only two publications have yet to confirm that they're pulling their articles."

"That's amazing, man. You must be so relieved."

Emma loses interest in the crackers again. Before she can launch onto my back, I hand her a sensory toy with a bunch of colorful domes to pop. She thumps down beside me and starts jabbing the toy like it's personally offended her.

"I don't think it's fully hit me yet. It's been an intense weekend. A lot of emotional extremes."

Rye nods in understanding, then asks hesitantly, "How's Eva handling everything? Not gonna lie, Lily and I were prepared to unplug the TV and hide her phone, but she seems... fine."

"I've been distracting her since we woke up. We only put clothes on ten minutes before you got here."

He makes a face. "Bleh."

My chuckle tapers into a sigh. "She's going to find out all the details soon enough. I wanted her to have a few hours of peace."

"Understandable. The news is awful."

I nod, having skimmed some of it while Evangeline was showering this morning. A lot of what I read wasn't surprising, but there was a summary of a joint LAPD and FBI press conference that I could barely stomach.

In a twisted coincidence, Clay was already on law enforcement radar in a big way, the added evidence from Seattle merely accelerating his arrest. The bulk of the charges are for white-collar crimes: fraud, tax evasion, money laundering, witness tampering, and the like. As with Conrad, Clay is taking others down with him, among them a well-known music producer, a local politician, a judge, and two other lawyers.

But there are other charges against Clay, ones for far more egregious crimes: multiple counts of sexual assault of a minor and production and distribution of child pornography.

That, I know, is what will fuck Evangeline up the most, not to mention Kendra.

Clay's victim was sixteen when he targeted and coerced her with promises of fame. He also recorded her without her knowing, then threatened to release the videos if she ever told anyone about him. Not only was the footage found on his home computer, there was evidence of it being sent to multiple people.

Now twenty and famous, the victim allowed herself to be named in connection to the case, which is why the story is breaking nationally.

Poppy Cole, Grammy-winning pop star, has vowed

to use her platform to spread awareness to her young fanbase about how to recognize and defend against predators.

"I hope he gets prison justice," Rye murmurs.

I nod somberly. "Same."

Emma squirms, huffs in annoyance, and promptly chucks the sensory toy across the room. Rye and I share a knowing smile.

Facing Emma, I widen my eyes. "Who wants to go for a walk and collect flowers for their mommy and Aunt Eva before lunch?"

"Me!" she screeches, jumping up and down. I catch her as she nosedives off the couch.

evangeline

THREE WEEKS LATER

My pen scratches over a page in my journal, the words sloppy, almost illegible. But I don't suppose it matters. I already know I'll never read this one again.

I'm barely cognizant of what I'm writing, only the effort and necessity of it. My aching fingers. Shallow breaths. Sweaty palms. The unknown force that wakes me each morning and propels me into the office downstairs, where I spend an hour or more metaphorically bleeding onto a blank page.

Pausing to stretch a cramp from my hand, I look at

the sticky notes lining the top of the desk. A new one appears every day, all of them various quotes in Wilder's handwriting.

The newest reads:

> "FORGIVE YOURSELF FOR NOT KNOWING WHAT
> YOU DIDN'T KNOW BEFORE YOU LEARNED IT."
> —MAYA ANGELOU

I'm trying.

Fuck, I'm really trying.

Talking to Kendra has helped, as have conversations with my mom, Rose, and Wilder. Each of them has experience with where I find myself—at the intersection between anger, guilt, and self-forgiveness. Between them and twice-weekly video calls with my new therapist, I'm learning how to navigate my jagged internal landscape.

I do my best to stay focused on the present and grounded in gratitude for my life. For the opportunity to learn and heal and *feel*. For Wilder, for the love and forgiveness of my family and friends. For the Glow album Lily and I are recording, and for the magnanimity of Cory Donovan at Indigo Records, who accepted my stumbling, heartfelt apologies and didn't hesitate to offer us a new contract.

And I'm deeply grateful for Poppy Cole, who

reached out to me after a video I posted on social media went viral. In it, I spoke candidly about Clay's emotional abuse, my shame and struggles to recover from it, and my disgust for his actions. I also said I hope his dick falls off and he never sees the sun again, but Anita made me cut that part out.

Poppy's and my first conversation started off painfully awkward and ended with tears. She shared that a week or so after I left Clay and disappeared, their paths crossed at a charity luncheon. Over the years, she'd grown numb to seeing him at events, but this time he was baldly attempting to charm a seventeen-year-old singer just starting out in the industry. Overcome with rage, she intervened. He later pulled her aside and threatened to release the videos of her at sixteen if she stepped out of line again.

The interaction sent her into a week-long depressive episode that ended with what she called, "the mother of all 'fuck it' moments."

Turns out that Poppy, like Kendra, kept receipts. Emails. Text messages. Voicemails. Photos. All damning, all proving that not only did Clay manipulate her into thinking he was the ticket to success in the music industry, he coerced her into having sex not only with him but several others. All when she was barely sixteen, newly emancipated from her parents and fresh off the bus from a small town in Colorado.

Through untamed sobs, I told her how sorry I was, that I was in awe of her, and that I hoped she knew how unbelievably brave she was. She broke down too, then said something that cemented her a place in my heart forever.

"In one way or another, I've been a victim my whole life. Of people like my parents, of men like Clay, of a world that taught me that my worth was measured by how pleasing I was to others. I'm done with all of it. No more contorting myself to fit into the tiny box they forced me into. I want to be free."

We've talked almost daily since, and I've basically adopted her as my little sister. She's visiting Seattle soon; I'm flying down to support her when she's called to testify. Lily and I have also committed to partnering with her on her campaign aimed at empowering young women.

None of this has been easy, but every day I find a little more space in my heart for acceptance of the past and of myself.

Closing my journal, I scan the collection of sticky

notes. My lips quirk at the randomness of Wilder's small, daily gifts.

"LIFE IS PAIN... ANYONE WHO SAYS DIFFERENTLY
IS SELLING SOMETHING."
– THE PRINCESS BRIDE

"MY EGO IS NOT MY AMIGO."
– SOME DUDE IN AN AA MEETING

"A HUNGRY FAIRY IS A GRUMPY FAIRY. COME
EAT BREAKFAST."
– WILDER

When I read the last one, my stomach growls. A glance at the clock startles me—it's almost ten. Usually by now, I'd have heard Wilder singing in the kitchen, as he does whenever I lose track of time writing and breakfast is getting cold.

I tuck my journal and pen into their dedicated drawer, then poke my head into the hallway. Silence greets me, and a sniff confirms the absence of the French toast he promised to make for my birthday.

Rather than disappointment, giddiness fills me at the possibility he might still be asleep. He doesn't sleep in often, and since my own sleep has drastically improved, I haven't had as many opportunities for my favorite challenge: seeing if I can make him orgasm before he wakes up.

I take an eager step toward the stairs, then stop abruptly when a flash of bright yellow catches my eye. A few feet down the hallway, a sticky note is attached to the wall. There are no words, just an arrow pointing toward the kitchen.

With a rueful smile for the lost opportunity, I follow Wilder's prompt. Given his caginess over the last week whenever I brought up ideas for celebrating my thirtieth, I should have known he already had something planned.

Sweet, sneaky man.

I find the next note attached to a tumbler of coffee, beside which sits one of the lemon-blueberry muffins we made yesterday.

Humming in delight, I take a bite as I peel off the note.

WHAT IS ROUGH BUT SMOOTH AND ALSO
SUSPICIOUS?

Laughing softly, I grab the tumbler and head out the back door into the morning sunshine.

Despite my rising excitement, I walk slowly, enjoying

the fresh air as I nibble on the muffin and sip delicious coffee. Each deep inhale brings a bouquet of scents I've come to associate with peace and happiness: salty air, pine, and petrichor mingling with the faint sweetness of lilacs and lilies.

I'm mid-swallow when I reach the small clearing and see who's sitting on the sex stump. I promptly gasp, then choke, and end up bent over and coughing uncontrollably. Footsteps rush toward me and a broad hand pounds my back—a completely unhelpful and yet utterly reassuring gesture.

"Dad?" I wheeze, straightening and wiping my tearing eyes with the back of my hand. "What—what are you doing here? How did you get here?"

Pale eyes sparkling warmly, he hands me three bright red tulips. "Wilder opened the side gate for me. Happy birthday, pipsqueak."

I snort at the ancient nickname. "Thanks. Is Mom here? Where's Wilder? I'm so confused."

He grins. "It'll make sense eventually. Will you sit with me for a minute?"

Smiling uncertainly, I nod. He returns to the stump and I settle beside him, hoping my coughing fit is a sufficient explanation for my red cheeks. Privately, I vow to punish Wilder, as I have zero doubts he suggested this location to my dad just to mess with me.

Especially since the last time I was naked here was *yesterday.*

Oblivious to my inner freak-out, my dad says, "There's something I wanted to talk to you about."

At his serious tone, my tumbler stalls halfway to my mouth. I lower it back to my knee, belatedly registering his tense shoulders, fidgeting fingers, and tapping feet. All rare signs of nervousness from a man who normally drips easy confidence.

I clear my throat weakly. "Sure, Dad. I'm all ears."

"This may sound random at first, but bear with me." He takes a deep breath, his gaze lowering to the forest floor. "I had a pretty great childhood. Lived in a good neighborhood. No abuse, no financial or food insecurity. No major trauma besides my dad splitting when I was eleven, which was honestly a good thing for all of us. Plus, your grandpa Bill came along a few years later and he was an amazing stepdad. And I'm sure this next information will come as a surprise, but I was also popular in high school."

I gasp dramatically. "No way!"

He chuckles. "I had a ton of friends, and don't tell your mom, but I've always been a hit with the ladies."

My laugh is mostly a groan. Growing up with a sex symbol for a father was both aggravating and hilarious. It wasn't uncommon for my friends to blush and stammer in his presence, thanks to easily accessible old photoshoots of him in his underwear. Their moms weren't much better and in a few cases, they were a lot worse. Talk about awkward.

My mom truly is a saint, though my dad does deserve some credit for making her feel secure. He's never been shy—in fact, he can be downright obnoxious —about expressing his devotion to her in public.

"I met Julian and the guys right after graduation, and within two years, we were famous." He pauses, the vestiges of humor fading from his face. "Nothing was ever really *hard* for me. I wouldn't say I was oblivious to pain or struggle—I had my fair share of disappointment, heartache, and the like. But I was seriously lucky on a lot of levels. And for the most part, I stayed that charmed, clueless kid until my early thirties."

He looks up at me, his expression anguished. Fine hairs lift on my arms, my awareness narrowing to the pain in his eyes. Though a breeze teases strands of my hair against my cheek, I can't feel the tickle. Nor do I register the wood beneath me, the white-knuckled grip I have on the tumbler and flower stems, or the air trapped in my lungs as I hold my breath.

"The thing is, Eva, I'd never experienced true grief until your mom and I lost your older sister to a miscarriage. And I'd never felt real fear until the day I found out Sophie was pregnant with you. From the moment you were born, I've been terrified of something happening to you. When you were a baby, I'd watch you sleep to make sure you didn't stop breathing, then pass out in the morning when your mom woke up. As you grew up, the fear ebbed and flowed. Some ages were easier than others."

I stare at him, completely blindsided but also... not. He's always been protective of Hunter and me, but especially me—to the point it became a running joke among my friends. At varying times, I've appreciated and resented him for it. But while I've always suspected the loss of my older sister had something to do with his status as a worrier, I had no idea the underlying fear was so extreme.

He continues hoarsely, "It got really bad after you moved out at eighteen. I'd wake up in the middle of the night freaking out that something was wrong. More than once, your mom had to stop me from calling you or driving to your place to make sure you were okay. She eventually bullied me into talking to a professional."

Despite the gravity of the moment, my lips quirk. "You mean she casually suggested it?"

His eyes crinkle as he nods in concession, but his expression swiftly sobers.

"I started seeing someone again a couple of years

ago. They've helped a lot. I'm not perfect yet, but I'm working on it. All that is to say, I'm sorry for being a controlling, overbearing ass of a father. I'm sorry for not being strong enough to fight the fear that told me I had to shelter you from a world that could hurt you, even if it cost me your trust. All you ever needed was my compassion and love, and I..." His eyes redden, tears welling. "I failed to give you what could have actually protected you."

The words drop inside me like boulders, the ensuing ripples spreading and illuminating my father in a new and profound way. Moreover, I see myself and so many others inside him, our experiences different reflections on the same water. And for an instant, I also glimpse something bigger than all of us.

I see *love*—the complexity and potency of it. The brilliant light it casts and the shadows that light naturally creates.

Trust. Tenderness. Peace.

Guilt. Worry. Fear.

I set down the tulips and my coffee, then grab my dad's hands.

"You know what I remember about growing up with you as my dad? Nature walks, making forts, and epic scavenger hunts. The countless times you read me another book when I asked, even though it was past my bedtime, and all the funny voices you did for different characters. I remember your endless patience when teaching me how to swim, how to play guitar, how to drive. I remember how much we laughed—you made me laugh so, so much. Mostly, though, I remember feeling safe."

Tears spill down his cheeks. Down mine, too. I squeeze his hands harder.

"You are and have always been exactly the father I need. I've never once doubted that you loved me. Don't you see? You did protect me, Dad. I'm here. I'm okay—more than okay, actually. I'm *happy*. And a huge part of why is that I finally found my way to something you taught me was possible. The ultimate prize on your greatest scavenger hunt."

"What's that, pipsqueak?"

Emotion overwhelms me. I don't fight it, instead letting it emerge as a tear-soaked laugh.

"Joy, Dad. You showed me the way to joy."

CHAPTER FORTY

The piano bench creaks as I sit with a huff and check my watch for the tenth time in the last five minutes. Unfortunately, I'm once again shown that my racing thoughts haven't affected the rotation of the planet, which continues at a snail's pace.

What the hell is taking so long?

Before leading the people I roped into Evangeline's first birthday surprise to five different, memorable-to-us areas on the property, I made sure they knew to keep each visit to ten minutes or less. Matt texted me over two hours ago when he saw her approaching him from the house, but I haven't heard from anyone else. Has she seen Martin yet? Rye and Lily? Her mom and Hunter? My parents?

Unable to stay still, I spring to my feet and start pacing again.

If all she had to eat was the muffin I left for her, she's likely starving by now. I should have had everyone give her little snacks instead of flowers. Or flowers first, then a snack when they gave her the next clue.

Pausing near a couch, I press the heels of my hands into my eyes and groan. Maybe this was a bad idea. Just because she used to never shut up about her dad's scavenger hunts as a kid doesn't mean they're still important to her.

I should have stuck with French toast and orgasms for her birthday morning and kept with my original plan of a surprise dinner party tonight. The party is still happening, but at this point I won't have enough time to make the focaccia from scratch.

Five minutes later, I've walked around the studio another few times, reworked the grocery order in my head, and am halfway through scripting an apology for fucking up her birthday when the door of the studio swings open.

My stomach does a backflip.

I spin around.

The first thing I notice are the flowers I cut this morning, now an impressive bouquet. Then I see her teary, mismatched eyes. Finally, I take in her bright, gorgeous smile.

Air rushes from my lungs. Relief turns my legs viscous, gluing me to the floor.

"Happy birthday, Fairy," I croak.

Evangeline closes the door, then sets down the bouquet and a small stack of yellow sticky notes. As she walks toward me, her smile softens, changes, until it's *my smile*.

She's every sunset and sunrise.

Moonlight on a moving river.

Wind in a desert canyon.

Music on the precipice of sleep.

When she jumps into my arms koala-style, I catch her with an "ooof" that makes her giggle. She peppers kisses all over my face, then hugs the shit out of me.

"Thank you, Wilder. It was perfect. I love you so much. You did so, so good."

Warm, fuzzy bliss spreads through me. Melts my anxiety. Relaxes my muscles.

Huh. Guess I'm a praise princess, too.

"Isn't that my line?" I rumble.

Her smile curves against my ear. "Not this time. Carry me to the couch, please."

There's a rasp in her tone that my body hears before my ears, sending a rush of blood south. I do as I'm told, dropping onto the cushions with her in my lap. She makes soft, happy sounds as she trails hot kisses over my throat.

When her hips start to move, I groan and grab her waist. "While I'm completely on board with this, I want to make sure you—"

"Yes, Wilder." Her kisses move over my jaw toward my mouth. "I know there are eight people waiting for us at the house. Our dads are making lunch for everyone, but we should probably hurry."

"Say no more."

Our lips brush, smiles meeting. Despite our words, our kiss begins softly, slowly. A tender exploration sprinkled with sighs. But when our tongues touch, fire meets oxygen.

We ignite.

My jeans are unzipped, my cock seized by strong, delicate fingers. I pull off her baggy shirt, then tug the cups of her bra down to expose her breasts. The decision backfires, immediately distracting me from my primary purpose. I twist us to the side and lower her to the couch, then shimmy down to feast on her nipples.

I barely get a taste before she tugs my head up. Blinking in confusion, I take in her glazed eyes, flushed cheeks, and swollen lips that curve into a knowing smile as I watch.

"Inside me. Now. Kiss me as you fuck me hard and fast."

I surge upward, claiming her lips. She opens to give me her tongue. I suck on it, swallowing her thready moan as I fumble for the waist of her cotton bike shorts. She tries to help, lifting her hips so I can pull them down, but ends up almost kneeing me in the balls. Her gasp and my chuckle are joined by the sound of cotton tearing.

"Oops," I mumble, tugging the now-loose fabric away from her body.

She fists my hair. Kisses me harder. Writhes beneath me, soft and warm and silky. Her legs frame my hips.

We move like music. We *are* music. Mesmerizing and melodic, electric and haunting. Transcendent.

As I sink inside her, I surrender myself to our song. To her. Only now when I give her all of me, she gives me all of her in return.

Every note, breath, and word.

Intro to outro.

First verse to last chorus.

EVANGELINE

ONE YEAR LATER

"Did everyone have fun tonight?"

The roar that answers me raises the hairs on my body and buzzes beneath my skin. I look across the stage at Lily, who grins back from behind her DJ deck.

"I think that's a yes," I tell her.

She leans toward her mic and says with mock seriousness, "I'm not convinced. Let's try that again. *Horizon Fest, did you have fun tonight?*"

The volume of sound almost doubles, drowning out my laughter and filling me with effervescent joy. The stage lights flash, purple and blue beams obscuring the stars overhead and strobing across a sea of twenty-five thousand screaming faces.

A subtle, atmospheric beat begins courtesy of Lily.

"You've been amazing," I tell the crowd. "We have one last song for you. It's a new one you might have heard recently."

I pluck a series of chords on my guitar, and the crowd responds immediately to the melody of our newest single's chorus.

Lily's beat silences abruptly, the light display freezing.

"Wait a sec," she says. "Aren't we missing something?"

I look offstage, my heart skipping when I see Wilder already watching me.

"You're absolutely right. Hey, Night Theory, are you guys too tired from your set last night or can you help us out?"

The crowd goes berserk as the men walk onstage. Wilder angles for me, Zander beelines for the baby grand piano, and Jax takes a seat behind my cello. Eddie walks out last and wanders in exaggerated circles until Lily offers him a set of maracas.

"I handle the beats on this stage," she says sweetly.

As the crowd laughs and screams, Wilder's hand

slides across the bare, sweaty skin of my lower back. When his fingers clench on my hip with dark promise, my small, involuntary gasp is amplified. Which, naturally, the crowd loves.

Wilder's soft chuckle floats around the amphitheater, followed by low words that drip suggestion.

"I'm always available to help you, Evangeline."

Catcalls fill our ears as I roll my eyes. "Flirt with me later. We have a song to sing."

"Actually, there's something I have to do first. It'll just take a minute."

My lips part in shock as he steps back. He looks offstage and nods at someone I can't see.

"What's going on?" My question falls flat, the mic in front of me having been turned off remotely.

Lily's mic, however, is still on. She says lightly, "No problem, Wilder. Take all the time you need."

I whip around to see her grinning at me. Quick glances confirm that Jax, Eddie, and Zander wear similar expressions of conspiratorial glee.

My heart stampedes.

My breaths turn shallow.

I spin back toward Wilder right as the stage lights go out completely. Momentarily disoriented, I seek the ever present glow of phones in the crowd.

But what I see isn't an ocean of bobbing, tiny white

dots anymore. Floating on the surface are hundreds, possibly thousands of bright blue LED lights. They're organized into wavy, imperfect lines. Creating letters. Forming two words.

M-A-R-R-Y

M-E

The crowd begins to chant.

"Say. Yes. Say. Yes."

Sparkles line the edges of my vision, then grow brighter. It takes me a second to realize the stage lights are slowly rising. My body feels heavy, unusually clumsy as I turn fast, almost taking out the mic stand with the headstock of my guitar.

Wilder is down on one knee.

I absorb him in sequence, like dramatic notes of an incomparable song. Messy dark hair, strands dancing in the wind from a nearby fan. Golden, inked skin. My sunrise smile, one dimple deeper than the other. Enchanted forest eyes radiating hope and love.

My gaze finally falls to his uplifted hand and the glittering ring pinched between two fingers.

The chanting is so loud he has to shout. "Evangeline Marie Sullivan, my Fairy and muse forever, will you marry me?"

I'm already nodding—laughing and crying—as I fumble to unfasten the strap of my guitar from its pins. Thankfully, Eddie steps forward to help and in seconds I'm free.

I launch at Wilder, catching him as he starts to rise and propelling us both to the ground. He shakes with laughter beneath me. Squeezes me tightly. Lifts my hand, slips the perfectly sized ring on my finger, then grabs my face for a kiss.

"Aww," coos Lily. "I think that's a yes!"

A mighty wave of sound crests and crashes atop us. Swirls and cocoons us. I savor the remains of Wilder's smile. Drink our mingled tears. Revel in the harmony of the small, perfect space we create in the universe.

"I love you," I mumble against his lips.

I feel rather than hear his hum of satisfaction. His hold shifts, hands lowering to my hips as his tongue dips inside my mouth.

"Hey, now!" hollers Zander. "This isn't that kind of show."

Wilder chuckles and gives me one last kiss. Then he sits up, bringing me with him. I'm grateful when he does most of the work getting us back to our feet.

Hands cupping my shoulders, his eyes twinkle down at me.

He asks, "Will you sing with me?"

The nearby mic is back on, projecting his question and my answer: "Always."

He retrieves my guitar from Eddie, and I cradle the comforting weight as he reattaches the strap. When the instrument is secure, I quickly wipe my eyes, then step back into position with a small, ecstatic laugh.

Over deafening cheers, I say, "I think it's safe to assume I'll never forget tonight. Thank you all for being a part of it."

The audible strain in my voice sends my barely recovered pulse racing anew. Swallowing heavily, I look imploringly at Wilder. I'm supposed to introduce the song, but I need a minute if I have any hopes of doing it justice. And my emotional overwhelm is his fault, anyway.

Wilder reads the request in my eyes and doesn't hesitate, grabbing my reaching hand and stepping up to the mic.

As he speaks, I slow my breathing and stretch out my neck and shoulders. The last few minutes go into a box in my head—a temporary one that I'll gladly revisit when we're alone. When I can break down in the privacy of our trailer. Actually look at the ring he put on me. Let him hold me while I cry through the endorphin crash. *And* maybe yell at him a little for blindsiding me before tearing off his clothes.

"Horizon Fest, your energy is fucking nuts. I love it. I want to say a quick thank you to my blue-light volunteers. You guys came through for me in a big way. I'll be forever grateful. Unfortunately, you're still not invited to the wedding."

Laughter and whistles float toward the stars. The joyous sounds are a magic spell on my nervous system, leveling out my energy and relaxing my throat. With a sigh of relief, I squeeze Wilder's fingers to let him know I'm good to go. He squeezes me back, and another shot of calm hits my bloodstream.

"Eva and I wrote this next song together. It's dedicated to two amazing, brave women who happen to be here with us tonight. Everyone say hello to Poppy Cole and Kendra Monroe!"

The screens around the stage switch to a crowd view, zooming in on the VIP section where Kendra, her wife, and their twins are screaming and jumping. Next to them stands Poppy, casually dressed and makeup-free. Her response is genuine but more subdued, a smile and a small wave.

Wilder winks at me, then releases my hand and shifts into position for backup vocals. The stage lights dim, and the multi-tonal roar of the crowd tapers to an expectant thrum.

As I make a final adjustment to the pedals at my feet,

Jax plays a few spine-tingling scales on the cello, and Zander teases the song's piano intro. Not to be excluded, Eddie shakes a maraca near his brother's microphone.

I glance over at Lily. We share a giddy smile. As I turn back around, a deep breath creates space in my lungs, in my heart. I gaze out at the crowd, a writhing sea of light and shadow.

Wilder's fingers graze my back.

"Thanks again, Horizon Fest. We're Glow, these guys are Night Theory, and this song is 'Accidental Grace.'"

Lyrics of "Accidental Grace" by Glow

Album: *Find Her Tomorrow*

She rests between stars

Dreams of water and wind

Until her patience thins

And she wakes

The world will shake

The chains will break

Find her tomorrow

Where the river begins

Listen for mayhem

A storm in the wind

Her tears, they'll carve canyons

Bring life to our wastelands

So find her tomorrow

Where the river begins

Listen for mayhem

A storm in the wind

She's coming

Oh listen, she's coming

Accidental grace

Claiming her place

Not ready to say goodbye to Evangeline and Wilder? Download an extended epilogue with four, full-length bonus chapters.

afterword

For six straight months while I wrote this duet, Wilder and Evangeline were my solace and escape. They've earned an eternal space in my heart, and I'll be daydreaming about their lives for the rest of mine.

I'd like to briefly address the two heaviest themes in the duet: addiction and emotional/narcissistic abuse. If you read the afterword of *First Verse*, you know I have firsthand experience of the former. I also have firsthand experience of the latter.

There's a famous quote commonly attributed to Earnest Hemingway that comes to mind. You've probably read it before: *"There is nothing to writing. All you do is sit down at a typewriter and bleed."* Suffice to say, I've bled my heart into these pages. My trauma, too.

If Wilder's struggles with addiction or Evangeline's

experience in *Last Chorus* resonated with you, **you are not alone.** Here are some resources to be used when it's safe to make a phone call:

National Domestic Violence Hotline
1-800-799-7233

National Drug Helpline
1-844-289-0879

The jumping-off point for change is scary as hell, but I promise—*I promise you*—there are hands outstretched to catch you. All you have to do is keep your eyes on the horizon and reach.

And you'll fly.

Laura

acknowledgments

To you, the reader, 'thank you' isn't enough to express my gratitude for coming on this journey with me. I know it hurt at times, but I hope the landing was soft.

Thank you to my extraordinary alpha and beta readers: Shan, Heather, Danielle, Michelle, Jessie, Jaime, Amanda, Jen, and Dawn, and to my editor, Emily.

To all the new-to-me readers who took a chance on this duet, I'm sending you extra hugs. There are so many talented indie authors to read out there, and I'm so grateful you gave me a try.

Big thanks to Shauna and Becca at The Author Agency for once again handling ARCs and release shenanigans for my hot-mess self.

To Kim Gilmour at Lyric Audio—thank you for holding my anxiety-prone hand through my first foray into duet narration. Isabelle and Austin, you brought these characters to life. There are no words to express how blown away I am by your talents. *Thank you.*

Shout out to Kristina (Instagram: @madmire_) for

her stunning work creating character art for the duet. Thanks for being such a lovely human.

Sydney—my fellow lioness, thanks for speaking my language. S4L—I love you ladies. Stephanie—never stop sending me memes; someday we'll laugh together in person.

Dave, thanks for being you.

And finally to Stella, my magical little human. I have a feeling you'll read this someday (hopefully many, many years from now). In case I haven't told you enough, here are some reminders in print:

- I'm sorry Mommy's brain melts after six p.m., especially when I'm on a deadline.
- Yes, I'm *for real* taking the summer off. And yes, we're going to paint your room.
- I love you more than all the stars... but you still can't have another kitten.

Until the next book/song,
Laura

www.lmhalloran.com
lm@lmhalloran.com

playlist

"Can't Get You Out of My Head"—Johnny Goth

"You Broke Me First"—Tate McRae

"buzzkill"—MOTHICA

"Girls Like You"—The Naked And Famous

"Wasted Youth"—goddard, Cat Burns

"War"—Chance Peña

"Darkside"—grandson

"Oxytocin"—Chandler Leighton

"Your Touch"—Foreign Air

"My Perfection"—Tokyo Project

"Toxic"—Omido, Rich Jansen

and more…

breaking love series

FAMILY TREE

BREAKING GIANTS

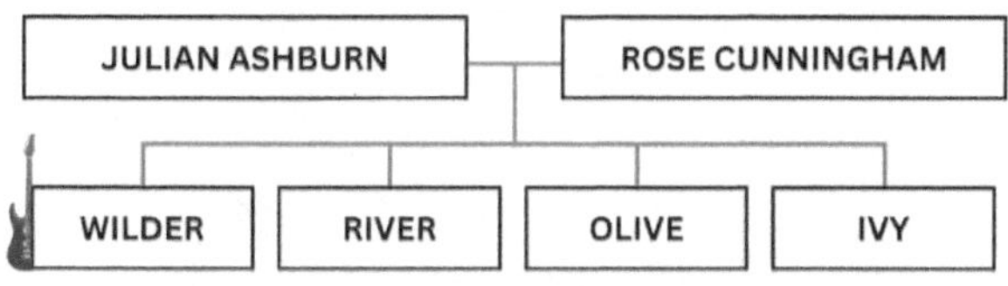

BREAKING SILENCE

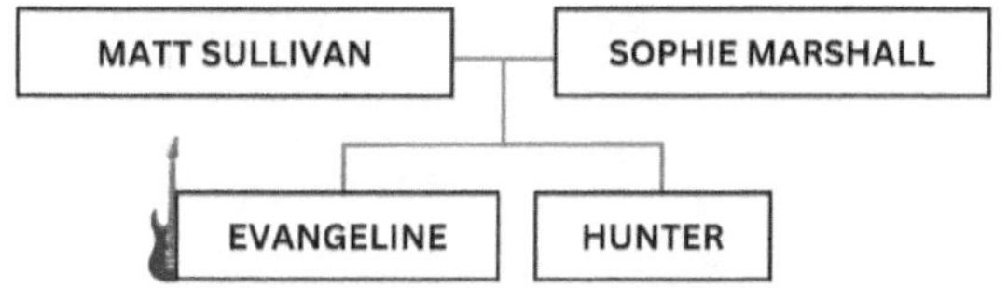

OTHER BAND MEMBERS

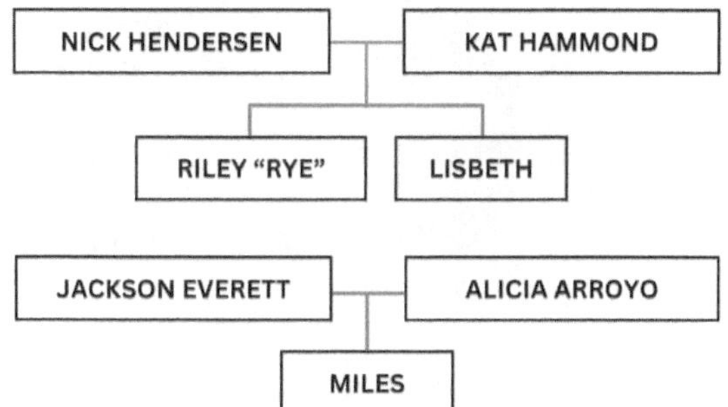

about the author

When not writing or reading, the author can be found daydreaming or trying to keep up with her daughter. Some of her favorite things are puzzles, podcasts, and small dogs that resemble Ewoks.

Home is the Pacific Northwest.

lmhalloran.com